For —

With love in Christ
our Salvation,
Alicia

The House of Mercy

ALICIA ROQUE RUGGIERI

The House of Mercy

Copyright © 2013 Alicia Roque Ruggieri

All rights reserved.

Scripture quotations are from The Holy Bible, English Standard Version® (ESV®), copyright © 2001 by Crossway, a publishing ministry of Good News Publishers. Used by permission. All rights reserved.

ISBN-10: 1492926205
ISBN-13: 978-1492926207

FOR MAMA-BEE
"Her children rise up and call her blessed."

FOR JUDGMENT IS WITHOUT MERCY TO ONE
WHO HAS SHOWN NO MERCY. MERCY
TRIUMPHS OVER JUDGMENT.
JAMES 2:1

PROLOGUE

Dunpeldyr, Lothian
486 A.D.

From the top of this lone hill, Hamish felt bodily—though not emotionally—distanced from the fort. Enough so that he could swing his mount around and pause, gazing at the smoldering stronghold. His heart wrenched as he heard the faint lamentation echoing through the valleys.

My kinsmen.

Many had lost their lives in the days-long siege of Dunpeledyr, "hillfort of the spears." Hamish's people, the Votadini, had made Dunpeledyr their home for as long as the memory of these northern lands stretched. And they had called one, Eion, son of many noble men, their royal chief for a dozen years now. Wisdom crowned that man's brow as visibly as any diadem. A well-skilled leader in war, poetry, and the honor of the gods.

And yet he was no more. Southern forces, led by that clever butcher Weylin, had ravished the ancient holding, slitting the throat of Dunpeledyr's chief. The message from the South was clear: Total destruction would result if a leader refused to submit to the young warlord Arthur Pendragon. As Hamish's eyes riveted to the smoking fortress, grief clenched his jaw afresh. Hardened warrior that he was, the sight forced him to turn away.

To turn away and look down upon the dirty, sleeping face of the young child strapped to his chest. Hamish recalled how a short time earlier, the walls of Dunpeledyr ready to give way, Lady Seonaid had pressed the child into his arms…

"Take my son!" she choked. "Take Padruig to Arthur."

Hamish looked at her, puzzled. "To Arthur, my lady? He has caused all of this. Why would I take your child to him? 'Tis taking him to his death!"

Seonaid shook her head. "Arthur will protect him. He will be good to him. An orphan himself, he will shelter my son."

"My lady, why are you still here?" Hamish glanced around at the flying arrows, some tinged with orange flame. Panic rose within his chest. "You must go now! A horse stands ready at the southern wall. Go, Lady Seonaid. I beg you. Take the child and go!"

Coughing, Seonaid pressed the little boy into the fighter's capable but reluctant arms. "I must stay with Lord Eion. Take the child, Hamish. Please." Her eyes begged him.

Hamish hesitated for just a moment, then nodded. Duty and oaths required his obedience. "All right, my lady. The child shall arrive at Camelot safely by my hand, if the gods spare me. I swear it."

CHAPTER ONE

Late Summer, A.D. 502
West Lea, Southern Logress

The air felt freshly washed, like it had been pounded and scrubbed in the swift stream running near the cottage. Bethan breathed in deeply, her eyes moving over the wheat fields. Or what was left of them.

"Come, Enid, I'll race you back home," she said, trying to turn her mind away from the mounting problems evident all around her. Her little sister grinned and rushed forward, paying no attention to the still-melting hail. Bethan let her get a head start, and then ran forward, feeling the crunch of crushed wheat beneath her bare feet.

The second harvest is gone. She could think of nothing else as she kept a pace or two behind Enid. *God, help us. The second harvest is gone. In one late-summer hailstorm, our lives are set ajar... again.*

~ ~ ~

"How bad is it, Burne?"

With half-closed eyes as she snuggled next to Enid on their pallet, Bethan saw her mother kneeling beside her father. The dim firelight illuminated their sober faces.

Papa reached over and cupped Mama's chin with his hands, studying her. Finally, he began, "Wife, you know too well that we've lived on the knife's-edge of survival for long years. Times have been better with Arthur reigning over all the island, keeping peace from east to west, north to south, halting the Saxon raids. The battle of Badon assured that two summers past. I had hoped that this crop would raise us a bit, enable us to pay back some of the debt we owe Lord Drustan."

"And allow Bethan to marry Garan, aye?" Mama put in quietly.

Papa sighed. "Aye. Her marriage has been put off for one year already. Another year and…" He paused, and Bethan held her breath.

"You're afraid that the priest may find another wife for his only son."

"Aye."

The pair sat, Mama stroking Papa's hand with her tough fingers.

"What are we to do about Lord Drustan, Burne?" Mama broke the silence.

Papa grimaced. "He has been gracious to us these past years, and I hate to continue using land we can't pay for…"

"Will he seize the land?"

Papa hesitated, then finally said, "I don't know. He may. 'Tis his right, Lowri. Thus far, he has granted us protection in exchange for a portion of our harvest. But what benefit is such an arrangement to him if there is no harvest to speak of? And we need the protection from raiding bands. Arthur's reign has stopped them for now, but if they begin again, where could we flee for refuge?"

Silence descended like death over the face of a corpse. Bethan thought about her sleeping sister Enid, whose quiet breathing told of undisturbed repose. How she wished she, too, was seven years old again and could relax into sleep with an unworried heart!

"Is there no way, then?" Lowri spoke against the agonized hush.

Again, Papa hesitated. "There is one way I can think of. But 'twill mean a sacrifice on Bethan's part."

Bethan listened closely.

"Do you remember when Winfred's mill burnt to the ground last year?" At Mama's nod, Papa continued, "Winfred's daughter went to

Oxfield to work as a dairy maid there. To compensate for her services, Lord Drustan gave Winfred new millstones and enough cut wood to rebuild the mill."

Papa paused and watched his wife's face to see if she had caught his suggestion.

After a moment, Mama said, "You want Bethan to go to Oxfield, aye, Burne? To work off our debts?"

Bethan felt tremors through her body. She looked at Papa's sun-browned face, loving him and yet aching at his words. Never had she thought such a thing would be asked of her. *I do not want to go! I do not want to leave. Everything I hold dear, everything familiar to me, lives in this valley. Why must I be the eldest?*

"Lord Drustan always needs more servants," Papa said.

"If I remember, Winfred's Edna would have stayed at Oxfield, if they had not needed her at home," Mama added thoughtfully. "'Tis a good notion."

"Aye." He paused. "My only reservation lies with this betrothal, Lowri. We promised Bethan to Garan as soon as the second harvest finished. He is too good a match and too good a man for us to risk losing."

"If she goes, she must return in the spring to marry him," answered Mama.

Bethan's mind froze in resignation. She knew that she would not be asked if she wanted to go; she would be told 'twas her duty.

After a moment, Papa stood, shoulders wearily bowed. "Alright. I shall send a message with the next traveler who passes this way toward Oxfield."

With a puff, Papa blew out the lamp at his elbow, and Bethan saw his and Mama's shadows move toward their bed on the far side of the small room. Her mind running faster than a spring rabbit, Bethan turned over on her back and stared up at the moon-streaked rushes. She pictured Garan's intelligent, pale face, set with restless eyes. Her breath caught in her throat, and the smile fell from her lips.

Will he wait for me?

CHAPTER TWO

Oxfield

"You must have this letter in the high king's hands by sunset three days hence, lad. Understand?" For emphasis, the lord held up the sealed parchment scroll and looked his attendant full in the eyes.

The young man standing before him met his gaze with confident green-blue eyes and received the scroll quietly, tucking it away into his leather traveling pouch. "Aye. 'Twill be done, my lord. Is there anything else that needs my attention while I'm away this time?"

"No, that is all, but 'tis most important, Deoradhan. It regards a nephew of mine, Lancelot du Lac, who arrives shortly from Gaul and desires a place among the Pendragon's warriors."

"If he is an able-bodied man, not prone to excess, the king will not hesitate over him, I'm certain. What with the border skirmishes, Arthur needs every warrior he can muster," Deoradhan answered honestly.

Lord Drustan nodded his agreement as the two moved toward the door. His hand on the latch, the lord paused. "Oh, aye. There was one more thing, Deoradhan. A new maidservant comes from the village in our West Lea. Get her while you are returning."

"Whose daughter is she, sir, that I may know for whom to inquire?" Such a task was not unusual for the lord to request. Maidservants came and went like dew on the morning fields, useful but transient.

"She is the daughter of Burne, a wheat farmer. I think she'll be a kitchen maid." Drustan opened the wooden door, built to withstand heavy blows from the outside. "Take sufficient supplies for your journey, lad, and may God go with you." His lips twisted. "Though pagan that you are, you may wish for me to ask the gods' blessing, instead."

"I wish for no such thing, my lord," Deoradhan evenly replied, his usually cheerful countenance hardening. "I do not believe in your Roman God, so your first blessing will not rest upon my head. And the gods of my land have turned dark eyes upon me. Thus, I do not expect their favor, regardless of the one who blesses. But," he added with a smile, "I thank you for your own good will. As for the rest, I fear that I must guide my own steps and those of my mount. Farewell." He stretched out his forearm, and Drustan grasped it.

"Farewell."

~ ~ ~

Deoradhan had rode hard, demanding of his horse as much as his natural humanity would allow. Now, nearly a week later and returning to the high walls of Oxfield, he slowed to a trot and set his teeth in frustration. The journey had borne no fruit, at least for him. He had not had the courage to ask for an audience with Arthur. As usual, he had handed Lord Drustan's message to a guard at the gate, not even entering the stronghold of Camelot.

Wait, Deoradhan. What harm will it do you to wait a little longer? Who knows, in a month, six months… Today, he could not bear his own reasoning and tried to distract himself by looking at his surroundings.

'Twas lovely countryside, this western valley, though haunted by the failure of the wheat crops. Hills rose in the distance like verdant suns. Dabbing across the emptying fields, cottages stood firmly, neatly bordered by kitchen gardens. Each rooted itself on its land, Deoradhan thought, as if to say, "We may be humble abodes, but we're built to last, built to stay put." Like the peasant farmers themselves, unwilling to give up despite opposition all around.

Like myself. I will never give up.

The autumn heat penetrated even through his linen clothing. Deoradhan pushed his curly auburn hair off his forehead and squinted at the horizon. He was approaching one of the villages. Yet another young girl awaited him to bring her to service at Oxfield. Deoradhan set his teeth. *I hope she doesn't talk too much. I'm in no mood for it today.*

~ ~ ~

Lowri swept the stone path with firm strokes of her twiggy broom. Dinner bubbled in the pot over the cook-fire, little Enid sat steadily sewing patches on items from the family mending pile, and Bethan kneaded dough in the cool house. Burne was helping with the harvest in some fields down the road a piece, fields that had been spared the hailstorm. All the family was accounted for and safe.

I wish to the gods that I could keep them so. Bethan's eventual departure for Garan's household, she did not mind, though he was a priest's son. Every maid must marry, and the sooner the better, for old bodies could not bear children so well. But to leave for Oxfield first, unmarried . . . Well, let it suffice to say that she wished she could keep Bethan at home for now. An unwed girl should not travel far from home, far from under her mother's watchful care, from her father's strong protection. *I am afraid for her, for all of us...*

She would pray each morning to the gods for their guardianship of Bethan, Lowri decided. With a decisive snort, she turned toward the cottage. This Roman God was not for her. Let the nobles take that deity for themselves if they cared for Him. Holy and pure, mighty to save their souls. As if a peasant woman had time to worry about her soul. *Her* gods were those of the wind and rain, stream and wood. Let the nobility redeem their souls; Lowri needed nature's ancient gods, who saved harvests and bodies, whose bonfires she could help light at Beltane and Samhain. This last hailstorm proved that. Indeed, she wondered if it had not been a judgment against her own husband, who clung with perverse tenacity to faith in this new Roman God.

~ ~ ~

Bethan knelt by the bubbling stream and splashed a handful of water on her flushed cheeks before dipping her bucket into the clear liquid. Sighing with refreshment, she leaned back on her heels, feeling the cool squish of mud under her feet. *I wish it could be so pleasant, so peaceful always.*

"Lass?"

She started, almost knocking her bucket over, and jumped to her feet. A young man stood perhaps ten feet away, right in the middle of the forest path. He wore dusty attire and held a long-legged gray horse by its bridle. On her guard, she readied herself to run, if necessary.

The young man smiled kindly, evidently to reassure her. "I apologize. I startled you."

Having regained her composure, Bethan shook her head but retained her place on the damp bank. "No, it's all right." She waited to see what this mannerly stranger wanted. "Please, feel at liberty to water your horse," she offered.

"Thank you." The young man led the quiet mount forward to the bank. Bethan watched as the animal lowered its neat head on its smooth neck and assuaged its thirst in slow gulps. Its human companion lowered his own mouth to the deep stream and drank as well. At last, he raised a refreshed countenance to Bethan. When he did, she had a question of her own.

"Are you hungry?"

He opened wide surprised eyes. "Yes, I am, but I've plenty to eat in my pouch."

"What, dry bread and cheese? Please, you and your animal are welcome to enjoy our ripe apples. My father would wish it."

"Why?"

Bethan smiled. "Surely you know the words, 'For I was hungry, and you gave me food, I was thirsty and you gave me drink, I was a stranger and you welcomed me.'"

The young man stood silent for a moment, a mixture of cynicism and interest flitting over his face faster than robins across the morning sky. Finally, he spoke, ignoring her offer. "I'm a messenger from Lord Drustan. Can you give me directions to the home of Burne? I believe he's a farmer of this village?"

Through the scratchy wool of her long tunic, Bethan felt her heart beating so heavily it nearly hurt. *The day has come.* Her limbs felt like icy water poured over them. *Be strong and let your heart take courage... Oh, Lord be with me wherever I go!* Swallowing hard, she whispered through a tight throat, "I am Burne's daughter, the one whom you are taking to Oxfield. We've been expecting you."

Clearly relieved to complete his mission so easily, the young man smiled again. 'Twas a nice smile, and it somehow calmed Bethan. It contained no guile, only kindness and, Bethan suspected, a certain measure of concealed grief.

"Please," she continued, "follow me. I will show you to my father's house." Bethan turned and climbed up the dappled bank, leading the way out of the forest and into the sunny meadow beyond.

Reins in hand, Deoradhan followed the determined footsteps of the young girl before him. To his eyes, she appeared around fifteen or a little older perhaps, fair, but lacking the fineness of features that would have made her beautiful. Her chestnut braids swung down to and fro, the uneven ends brushing her knees. Like most peasants, she wore a rough woolen tunic, belted at her waist. Her dirty bare feet moved noiselessly over the dry grass, contrasting with the crunch of his boots and the heavy hooves of his horse.

Shortly, they reached the farm cottage, its low thatched roof shining brightly in the sunlight. A few feet from the doorway, the young woman paused. She drew breath, squared her shoulders, and turned around to face him. Deoradhan saw her eyes brimming with unshed tears and realized how much this departure cost her. *Poor girl.*

"Wait here a moment, please," she requested and disappeared into the dark opening. He waited patiently, hand resting on Alasdair's neck.

Soon, the girl reappeared, accompanied by an older woman. She addressed Deoradhan. "I am Burne's wife, Lowri. You are the lord's messenger?"

"Yes. I am called Deoradhan. Lord Drustan commanded me to escort your daughter to Oxfield. I understand that she is to be a maidservant there," Deoradhan answered gently. The woman's tight mouth and creased forehead indicated her worry over her child. *Did my mother look thus when she sent me away?*

"I see." Burne's wife stood quietly for a moment. "Bethan, get your things together quickly. Bid Enid farewell."

"Yes, Mama." The girl disappeared again into the house.

Deoradhan and the woman stood silently until her daughter reappeared, clutching a small bag. He knew it probably contained all of her worldly possessions. She kissed her mother tenderly and then turned to Deoradhan.

"I…I am ready," she told him.

He nodded, and swung himself up onto Alasdair's broad back. Then he reached down, pulling Bethan up behind him with strong arms.

"Thank you," he heard the girl say softly to him.

Her mother reached up to touch the girl's cheek. "May the gods protect you," she murmured.

"Goodbye, Mama. I love you," came the reply.

The woman nodded, her lips pressed together tightly. "Good day, my good woman," Deoradhan addressed her. He heeled Alasdair into a quick trot.

The horse paced along steadily. As the animal moved beneath her, Bethan felt the sun's heat, sharp and harsh on her face and arms.

She gripped the young man's shoulders with both hands, afraid that she might fall off and disgrace herself. *The last thing I need.* She breathed deeply, bringing under control her shuddering emotions. There had been no time to tell Garan that the day of her departure had arrived. She knew Papa would get word to his family and hoped he would understand. *Garan is a good man,* she reassured herself.

"We should be at Oxfield by nightfall," the messenger commented, interrupting her thoughts.

Bethan suspected he was trying to make her feel comfortable. *I should make an effort to be friendly,* she thought. *He'll think I'm rude.* "Have you worked for Lord Drustan for many years?" she asked.

"No. I came under his service when I was sixteen, only a few years ago. I... did other things before this."

His closed tone did not invite further questioning on the subject, so Bethan turned to another topic. "Have you any family?"

Deoradhan was silent for a moment. "I have a mother still living," he finally said, "but I have not seen her face for many years."

Bethan did not know what to say. This subject, too, appeared unapproachable. At last, she offered, "She must miss you."

"Aye."

~ ~ ~

When the sun rose high, Deoradhan guided their mount off the dusty road and into the wood. Bethan sighed, relieved to feel the cool shadows wash over her face.

"My horse is thirsty, lass, and I think both of us are as well. And hungry, I would guess," Deoradhan commented. "We'll come to a stream soon now. The water is good here, and I have some bread and cheese in my sack."

Shortly, they did come to the stream, its deep running water gushing over glossy brown boulders in its bed. Deoradhan dismounted first, then reached up for her. Bethan realized how strong this young man was as his powerful hands set her down barefoot on the plush green moss. She met his eyes momentarily and felt glad that the owner of that gaze was her protector, rather than her adversary.

The young man turned his attention to his horse. The gelding was thirsty, indeed, and Bethan watched as he swallowed repeatedly, his long neck stretched out. Deoradhan stood with his hand stroking the animal's shoulder, patiently waiting for him to finish his drink. After a moment, he looked up at Bethan.

"I've that bread and cheese in my pouch yonder," he directed. "I'll be finished with Alasdair in a trice, then we can refresh ourselves."

Bethan nodded, admiring his kind way with his beast. Many men she knew, even or perhaps especially, those who professed the Christian faith, would not exercise such benevolence toward their animals. Some treated their inanimate tools more gently than the dumb companions who faithfully served them. *I'm glad Garan is a kind man.*

Turning, she found Deoradhan's leather sack lashed to his saddle pommel. She untied the leather cords and brought the bag to a patch of dry grass. One by one, she withdrew the food items: a loaf of fairly fresh bread, some oatcakes, several apples, and a large chunk of strong-smelling cheese.

As Bethan finished arranging their meal, Deoradhan joined her, crisscrossing his sturdy legs. He had left the horse to graze by the bank a dozen paces away. Even while settling himself down for his meal, however, Deoradhan appeared watchful and a little restless.

"My thanks for laying it out," he commented, taking out his knife to cut the bread and cheese. He sliced both into several chunks, giving Bethan and himself good-sized portions.

"My thanks to you for bringing it, otherwise we should go hungry," she answered. "Will you bless the meal, Deoradhan?"

He paused, and then looked at her frankly. "I don't think you'd want my blessing on your food, Bethan. I am neither Christian nor true pagan."

Bethan stared, disappointed at this turn in such a good-natured young man. Yet, a part of her grudgingly admired his boldness, his honesty. At least, he was no fraud. Finally, she said, "May I ask the blessing, then?"

He shrugged. "If you like. It doesn't bother me. I just don't think it does any good, lass." His tone held a bitter tang as Bethan's ear tasted it.

Bethan paused a moment, then bowed her head. In a few short words, she thanked her Lord for the meal and for His protection on their journey. When she raised her eyes, Deoradhan sat stoically, a study in nonchalance. *Deep ravines lie within that man, where many a wild beast must prowl.* How different from Garan, whose light blue eyes always shone with tranquility!

Deoradhan remained morose for a little while but then talked readily enough when Bethan began to ask questions about their journey and Oxfield. He identified several forest birds by their call alone and described the servants at the manor, telling her their names and specific work. He clearly enjoyed conversation and spoke well, hinting at an intentionally-acquired education. Bethan studied him as he talked, taking in the well-made deerskin trousers and boots, the fine linen tunic that draped his rugged but graceful frame. Out of a sun-browned countenance, his blue-green eyes narrowed in thought one moment, then opened wide with laughter the next. His similarly mobile mouth smiled often. He was not exactly handsome, Bethan decided, but his manner added attraction to his imperfect appearance.

As soon as they had wiped the last crumbs from their mouths, Deoradhan stood. "We'd best be on our way, lass, if we want to arrive by nightfall. Come, I'll help you up."

With that, he mounted the gray gelding and reached down to pull Bethan up behind him. A nudge of his heels sent Alasdair into a swift trot out of the wood and onto the road once more.

CHAPTER THREE

She woke to the sound of clanking iron. *I must have fallen asleep!* Bethan thought in surprise, raising her head from where it rested against Deoradhan's broad back. Torchlight, shimmering in the dusk, flooded her eyes, and she felt the horse halt beneath her.

"Are you awake, Bethan?" Deoradhan questioned, his voice quiet.

"Aye. Where are we?" Bethan asked, though she already guessed.

"We've come to Oxfield. 'Tis just after supper; we've made good time." Deoradhan swung his right leg over the horse's withers and slipped to the ground.

Bethan blinked in the flickering light and saw that they stood before a heavy iron gate, flanked by stone towers on both sides. She wondered who would admit them. When she glanced down at him for a hint, Deoradhan stood waiting patiently. Suddenly, a voice echoed out of the darkness, from one of the towers, she thought.

"Who requests entrance?" the voice demanded in a tone that chilled Bethan's stomach.

Deoradhan appeared unaffected by the intimidating, invisible speaker. "'Tis only our lord's messenger, Deoradhan the Red, and a new servant," he called back.

Immediately, the gate creaked open on its weighty hinges. It revealed several armed guards, one of whom strode forward. His solid jaw broke into a wide grin at the sight of Deoradhan, and his hand dropped from his sword hilt. "Deoradhan, lad! I've not seen hide nor hair of you in days. Where have you been?"

Safety enveloped Deoradhan and Bethan as they entered the stronghold. "On the lord's business, Calum, as usual," answered Deoradhan.

"Aye. 'Tis good to have you back." The tall guard turned his eyes, bright in the torchlight, up toward Bethan. "And what pretty maiden have you brought back with you?"

"A new servant for the kitchens. Bethan of West Lea, daughter of Burne." Deoradhan reached up and brought down Bethan from the saddle, setting her on her feet. "Bethan, I'd like you to meet my friend Calum, the commander of Oxfield's guards."

Brushing the dust from her rumpled dress, Bethan glanced up at the man. He looked no more than thirty years and had the defined features of a handsome man, though several deep scars across his cheeks had twisted an otherwise comely face. Hazel-blue eyes, shadowy in the torchlight, met her own with a gentleness that she had not expected from a battle-hardened warrior.

"Pleased to make your acquaintance, Calum," she smiled.

"As I am yours, Bethan. You'll show her to the kitchens, Deoradhan?" he inquired of his friend.

"Aye, I will. Are you on night watch?"

"Aye. Come to the tower after you bring her. I'll take Alasdair for you now."

"My thanks. I'll see you in a bit then. Come, lass," Deoradhan spoke and led the way through an open space, leaving his horse with the rugged guard.

Bethan followed a pace behind him. She shivered in the night air as they made their way around numerous stone buildings, their outlines alternately vague and sharp in the darkness. Several lights shone from the main structure's towers, casting deep shadows all around them and making Bethan feel dwarfed before such strangeness. She heard snatches of songs slurred out from what she took to be the stables. Still Deoradhan walked on, his strides unwearied.

Deoradhan glanced behind him. The young girl felt tired and cold, that much could be safely deduced. Compassion stirred in his chest, and he stopped, removing his woolen cloak. She stumbled into him, her eyes to the ground.

"Oh, I'm sorry!" she exclaimed softly, stepping back.

He smiled. "It's I who am sorry, Bethan. I should have taken your weariness into account. Here," he directed, draping his cloak around her bowed shoulders.

"Thank you," she accepted, and Deoradhan led the way once more, this time walking by her side, slowly, though he wanted to run forward.

They came to a wooden door set in the main building's wall. It was as familiar to Deoradhan as the hooves of his mount. "The kitchen," he said when he saw Bethan give him a questioning look. He applied his fist heavily to the door, explaining, "It's where you'll be working and living at Oxfield."

She nodded as the door creaked and swung open. There stood the head of the kitchen, known almost universally as Cook, stout, perspiring, and greasy as always. Her thin lips split into a toothy, brown-stained grin at the sight of him. "If 'tisn't my own Deoradhan!" She opened her fleshy arms toward him, and he embraced her, ignoring the heavy odor that clung to her clothing and skin. This was the woman who had nurtured him when he felt that he had no place to rest his head.

After a moment, he stepped away and turned Cook's attention to Bethan, who had been hiding in Deoradhan's shadow. "I've brought you a new servant, Aunt Meghyn. Her name is Bethan of West Lea."

Cook's small black eyes flew to Bethan. Deoradhan saw the woman sizing up the girl from toenail to forehead; he held his breath. Cook often stuck with her first impressions. For Bethan's sake, he hoped Cook would take a liking to the lass.

"Well, then, you'll be joining us in the kitchen, Bethan?" Cook took the girl by her hands. "Good. Strong, capable hands. I think you'll do well."

Deoradhan sighed, relieved. "You'll see to her from now on, Aunt Meghyn?"

"Aye, that I will," she responded, smiling at Bethan, then directed her gaze to Deoradhan. "But, you, my boy, are not thinking of sneaking off already? With only a hello and goodbye for your Aunt Meghyn?"

"Aunt Meghyn, I have things—" he began, already feeling happily defeated.

The older woman waved her hands as if to sweep away all obstacles. "Things more important than your old auntie? Come along. Have a cake, and make Bethan feel welcome among us tonight. There's plenty of time for your things tomorrow."

Deoradhan grinned and raked a hand through his auburn hair. "All right, then. You've conquered me." He passed through the low doorway, following Cook and Bethan. The girl glanced back at him once or twice, shyly, seemingly glad that someone familiar accompanied her into this strange new place. To reassure her, he offered a smile. He knew all too well what it was to be an outsider, though the feeling would soon pass for her, as the other kitchen maids were sure to accept her. As for himself, he feared that consciousness would never cease.

Cook led them down the short curved hallway, its walls thick with cold stone. Before they reached the main kitchen room, Deoradhan could hear female voices chattering and giggling, answering one another and clamoring to be heard. Beneath it, he could make out the sweet lilt of a flute playing an ancient tune.

Aine. Before they entered the room, his mind saw her, curled up before the fire. Her black-fringed eyes would be gazing into the flames, half-closed in pleasure at the sounds she coaxed from her carved instrument. Almost every time he had come to this room at dusk, she knelt quietly there, her dark locks cloaking her thin shoulders, her white complexion glowing in the heat. Deoradhan's heart began to pound in anticipation like northern drums before a battle. His eyes lit as they entered the warm, shadowy room.

There she was. Surrounded by a half-dozen girls chatting as they sewed, Aine sat playing her flute, just as he had imagined. *My Aine.* He could dare only to think it.

"Look who I've brought you, girls," Cook announced as they entered. "A new workmate and your favorite messenger lad."

At the sight of him, all the girls sprang to their feet, faces beaming and voices eager. They competed for his attention, pulling at his tunic, taking him by the hand, urging him to sit down. All except for one, the one who mattered to him. Aine alone remained by the tossing fire, a quiet smile playing on her pink lips.

"Goldie, bring some bread and ale for Bethan and Deoradhan," Cook instructed. "Come, Bethan, I'll show you where to put your things." The gangly youngster hurried to accomplish the command while Deoradhan eased himself onto a stool as near the fire as possible. *As near to Aine as I can get.*

When she turned toward him in welcome, he decided to risk it. "Aine," he whispered, "I've missed you."

He held his breath, waiting for her response, glancing toward her and then away, then back again. Her cheeks deepened to peony, and her expression told him that his words had pleased her. Deoradhan reached down and took her hand before proceeding recklessly, "Aine, I wish to win your heart. You know that, don't you, lass?"

Only a moment passed before the other kitchen maids gathered round them and Aine quickly withdrew her hand. But before her small hand left his, Deoradhan felt her squeeze his fingers in confirmation.

CHAPTER FOUR

"Up, lazy bones. Breakfast won't wait for you," a voice broke into Bethan's heavy sleep. She struggled to orient her thoughts as she opened her eyes to the dimly-lit room. Turning on her side and half-rising, she saw one of the older girls standing before her. A contemptuous expression reigning in her eyes and mouth, the speaker reinforced her words by pulling the blanket off Bethan. Then she waited, hands on her hips.

Bethan shook her head in an effort to rouse herself. "It must be early yet," she muttered in a sleep-soaked voice.

The girl snickered. "Perhaps for you. For those of us used to working, 'tis late. The sun already rises."

From her mat on the stone floor, Bethan scrambled to her feet, brushing off her tunic. She had slept in it for warmth. "What should I do first?"

The girl shrugged. "I don't really know. We've already done almost everything."

"Oh, Winter, you know 'tis not true," another girl put in. She straightened the bedding as she spoke. "Don't worry, Bethan. We've only been awake a little while. Anyway, Cook asked us to let you sleep. You had a long journey yesterday."

Bethan returned the girl's smile, relieved that she was not at fault. Winter raised her eyebrows and moved away.

The other girl stepped toward Bethan and took her by the hands. "Come along, Bethan," she continued. "I'll show you where you can wash your face and hands. Then, you and Aine will bring breakfast out to the rest of the servants."

Bethan followed her to the bowl of water already used by the rest of the servants. "And you," Bethan inquired as she washed, "what is your name?"

The girl smiled again, displaying a row of square buckteeth. "You may call me Amy. Come, Aine will have the gruel buckets ready."

~ ~ ~

The rising sun cast a burning hue across the roofs as Bethan and Aine carried the brimming buckets of brown gruel into the yard. Each also bore a large basket of broken loaves, left over from last night's meal.

Bethan felt the cool dust of the yard beneath her feet and took in the sights around her with wide eyes. Last night, dusk had cloaked the manor and her vision; now in the waking daylight, she saw this strange place clearly. And there was much to see.

Built of thick, heavy gray stone, numerous buildings spread across a wide courtyard, including the old Roman barracks, now used for the servants' sleeping quarters. Packed dirt served as the foundation for the stone walls surrounding the stronghold. Bethan saw several guard towers similar to the two that had flanked the gate she and Deoradhan entered last evening.

Though still so early, noise rose from every quarter as the inhabitants began their day. Many servants clustered near the kitchen entrance, some of the stableboys pulling on their ragged shirts and yawning. Dairy maids stood combing their fingers through their hair, trying to unknot and plait the oily locks. A few guards leaned against hitching posts, dozing. Bethan recognized Calum among them. He smiled at her when their eyes met. She returned the courtesy, glad to see a familiar face.

"They wait for us," Aine murmured to Bethan. With lithe

hands, she set down her basket of bread, and the servants moved eagerly toward the two girls, settling into irregular lines.

Bethan took her place beside Aine, carefully following the experienced girl's example. Every servant took a piece of dark bread, and most also brought a bowl to receive the scoop of nourishing gruel Bethan and Aine offered. Bethan began to glance around, wondering if she would see Deoradhan's familiar face. She had known him for only a day, but even a day's acquaintance made his kind presence welcome to her. In a way, he reminded her of Garan, with his aloof otherness. As her eyes searched the crowd, the question of whether he would welcome seeing her again flitted through her mind and caused her to blush.

As she filled a bowl with gruel, her head bowed, she heard Deoradhan's mellow tenor voice. "Good morning to you, lassies."

A smile rose to Bethan's lips, but as her eyes lifted to Deoradhan's face, she saw that, though his words were for them both, his gaze was for Aine alone. Bethan felt disappointed but could not be surprised. Aine was a rare beauty, a lily among thorns, as the Holy Book said. Of course Deoradhan would be taken with Aine; a man, he would judge and be pleased, at least initially, by appearances. And Aine certainly was comely in every way, Bethan regretted to acknowledge as she compared her own paltry beauty with that of her companion. She looked to see how Aine would respond to Deoradhan's obvious regard.

Aine's plush lips curved up in pleasure. "Hello, Deoradhan," she replied softly, her eyes shyly meeting his. "Are you wantin' some breakfast, something to refresh you?"

He shook his head and glanced around. The rest of the servants began to disperse, heading toward their daily tasks. Deoradhan picked up the girls' buckets and stepped next to Aine. As they moved back across the yard toward the kitchen's outer door, Bethan heard him quietly answer Aine, "Seeing you is all the refreshment I need, lass."

Aine's round cheeks flushed. At the sight of her delight,

Deoradhan's own smile deepened.

Seeing them thus, Bethan felt a little hurt. She liked him, this messenger lad with eyes the color of the far-off sea, an easy smile, kind manners, and more than a hint of polish. He embodied much that she admired and hoped to see in Garan. *So in a way, when I like him, I'm really liking Garan,* Bethan reasoned, trying to ignore the guilt rising up within her.

Deoradhan and Aine strolled close together, his eyes on her bowed head, seeming to nourish himself on the sight of her bonny countenance raising itself to his every few moments. Walking a bit apart from them, her heart restless, Bethan roused suddenly, astonished at her own thoughts. *He's courteous and pleasant, aye, but he can't cause these tender feelings in my heart. I'm promised to Garan. I must be faithful to him. Besides, this man serves other gods.*

'Tis wrong.

Oh, Living God, she prayed, dropping a pace or two more behind Deoradhan and Aine, *help me not to falter! May my heart obey You alone, as my father taught me.*

CHAPTER FIVE

Amy grasped Bethan by the arm, startling her so that the dough nearly fell off the table. "Bethan, you'll never guess!"

Bethan tried to look stern. "I probably won't, and it had better be something worth hearing. I almost lost that bread dough, and if I had, I would have lost my head, most likely, when Cook found out."

The lively fifteen-year-old's eyes sparkled like sunlight on water. "Oh, it's worth hearing, Bethan. Are you ready?" When Bethan nodded, she went on. "There's to be dancing tonight in the stableyard."

Excitement rose in Bethan. She would welcome a diversion from the melancholy that had crept up in the past few days she had been at Oxfield. "Dancing? With whom?"

"With the young men around the estate, of course. None of the uppity house servants will come, except for Deoradhan, but most of the stable boys and herds and some of the guards will attend." Amy began to work the dough with Bethan.

Uninvited, a thrill ran through Bethan's spirit when Amy mentioned the messenger. Pushing away her guilty conscience, Bethan inquired, "Deoradhan will be coming?"

"Aye." Amy plucked a handful of flour from the sack beside them and dusted it across the rough-hewn table. She began to separate the dough into loaves before speaking again. "You favor him, Bethan?"

Bethan felt her heart bang against her ribs and her face grow hot.

She swallowed hard. "No, I ... I just don't know very many others here yet, and I always think of him as sort of a friend. He's the first person I met from Oxfield, you know."

Amy nodded. "I just wondered. I wouldn't have blamed you if you did fancy him, though. Most of the kitchen maids do. I've even seen Lord Drustan's wife smile a little too warmly at him when I served in the hall once a long time ago. But don't say I told you that."

"How long has Deoradhan been at Oxfield?" Bethan asked in a voice she hoped sounded nonchalant. "Or was he here before you?"

Amy bit her lip, remembering, then shook her head. "No, he came just a little while after I did, more than two summers ago now. I had just turned thirteen at the time." She laughed. "I remember being out in the courtyard when Deoradhan first rode in on his horse Alasdair. When he cantered through that great iron gate, all the servants turned and stared, especially the lasses.

"Mind," she said, shaping the loaves, "Deoradhan's not handsome in the usual way. He hasn't got great dark eyes or a fair countenance, and he's not tall and elegant like some. But I remember that from that first day, he rode with such a look of purpose to his eyes and in his way of carrying himself, it attracted everyone to him. Now, I'm sure he's got those who don't like him, same as everyone does, but there's something about Deoradhan that draws you. It's the reason all of us kitchen girls get excited when he comes. You must have felt it, too, or you wouldn't be asking me about him, now would you?" Amy smiled at Bethan, her mouth showing a gap where she had lost a tooth.

"But," Amy sighed, "We've no chance with the lad, now, Bethan."

"What do you mean?"

Amy raised her thin eyebrows. "Surely you've noticed how he looks at Aine. Hangs on her every word, he does. Not that they're many or very clever." She snorted.

"Why do you suppose he likes her?" Bethan asked, even though she already guessed the answer.

Amy shrugged. "Why do you think he does? She's pretty and that's enough for most men, even for Deoradhan."

Bethan nodded, knowing Amy spoke accurately. "She is pretty. I can't argue with that." Aine was as beautiful as the sun rising across the dew-laden meadows back in West Lea. Bethan felt jealousy stab her, knowing she could never compare with the dark-haired kitchen maid.

Suddenly, she realized how unattractive her feelings were. Dusting off her hands, Bethan laid the last of the loaves aside and covered them with a sheet. She grasped Amy by the hands. "Come along with me."

"What?"

Bethan tugged her along toward the door. "Come along. Those loaves must rise, and so we've some time on our hands." She stopped and smiled sincerely at Amy. "We two may not have Aine's rosy lips or her graceful limbs, but we *are* going to look very pretty indeed for the dancing tonight, if I have anything to do with it."

Amy's green eyes lit like fireflies. "Lead on, Bethan."

~ ~ ~

The night was clear and crisp with the scent of autumn. Deoradhan made his way across the courtyard toward the stables. Dancing tonight, then his conference with Lord Drustan to see whether he could be spared to travel north. Again.

Six times in the last year he had made the dangerous journey up the island, eluding robbers and wild beasts, avoiding notice while scouting for information. *At this point, I would welcome any change, no matter how it came. Any wisdom, as long as it allowed me to regain what is mine by right.*

Frustrated, Deoradhan turned his mind to other, more pleasant matters. Such as Aine whirling to the music of pipe and drum, her every movement a stream of grace and beauty. Her small feet would be bare, her dark hair like a flock of black sheep running down her shoulders, her teeth white like northern mountain peaks. She would smile with pleasure at every word he whispered.

His mind saturated with thoughts of the girl, he decided. *Tonight, after the dancing, I shall ask her.*

Her arm tucked into that of Winter, Aine tried to match her steps to those of the taller girl. In the glowing dusk, she glanced up at the profile of her companion, envying her careless audacity, her certainty that she knew what she wanted and how to get it. Brazen at times, aye. Cruel, often. But confident.

As different from you as day from night. Aine could not seem to settle on anything to satisfy her, to take away the longing that ate away at her being. Some nights, as she lay on her hard pallet, thin woolen blanket pulled up to her frozen chin, she tried to think of what could absorb her loneliness, what remedy would assuage her yearning for something . . . *more.*

Far off, a robin sang out his ancient song, practiced since the beginning of time. Mama had loved the evening songs of the birds, Aine recalled now. She could remember her mama's face turning toward the window of their cottage as darkness fell. She might be in the middle of something important, might be bathing little Currier or churning out butter, but at the voice of the red-breasted bards who carried their instruments internally, Mama would rise, handing over the task to a willing Aine. With eyes infused with pleasure, the older woman gazed into the gloaming, her tired lips blossoming into a mysterious smile. For a few unfettered moments, Mama regained and exceeded the loveliness of her youth. There in the evening hours, her mama's deep soul-beauty appeared, coaxed into blooming by the siren-sounds from the wood. Night after night, Aine had watched in wonder while her Mama delighted in sonnets fresh from the hand of her God.

Walking across this courtyard, arm in arm with bright-cheeked Winter, Aine could not understand what Mama had found to solace her in the night songs. When the darkness approached, Aine wanted only to distract herself with such things as would take her mind off the horrible fears that invaded her mind and heart. Even now, with the shadows lengthening across the earth, chilly thoughts wrapped themselves around her thin shoulders. She shivered and moved closer to Winter.

Winter glanced down at her. "Cold? Don't worry, 'twill be warm inside the stable yard. The heat of the horses—and the laddies—will see to that."

Aine flushed scarlet, suddenly glad for the darkness. What things this girl could say! At the mention of their waiting partners, however, her mind ran to Deoradhan. As his sensitive sea-blue eyes blessed her thoughts, she wondered if he anticipated the sight and presence of her as much as she did him.

With unusual boldness, Aine dropped her arm from Winter's and began to scamper on slender legs toward the glittering lights that beckoned. "Come, let's hurry!" she called back, her heart racing past her feet to meet that of the spirited messenger.

The running girls caught the eyes of Bethan as she, along with Amy and Haylee, picked their way around the horse dung littering the ground near the stables. Squinting through the dusk, she couldn't recognize who they were.

"'Tis Winter with her lackey Aine," Haylee observed frankly.

"That girl will only bring trouble for the scared wee mouse," Amy put in. "I wish Aine would realize that. But I think she admires Winter, if that's possible."

Bethan nodded. She, too, had noticed the power and influence Winter exerted over Aine. "It's too bad, really. Aine appears so trusting and innocent, and—"

"Winter is anything but," Amy finished. "I know."

"Aye, Aine's not a wicked girl, really. I've tried to warn her, but she seems blind to Winter's faults. Or not willing to admit them," Haylee commented as they approached the buildings where the horses were kept. Invigorating music wafted through the cool air to greet them, and the three hurried their steps simultaneously.

At the door, the girls exchanged excited smiles. Gloriously pleasant hours stretched out before them like sun-filled meadows before energized horses.

"You look very bonny," Amy whispered to Bethan as they moved the doorway.

"So do you," Bethan replied sincerely, thinking of the time they had spent combing and plaiting their hair, scrubbing their faces, and brushing off their simple tunics in preparation for this evening. They both looked as fine as grooming could make possible, Bethan knew. Haylee, younger by a year, had used her time wisely after supper as well; her golden mane shone like a king's treasure trove and her limbs glowed from a hearty washing.

As they entered the stable area, Bethan breathed in astonishment at the yard's transformation. All the usual filth had been cleared away, leaving the square expanse open for dancing. Torches lined the yard, blazing warmly to illuminate. Three or four stable lads stood at the far end of the yard, equipped with the essential instruments: recorder, bagpipe, and drums. Already, they began to beguile the assembly with vigorous music, the inimitable sound of the pipe undergirding the high sweet whistle of the recorder, belted together by the drum's varying pulse.

At the instruments' call, the dance floor sprang to life before Bethan's widening eyes. Here, a guard swung a dairymaid round; there, a shepherd boy pranced to the laughing admiration of his kitchen maid partner. Bethan's spirit leaped at the prospect of such carefree merriment, and she, too, wished to join in similar wild abandon. *There is nothing evil here,* she thought. *'Tis only fun. Even Papa would surely permit it.*

Permit it, aye. And caution, as well.

CHAPTER SIX

Aine glanced this way and that, eager to glimpse a certain messenger's face in the crowd of servants. Running a hand over her loose hair, she decided to amble casually, looking for him as she went. Winter had rushed off with a rowdy bunch of guards and dairymaids the moment they entered the stable yard, and so Aine was at liberty to go where she pleased.

Excitement creeping through her arms and legs, streaming down to her toes and fingertips, Aine moved around the groups of chatterers and avoided the dancers' flying feet. She passed by the table laden with cakes and tankards of ale where weary revelers refreshed themselves. Deoradhan's smiling countenance flashed through her imagination. Each time she saw him, his gaze seemed to say that he cared for her more, that she was ever more important to him. What would he say to her tonight?

"Lass."

With a sharp intake of breath, she turned to the voice behind her, unable to do otherwise even if she had tried. "Deoradhan," she breathed. "I thought you would be here."

He smiled gently. "You look like a goddess of night, Aine." He moved closer to her and whispered, "If I take you in my arms for the dancing, will you vanish?"

She blushed and shook her head vigorously.

"Tell me," laughed Deoradhan, "is that a nay to the vanishing or to the dancing?"

His mild teasing and intent gaze overcame her. Tongue-tied, Aine shook her head again, her eyes to the ground. Then she felt his strong hand lift her chin with the kindness with which a shepherd would lift a wee lamb. Half-frightened, she raised her dark eyes to his and found herself breathlessly bound in unspoken communication.

His eyes spoke of things which she could not, did not want to understand: pain he felt she could mitigate, desires he wished her to gratify, expectations of whom he believed her to be. In the face of such a summons, Aine felt powerless. She knew herself unable both to resist and to fulfill his anticipations. *I cannot.* She knew that she would fail ultimately, for she knew how defective she was. Yet she knew also that she would try her utmost to succeed, to be all that he wanted and needed, if only . . . *If only he will love me.* And perhaps then the lonely valleys of her heart would be lifted.

After long moments, her chin held in his right hand, her eyes held by his, Deoradhan spoke. "Come, lass," he murmured, his voice a dry streambed, and led her toward the open yard.

Bethan observed Deoradhan and Aine with mixed feelings swirling together within her heart. Resignation held the throne largely. *He's not for you, lass. You knew that even before you saw he favored her. Papa would not approve. Besides, what of Garan?* Yet, Deoradhan was such a generous, kind young man, unlike any among her acquaintance. Though he did not embrace the Way, his spirit spoke of a natural goodness. This drew Bethan's heart toward him like a thirsty rabbit to clear water. She bit her lip, watching him delight in the company of his lithe partner. Aine looked up into Deoradhan's face with shy but equal rapture.

What fellowship has light with darkness? Papa's blue eyes, lined with concern, appeared in her mind's eye, beseeching her to think, to be led by the Spirit living within her. *Be careful, daughter.*

"Why are you standing here like a scared brown bird, lass?" The deep voice came at her elbow.

Surprised, Bethan turned to see who addressed her. A familiar man smiled down at her, his fierce scars softened by the torchlight.

"Bethan, isn't it?" he asked amiably. At her nod, he continued, "You might not remember me. I'm a guard, Calum by name."

"I remember you. I met you the first night I came to Oxfield," Bethan replied, glad for the diversion. "You're Deoradhan's friend, aren't you?"

"Aye, we're friends. I've known him since he arrived from Gaul."

Bethan's eyebrows rose. "I didn't know Deoradhan came from Gaul. By his accent, I would have guessed the north, even Lothian," she referred to the often-disputed territory between the wild tribal land and Arthur's southern domain.

"Aye, he was educated abroad, in a monastery, actually."

"A monastery?" Bethan's interest rose more quickly than a hungry sparrow's toward a beetle. "But…"

Calum smiled. "I know. Deoradhan isn't exactly of the Christian persuasion, is he, Bethan? But much has happened in his youth, I think, and he may yet turn. What do the Scriptures say? 'Tis not the healthy that need a physician, but the ill." The older man's eyes took on a sorrowful glint. "That the lad would see his infirmity and be healed," he murmured, half to himself.

"His infirmity? You mean his need for a Savior?"

Calum nodded. "Aye, a Savior. And a Friend who sticks closer than a brother. The only one who will fill the God-shaped hole in his heart that he's now trying to fill with Aine. Oh, I've nothing against Aine," he quickly added when Bethan's eyes widened. "She's a sweet girl, but I know from my own experience that nothing will satisfy us except for the One we were made for."

Bethan knew he spoke truly. She contemplated this man afresh. Prior to their conversation, she had looked on Calum only as Deoradhan's friend. Now, she saw him independent of Deoradhan, and he struck sincere admiration in her. Scarred as his face was, robbed of its natural beauty, his eyes testified to forgiveness received yet not earned; mercy and truth continually met on his countenance. *Though it holds deep sadness yet...* Calum's faith had given flesh and bones to the hope his Creator had thought into being. Deoradhan's self-confident carriage and pleasing appearance shriveled and dimmed into a flimsy illusion in the face of Calum's living conviction.

"Come, lass. Will you dance with me?" Calum offered her his hand, and she took it gladly, knowing both her fathers would be pleased.

After dancing past midnight, Aine begged Deoradhan through breathless laughter to allow her to rest.

Though his own energy was undiminished, her partner acquiesced. "Come, my Aine. We'll have a cup of ale." Still holding her small hand in his large rough one, he led her to the refreshment table.

My Aine. The words floated off his tongue, sweet and appetizing as early summer berries. He tasted and relished them and saw from her expression that she welcomed his endearing phrases. That she wanted to belong to him as strongly as he wished to possess her and so fill the cavernous space within himself.

He drank quickly, watching Aine sip her ale. Let the priests and deacons, monks and bishops have their far-off God, One who was strong to save, yet never did. His goddess stood before him, stainless and alive. A virgin spirit of nature she seemed to him in that moment, her dusky hair clouding the white star of her face, her limbs glowing with jubilant exercise.

Aine finished drinking, and Deoradhan took her cup from her, placing it on the table. "Come, Aine," he said gently. "I'll take you back to the kitchen."

She smiled, placing her hand in his offered one, and the two moved from the crowded yard, weaving around those whose dancing had taken a riotous turn as the night wore on and the ale flowed more freely and potently. Across the quiet courtyard, Deoradhan led his idol. They did not speak, each intent on the pleasure they knew awaited them at the other's hand.

They came to the kitchen door. Aine made a feeble attempt to enter, but Deoradhan stayed her with a hand to her shoulder. With a smile, he thought of how like the old stories this was: the dark night sky gleaming with half a hundred stars, the crisp aromatic wind nuzzling their faces, fallen leaves caressing their bare feet. With a deep breath, he gazed down into Aine's trusting eyes, treasuring the moment before he drank the perfume of his bloom.

As he kissed her, he knew why honeybees delight in intimately knowing a rose.

Aine broke away from their embrace first. "Cook will wonder where I am," she breathed, moving toward the door on slow legs, her eyes held by Deoradhan's gaze. "'Tis late."

"Aine, stay a moment." Deoradhan clung to her hands and swallowed. "Marry me."

"What?"

"Marry me. Within the month." She felt her heart pound in unison with his words. "I cannot think of living without you. I love you."

"Aye," Aine heard herself reply, her entire being dazzled with emotion. He desired her; he *loved* her. For the first time in her life, she felt benumbed with a restless bliss. Even as she felt it, she feared it would vanish, unreal as the mist streaming around the manor's walls.

"Aye," she affirmed defiantly and raised her face to kiss her worshipper.

CHAPTER SEVEN

'Twas Sabbath. Bethan knew it the moment she opened her eyes to the pre-dawn room. She inhaled the cold air of the room, grateful for her woolen tunic and blanket. She lay there quietly in the stillness, listening to the many-rhythmed breathing of her kitchen companions, thinking about the Lord's Days she'd spent at home in the West Lea.

This is the day that the LORD has made; let us rejoice and be glad in it.

Bethan felt her heart swell with peace as she remembered Papa's recitations. From deep within her, down to her very marrow, Bethan knew that she had a Mediator before the Throne of God. In her mind, she could see the God-Man Jesus standing before His Father, holding out nail-scarred hands with her name written on them.

Bethan rolled over onto her side, pulling the blanket up over her chilled shoulders. She closed her eyes and thought of her Papa. By this hour, he would be rising in their darkened cottage, anxious to secure long moments talking with His Friend and Redeemer before the animals required caring for. She could see Papa's lank form outlined by the rising sun as he meditated in the fields, like so many men of God had done before him. His eyes, lined with decades of toiling under that other servant of God, the sun, would close; his strong, bony knees would bend to the brown dust of the fields; and his large, rock-hard hands rise open-palmed in heartfelt worship.

"Bethan."

The whisper startled her. Snapping her eyes open, Bethan

peered into the now-gray darkness. "Who is it?" she inquired, rising on her elbows.

"Just me, Deirdre," the soft voice replied.

Bethan could picture the serious freckled face of the older girl. She did not know Deirdre well but thought of her as kind and patient with the younger servants. "What is it? Is something wrong?"

"No. You know Calum the guard?"

"Aye." Bethan waited for Deirdre to go on.

"He mentioned to me that you might like to come to our meeting this morning."

Bethan's interest rose. "Your meeting?"

"Aye. On Sunday mornings, the servants who are Christians meet together to worship the Lord. Would you like to come with me?"

"Aye!" Bethan eagerly replied. "Aye, I would."

"Calum said as much. We'll have to hurry, though. 'Tis nearly dawn. Come along." Bethan heard and felt Deirdre scramble to her feet. She threw back her blanket and quickly followed. Together, the two girls tiptoed barefooted over the cold earth floor, carefully moving around the sleeping kitchen servants. Noiselessly, Deirdre unlatched the door and slipped out, Bethan close behind her.

Into the fresh moist air they walked. As they strode, Bethan's heart soared with the song of the morning birds. Deirdre moved quickly, her longer legs pacing over the frosty dirt, a smile germinating on her pale lips.

"Where shall we meet the others?" Bethan asked, halfway through the courtyard.

Deirdre turned bright eyes toward her. "Outside the walls. They'll be gathering under the oak tree. Some will already be there by now."

"Why do you not meet inside the walls? From the little I know of him, Lord Drustan seems a reasonable man and would permit it, wouldn't he? I thought he was a Christian himself," Bethan inquired.

Deirdre raised her eyebrows. "Lord Drustan claims, or I should say, claimed, that he was a Christian, aye. But for the past decade, he has leaned more toward the pagan roots of his British mother than the Christianity of his Roman father. He no longer attends mass nor keeps a priest at Oxfield, except for Bricius, who serves only as his potter."

"So he will not allow you to meet inside the walls," Bethan concluded.

Deirdre shook her head, her curly braid bouncing across her slight shoulders. "No, he would allow it if we asked, I think. His wife holds to her faith in Christ yet, as well. But we *prefer* to meet at the tree."

"Why?" Shivering now, Bethan wondered why the group could not meet in the stables or by a fire in the hall. At least it would be warm there!

Deirdre turned her brown eyes to Bethan. "Because this way we can identify with Him who suffered outside the gate, separating Himself as a sin offering for us. As the Scriptures say, 'Therefore let us go to him outside the camp and bear the reproach he endured.'"

Bethan met the older girl's gaze in silence. This conscious effort to testify to separation by Oxfield's Christians humbled her. How often she had tried to conform as much as possible to her peers in her hunger to belong when really she needed to obey Christ only, honoring him with her loving allegiance! How frequently she had failed!

Deirdre led her toward a small door in the wall that Bethan had never noticed before this morning. "A guard always lets us in and out here. He's on duty patrolling the wall, and I think this gives him something to do in the quiet hours," she explained, smiling at Bethan. "He should be here any moment."

As they waited, Bethan could see a few others coming toward them from across the yard. She recognized some of them from the stableyard dance, others only by having seen them about their daily work. Deirdre greeted them each with a sweet smile and a whispered, "Good morn!" as they gathered around the small door.

They did not have to wait for long. Soon, a portly young guard waddled toward them, his leather armor strapped loosely around his girth. With a friendly hello, he unlocked the door, and the small band of believers hastened under the archway.

Once outside, the group moved quickly through the tall grasses, wet with frosty dew. In the east, the steadily rising sun dyed the horizon with stains of fire opal and garnet, gilded throughout with streaks of gold. *If the earth is the Lord's footstool, then that sunrise is the brilliant strap on his sandal,* Bethan thought. She breathed deeply of the cold air, glad to know that she was united in purpose with those who traveled with her, though she could not call most of them by name.

The potter who led the half-dozen across the fields broke into singing as he walked. One by one, the others joined him, their heartfelt voices rippling over the grasses like wind. Bethan recognized the song, though she did not know it by heart. She had once heard a travelling priest sing it in her village and now hummed along, wishing she had the words memorized and could join in heartily. Beside her, Deirdre harmonized as through the symbols of creation, the followers of Christ worshipped Nature's grand Lord:

> *O splendor of God's glory bright,*
> *O You who bring light from light,*
> *O Light of light, light's Living Spring,*
> *O Day, all days illumining.*
> *O You true Sun, on us Your glance*
> *Let fall in royal radiance,*
> *The Spirit's sanctifying beam*
> *Upon our earthly senses stream.*

Seated on the oak's heavy roots with several others, Calum saw the group approaching while they still had many steps to walk. His usually heavy heart swelled and lifted with delight as he heard the morning hymn wafting across the field, the mouths and hearts of his brothers and sisters engaging in the highest act of creation, the worship of their Father-Creator-Redeemer. Their gaze turned upward and outward, away from themselves, they could not help but have their hearts filled. Calum, of all people, knew this to be truth, though he did not always feel it.

Open your mouth wide, and I will fill it.

He noticed a new person walking among them, arm-in-arm with the Irish girl Deirdre. As the band neared, Calum recognized Bethan, the lately-arrived kitchen servant, her expression eager but a little apprehensive. Quickly, he rose from his seat on the oak's huge roots and went forward to meet her.

"Bethan! You are most welcome," he smiled, taking her hand in greeting.

She returned the smile a bit tentatively. "Deirdre invited me to come."

"I'm glad she did. Our worship is a little less formal than you might be used to; we have no building, no altar except our hearts; but we worship the same God now as we did under the Romans' influence."

The others began to settle themselves, some sitting on the extensive roots of the oak, others spreading cloaks on the ground before seating themselves. Bricius, the potter-priest, stood ready to open their meeting in prayer. Stepping under the wide canopy of the tree, Calum realized afresh that the ancient plant held neither god nor demon but grew in praise to its Creator. Bittersweet thanksgiving rose in his heart, his own hard memories combining with truth.

All is grace…

He spread his brown cloak across the hard ground. "Have a seat, lass. There's plenty of room," he invited Bethan, providing ample space for her to sit without bringing ideas to the heads of any matchmakers around them.

The young woman alighted beside him, smiling at him. He gave her a friendly wink and bowed his head, focusing his concentration on their upcoming Lord's Day celebration. Around him, the presence of other believers upheld him, encouraged him to press on, despite the mounting pressures from many in Logress who had begun to fall away. Even Lord Drustan had turned apostate, allowing and encouraging the old pagan ways to re-root themselves at Oxfield. Yet here, in the dawning light of the Sabbath, believers could rest their souls in Christ, confident that He would uphold them.

My Father, who has given them to me, is greater than all...

Aye, greater than the gods of the druids, who had long held Britain in dark chains and now eagerly anticipated their rise once more. Calum had heard one of them, called the Merlyn, swayed the high king himself.

And no one is able to snatch them out of the Father's hand...

His sister's face surfaced in his imagination, as he had last seen her, many years ago now. The pure countenance of one who had been redeemed and had nothing, no one, to fear.

Not even her murderers. His jaw set in painful memory; his eyes welled with the tears of one who had forgiven yet could not forget. Could not forget the part he had played in her death, that is. *O God, give me a chance to redeem a life for hers,* he silently beseeched his Father as Bricius began to offer thanksgiving aloud.

The sun had fully risen, a golden banner in the sky, when their worship ceased. Though now, three-quarters of a century after the Romans had departed, much of Britain had relaxed into semi-paganism again, most of the population still held Sunday as a quiet, restful day. The assembled group of Christians took their time journeying back to the walls of the stronghold, dividing into pairs and threesomes. Bethan noticed that Deirdre walked along with another woman, a pudgy, middle-aged dairywoman. Not wanting to be a nuisance, she ambled along alone, taking pleasure in the dawning beauty of the ripe meadow.

"What are you thinking of, Bethan?"

She glanced beside her to find Calum striding easily at her side. "Only that I'm glad that I was born in the country and not in the city," she replied, smiling.

"Well, I won't argue with that. Have you ever been to a city?" he asked.

"No, but my papa once traveled to Londinium. He said 'twas so crowded, he could scarcely breathe." Bethan shivered in the cool morning air.

"Sixty thousand people does make for cramped quarters," Calum remarked, smiling. "It may be out of context, but the Scriptures do say, 'In quietness and trust shall be your strength.'"

Feeling a kinship of spirit with this brother in Christ, taking pleasure in the breeze playing through her hair and around her face, Bethan laughed for the first time since she had left home.

His freckled cheeks glowing in the sunlight, Bricius observed the pair walking in front of him. His heart gladdened as he saw their mutual enjoyment of one another's company. *'Tis true, Calum has numbered a dozen winters more than she, but 'tis of no significance. The man deserves a good maid such as this for a wife.* Bricius nodded to himself in satisfaction as he moved slowly toward Oxfield, his arthritic limbs groaning. *'Tis what I prayed for, Lord.*

CHAPTER EIGHT

Deoradhan's keen eyes noticed the return of the little group through the narrow door. Smiling, Deoradhan shook his head and wondered if the band of Christians chose to use that little portal as a vivid reminder to themselves of their preferred way of life. He knew that they met outside the walls and took the communion meal for such a reason. He knew because he himself had once participated in their rituals, though in a different place and time. Once, his empty heart had cried out for the divine to fill it.

With my whole heart I seek you...

Bitterly, he drove his knife deeply into the apple wood and strove to put such thoughts from his mind. He had decided years ago that he would live by his own moral code, that he would stand or fall by his own honest ethics, hand-fashioned like this recorder by himself. The Christian God, the Roman God's code of honor, had failed him, just as the Romans had failed the Britons when they pulled their forces out of the island more than half a century past now. Now only scraps of their memory and culture remained, like a fading sunset.

He is a God for weaklings and tyrants, Deoradhan reaffirmed, satisfying his anger, justifying his rejection. *I have no need for such a God.* With a decisive whittle, he rose, sheathing his knife. It was high time for a conference with the Pendragon, time to make decisions for his own sake and now for Aine as well, whether the king wished it or not.

~ ~ ~

Like most of the kitchen staff, Aine had risen later than usual. The sun stood well above the horizon when she wandered outside, bucket in her bird-like hands. The stream flowed within the stronghold's walls, past the stables where Aine knew Deoradhan often tarried, and she secretly hoped that she might see her sweetheart as well as retrieve the needed water.

He loves me! The thought echoed through her mind over and over, chasing away the fears that she now regarded as childish. *I thought, oh, I thought that I was too worthless for such a man to desire me. But he does! Deoradhan does.* Her breath caught in her throat for joy. Was there any feeling in the world more exhilarating than this, knowing that someone treasured you and thought you precious? Aine shook her head. *Nay! And 'twill fill me.*

A guilty thought stole into her heart: *You do not love him, though, do you?* Shamed, she frowned and slowed her quickened pace. Anxiety clamped onto her shoulders. Aine bit her lip, turning its already pink shade bright peony. *Nay, but I like how he makes me feel. And all I ask is that he cherishes me. I care for nothing else. I only want to be loved,* she reasoned.

Conscience eased, she hurried her pace again, eager to let the hampering chains of guilt fall off completely.

~ ~ ~

In and out, out and in. The bone needle moved surely through the woolen fabric, hemming the edges. Past forty years of age, the woman known as Cook but whose given name was Meghyn could sew any garment put into her hands with unconscious deftness. She could not remember a time when she did not know how to create from fabric, and now she was glad for the occupation. It took her mind off her beloved foster-son.

In all fairness, Meghyn could not believe that the artless Aine meant to ensnare Deoradhan. A girl could not help being so pretty any more than a boy could avoid his attraction to such sweet visual nectar. The good Lord had created the fascination between lads and lasses at the beginning of the world, and He had said 'twas good. Who was Meghyn to argue over that with the Lord, much as she hated losing her boy to another?

But Meghyn's real anxiety grew from another root entirely. If Deoradhan's fondness for Aine had grown as she suspected, would he marry the girl? Would he bind himself to her permanently, seeking to satisfy his restlessness with one who was restless herself?

O Living God, You know all things, even the end from the beginning. Free my dear boy from his past. May he have a hope and a future grounded in You alone.

"Cook?"

Meghyn popped her eyes open. The brown-haired lass from the West Lea stood before her, sewing in hand. A kind-hearted, hard-working girl this one seemed, though time would tell if Meghyn judged rightly.

"May I sit with you?"

She patted the empty spot beside her on the bench. "I'd be glad for the company, Bethan. My thoughts are a bit gloomy right now, which cannot please the Lord. You may be a ray of sunshine sent by Him to clear the clouds from my soul, aye?"

Bethan smiled in response and seated herself. Meghyn saw that she was patching a tunic from the mending pile that always remained full, regardless of how much work the kitchen servants put into it. "You went off to the meeting Bricius holds outside the walls this morning, aye?"

Bethan's eyes rose to Meghyn's face in surprise. "Aye, I did. Deirdre invited me. I hope 'twas no inconvenience—"

Meghyn interrupted quickly to halt the girl's concern. "Nay, nay. Jesus is my Lord as well, Bethan. I was glad to see that you met with the others for worship. 'Tis a good witness to the others not to forsake the assembling of themselves, regardless of who occupies the country." She patted Bethan's hand in sincerity. "I would have been among you this morning, but my ankles swelled."

Bethan examined the woman's propped-up feet. Meghyn heard her suck her breath in quickly when she saw the purpled flesh, bulging with excess fluid. "Cook..." her voice trailed off, concerned.

Meghyn put a hand to the girl's mouth, smiling. "Hush, 'tis nothing serious. I've been doing a bit too much, 'tis all. I propped them up and have sewing enough to last me all afternoon. A body could not ask for more leisure than that."

Bethan seemed somewhat satisfied and settled in, picking up her own needlework. "What are you working on?" she asked.

Meghyn could not keep her lips from turning up. "'Tis a cloak for my Deoradhan. He'll need it this winter as he dashes across all of Logress, bringing messages here and there," she said, using the general name for the Pendragon's acknowledged territory.

Bethan returned the smile. "Your nephew is a busy lad, isn't he?"

"Aye, and a brave one. I brought him up, so I should know."

"You did?"

Meghyn nodded.

"Calum told me Deoradhan went to Gaul for his education, though," Bethan stated, looking confused.

They trod on sticky territory, Meghyn knew, but she gave Bethan an honest answer nonetheless. "Indeed, he did go to Gaul for an education among the learned men there, but he spent the first decade of his life with me. Then he went to Gaul." *Would that he had never gone!*

Bethan nodded. "What happened to his parents, if you don't mind my asking, Cook?"

Meghyn studied her sewing, averting her eyes from the clear gaze of her questioner. "They died," she replied simply, glad when the girl fell into sympathetic silence.

~ ~ ~

"Another trip up north, then?" Lord Drustan raised his thin eyebrows, set above frozen blue eyes gleaming from a leathered face.

Deoradhan stared back at him, his passions animated by the noble's coolness. This time, he would make some headway. "Aye."

The old warlord rubbed his hands together over the fire burning in the hearth. He maintained silence for only a moment, then asked, "And what good do you think that will do you?"

"I don't know. But... I can't just sit here waiting for years! Arthur must give me an answer sometime," Deoradhan growled in frustration. "I've waited long enough for something that should have been mine from birth."

"Listen, Deoradhan. Arthur's hands are tied. He—"

"If his hands are so tied, if he is so powerless, why should he style himself the Pendragon, then?" Deoradhan stopped himself with effort. His words smacked of treason, and both men knew it. He calmed himself before speaking again. "Forgive me. I respect Arthur as a king, as a man, as a friend." The lies came easily. "Which is why I don't understand why he will not establish my rightful claim—"

Drustan put a finger to his mouth to silence Deoradhan as a pair of guards strode down the hall, their boots thumping on the thick stone. When they passed, Drustan answered. "Much as I value your friendship and work, Deoradhan, I will not go against Arthur's policies. The land needs unity right now, not treachery, however small the form. If you need to know the reasons behind the king's delay, why don't you go to him and ask?"

"Ask him?" Deoradhan hesitated. If he asked the king straight out, the Pendragon could refuse him flatly. And Arthur seldom changed his mind once he had given an answer. His commitment to keep his word no matter what had helped to seal his leadership over all of Britain.

"Aye, go to Camelot. I've no need of you for a time. My nephew is due to arrive from Gaul any day now. I'll be much occupied with entertaining him, wild boy that he is." He chuckled, then continued. "I'll have no time for business. Take as long as you need."

"Thank you, m'lord." Deoradhan kissed his liege's smooth knuckles. "I appreciate this, truly."

~ ~ ~

Out of a twilight sleep, between waking and slumbering, Meghyn heard whispering voices. Slowly, her aging mind turned out of dream's confusing paths and into the difficult forest of consciousness. She lay still a moment, listening. After a moment, she distinguished two voices, one a rich birch-like voice—Deoradhan's, she knew—the other, a soprano wren, answering him. *Aine.*

Creeping up as quietly as her bulk and painful ankles allowed, Meghyn tiptoed barefoot across the kitchen toward the entry room, finding her way by long years' experience and the dim burning embers in the fireplace. At the doorway, she wrapped her woolen blanket around her shoulders and listened.

"What do you mean, you're going to Arthur? On the lord's business?" Aine asked, her voice sweetly perplexed.

"No, not the lord's business. My own," came Deoradhan's determined reply.

"But what do you have to do with kings, Deoradhan? You're a servant, like I am."

Silence.

"Aren't you?"

Deoradhan replied hesitantly, his voice pained. "I have known Arthur for many years. I...cannot risk telling you more now, Aine, until I see how this unfolds." Meghyn heard him sigh. "This may be the most important journey of my life. I have lived for its object for long years. I hold it more closely to my heart than anything else."

"Deoradhan, I thought..." Aine trailed off, but Meghyn could finish the thought for her, though she knew that Deoradhan could not begin to guess it.

She thought she was his single treasure, the apple of his eye. Meghyn smiled sympathetically. Surely, Aine had been idolized, but her value in his eyes held weight only momentarily until another god replaced her, another golden calf that Deoradhan hoped would lead him to the Promised Land.

Meghyn peered around the doorway. The main door stood open, silhouetting Deoradhan and Aine.

"Deoradhan, I don't understand," Aine's voice carried the tone of feminine hurt and fretfulness so disliked by men. "I thought—"

Meghyn saw their shadows join as Deoradhan kissed the maid in order to hush her, to stop the questions he did not want to answer.

When they parted, he kept his eyes averted to avoid Aine's beseeching gaze. "Trust me," Meghyn's foster-son stated. "I'll return soon."

"When?" she begged, clinging to his forearms.

He gently freed himself. "I don't know," he said simply and moved into the night, leaving her in the empty doorway.

Moving back to her bed, Meghyn pitied the maid. She knew too well what rejection, however temporary, felt like. Yet, 'twas her concern for Deoradhan that kept her eyes open deep into the night.

Why did he not tell me that he must journey to Camelot? He no longer places his confidence in me. Tears rolled down the sides of Meghyn's cheeks. *So wounded, yet he didn't come to you to be healed, Lord. Now, his heart, 'tis as calloused as his hands. He shuts out my voice. Can he even hear You now?*

From the guard-tower, Calum watched his longtime friend lead his mount toward the gate. He frowned. 'Twas nearly midnight. Only in times of distress would Deoradhan leave with a message at such a late hour. Furrowing his brow, Calum moved from his place at the window.

"Take my place a moment, Seisyll," he instructed his companion.

"Aye, Calum." The young man rose from his stool, yawning. His red hair caught the moonlight as he replaced his commander at the northern window post.

"Put your tiredness behind you now, Seisyll. You're on duty," Calum reminded the subordinate, his voice holding his trademark quiet authority. The young man straightened with alertness. Satisfied, Calum moved toward the stone stair leading down to the yard. He found his footing as well as any night creature, despite the lack of light, and soon stood waiting for Deoradhan's approach at the foot of the tower. The night lay calm around him, the chilly autumn breeze striking his scarred cheeks, the owls' hoots intermitting with the advancing clip-clop of Deoradhan's horse.

He stepped out of the heavy shadows into the torchlight. "Deoradhan, is something wrong?"

The younger man's face hardened in unnatural determination. "Aye." He paused, stroking the gelding's dappled neck. "But I go to right it."

Silently, Calum studied his friend, his eyes searching the other man's countenance for signs of goodness. Never before had he failed to find that glimmer of the Image, yet tonight he was hard-pressed to see it in Deoradhan's scowling face. Fear plucked at Calum's heart.

"Deoradhan, do not do anything you will regret," Calum murmured, clasping his friend's forearm in fidelity.

Deoradhan's jaw set. "I won't. I never do anything. That's the cause of my trouble." He mounted his horse. "Don't worry about me, Calum. I'll return or you'll hear from me within a fortnight, if all goes well."

"'If all goes well?' What are—?" Calum's concern increased.

"Don't fear for me," Deoradhan directed, smiling a little. "What do I have to lose? My life is worthless here anyway. A stale perpetual survival. Farewell."

"Where are you—?" Calum's inquiry died as Deoradhan heeled his mount forward toward the opening gate. Muscular arms limp by his sides, Calum watched his friend disappear into the darkness.

God, I am afraid for him. Watch over him; protect him for my sake and

Your own as his legitimate Father. Answer him before he calls, I pray.

Turning, the commander of Oxfield's guards meandered up the tower stair. *O You who save and redeem, not one of those whom Your Father has given You will You lose.*

CHAPTER NINE

"Bethan, someone is here to see you."

From her crouching position on the stone floor, Bethan twisted to look up at Haylee but continued to scrub the flags. "Who?" she asked, frankly curious. In the nearly two months since she had come to Oxfield, no one had come to visit her, and she didn't expect anyone.

Haylee set her heavy basket down. "A miller, I think. He said to tell you that Winfred had news for you. I met him on my way back with these apples. They're the last of this fall's crop. I thought the storm might knock them down." She pushed back the damp shawl covering her head and dried her moist face on her apron.

Bethan put her rag back into the soapy water. "Winfred?" she said aloud. "What news could he bring for me?"

"He didn't say." Haylee shrugged. "Hurry back, though. I need your help with coring these apples." Her golden hair wisped around her face, accentuating the younger, frailer girl's weariness.

Bethan nodded and rose to her feet, moving toward the door. "I'll be back as soon as I can," she promised. "Wait to do the apples 'til I return, Haylee. I think Cook has some sewing for you to work on." Bethan knew the needlework would give the younger girl a needed respite from the often-backbreaking kitchen chores.

At the entryway, Bethan paused to splash her sweaty face and arms with cool water from the bucket. Her skin felt relieved, but her mind burned. What news did Winfred bring? She feared 'twould be no good news to travel so far from home to Oxfield.

God is our refuge and strength, a very present help in trouble. Therefore we will not fear... At times like this, Bethan felt immensely grateful that her father had repeated his own memorized Scripture to her and her sisters as they went about their day and before they slept at night, even though her mother objected to it. She moved toward the door, willing herself to lift the latch and step outside into the cold October drizzle.

She saw Winfred standing under the ledge of the dairy roof, his knit cap snug around his fair-haired head. A descendent of the Saxons who had invaded Britain half a century ago, Winfred's heavy-boned frame towered a head above any native Briton, drawing the curious eyes of other servants. After a quick stare, however, they hastened on with their work, eager to escape from the pending storm.

Bethan ran toward the dairy and arrived breathless. She offered Winfred a hopeful smile. "Winfred! How is your family? What news from the West Lea?"

Winfred cast a nervous glance down at her, playing with the ends of his red-gold beard with the forefinger and thumb of his right hand. "My family is all well, but I fear the same cannot be said of yours, Bethan."

Her heart choked her. "What has happened, Winfred?" She knew their close neighbor would never have worried her with minute calamities. This must be something very bad, indeed.

He paused, as if to give her a moment to prepare herself. "Your mama is very sick with the fever, Bethan. A woman from the village has been nursing her, but now..." He sought for the right words before going on.

Bethan felt anxiety goad her. "Now...?" she pressed, catching his forearm in her hand. "Now, what, Winfred?"

His eyes, blue as the ocean his ancestors sailed over, grew soft with compassion. "Before I left for Oxfield, the woman asked if I would bring you home when I came to Oxfield with my payment for Lord Drustan."

"But what does Papa say, Winfred? Does he want me to come home?" Without warning, happiness, not dread, sprouted within Bethan. *I'm going home!*

Winfred looked puzzled. "Your papa left to work on some land north for the harvest. I thought you knew that."

Bethan's breath shriveled. "Nay, I didn't," she whispered, swallowing hard. "When do you leave for the West Lea, Winfred?"

"I have to speak of my contract terms with the lord first." He turned his eyes toward the sky, darkening and building into heavy clouds by the moment. "And I cannot leave until after the storm passes over. I came on foot."

Bethan nodded. "So perhaps in two days or so?"

"Aye," Winfred assented. "If Thor agrees," he added, referring to the one who Bethan knew to be the Saxon god of thunder.

"Alright. You know where to find me, aye? In the kitchen."

"Aye."

~ ~ ~

"Ready, lad?" Calum lifted the enormous leather bag with both hands and waited for the young guard to prepare himself. Moments earlier, Calum had filled the sack a quarter full of sand before adding the rusted chain mail tunic. He'd enlisted Marcus to help him with cleaning today, knowing that the exercise would build the dark-haired young man's strength. True, Marcus, the grandson of a Roman cavalry officer who had remained when the legions departed, already contained a sinewy power in his lanky arms, but Calum saw potential in this lad for leadership and wanted him to strive for excellence.

Six feet of the weapon house floor spread out between the two men. Marcus braced himself, holding his arms out, hands stretched widely. "Ready," he said, eyes focused on the sack.

With an easy movement, Calum tossed the sack to his assistant. Marcus caught it, staggering a little. "Heavy," he commented.

"Aye, 'tis," Calum smiled, knowing the sack weighed nearly half as much as the youth did. "But the sand will get the rust off that mail. 'Twill be good as ever. Throw it back," he instructed. The young man obeyed, heaving the bag across the short expanse.

"Good," Calum praised. Marcus smiled back, pleased, and readied himself again.

The boy's always on his guard, always prepared. It does my heart good to see that in him, for he'll need it if he's ever to take over for me. Marcus did not yet know of Calum's plan; none did, save the potter Bricius. *No one else need know for a while.* He would bide his time, waiting until an acceptable day arrived, when he would be at liberty to pursue his heart's desire. For now, he would work while he waited, prompt in doing what came to his hand to accomplish, whether 'twas cleaning rusty mail or sweeping out the guardhouse.

"Step back a pace or so, Marcus," he said aloud. "This is too easy for you. We'll stretch your abilities today."

~ ~ ~

Kick. Throw. Dip and smooth. Throw. Kick. The repetitive motions harmonized with the potter's muttered song:

"Be thou solely chief love of my heart,

Let there be none other, O High King of heaven."

And there was none other. At one time, he could not have sung the hymn with an easy conscience. But now Bricius sang with a heart unfettered by possession of people or things or knowledge. A heart at liberty to love as infinitely as any mortal could and yet never be owned by his passions.

Blessed are the poor in spirit, for theirs is the kingdom of heaven... And what was that kingdom but Love eternally, pulsing from the Creator's heart through the Redeemer's cross, paving the way to the throne of grace? How long Bricius had taken to learn such an easy lesson! How many never learned that the way to the Father's knee ran through His heart, not through His head!

The potter continued his movements, now as natural to him as any instinct, barely noticing when a shadow fell across the floor from the doorway.

"I'll be with you in a moment," he said, hands adding the last smoothing strokes to the pot. 'Twas a fine one, this, with thin walls and a slim neck, like the ones his great-grandfather had made in the days of the Romans. With a satisfied sigh, Bricius rose from his pottery wheel and turned to greet his guest.

To his surprise, Lady Tarian waited just inside the doorway. "Good afternoon, Bricius," she said, and the potter thought he heard a note of fearful courage in this woman's voice.

"Good afternoon, my lady." Bricius bowed and then waited for her to explain the reason for her visit.

Instead, she moved gracefully a few feet inside the workshop, her eyes intent on the pot on which he had been working. "You do fine work, Bricius. This is a lovely."

"Thank you, my lady. I'm honored that you think it so."

The noblewoman turned from the pottery wheel and met Bricius' gaze. "I have heard that you conduct mass outdoors each Sunday."

"Aye, my lady, I lead the worship."

"And what qualifies you to do this? Are you trained as a priest?"

Bricius smiled. "I lived as a monk for many years, my lady, and studied the Scriptures and the writings of holy men." He paused before gently continuing. "But as for what qualifies me, 'tis what qualifies any man or woman for the work to which he has been called. As the seer declares, 'I was no prophet, nor a prophet's son, but I was a herdsman and a dresser of sycamore figs. But the LORD took me from following the flock.'"

The young woman remained silent momentarily, then turned her imperturbable eyes to the potter. "I would like to join you at your mass," she stated. "This Sunday."

"We would be glad to have you, my lady. We meet at the ancient oak at the meadow's edge. I could have someone lead you."

"That will be unnecessary, thank you. At dawn?"

"Aye."

Bricius watched as the lady moved to the door. At the archway, she turned. "Thank you, Bricius. I shall look forward to this." With that, she stepped out, leaving the potter to scratch his beard in amazement.

CHAPTER TEN

Oxfield

Deoradhan's every sense informed him of the tiniest nuances in his surroundings. Around him, the once-verdant oaks and elms had shed their leaves, baring shivering trunks to the deep autumn wind, unmasking the forest. Alasdair's hooves moved with a muffled thud across the smooth, well-worn path, their sound combining with that of insects and soft bird calls. Deoradhan sniffed, and the scent of past winters' decaying leaves filled his nostrils, combining with the familiar smell of horse sweat and warm leather. He could taste the pungent odors with his tongue, nearly. His bridle reins fit smoothly, securely in his fingers, and he moved in unison with his horse as they traveled down the path.

He felt at home here in the woodland, as at peace as he had ever felt. Here, no mocking voice incorrectly called him the illegitimate spawn of the high king, intending to insult the Pendragon but injuring Deoradhan deeply. Or rather inflaming the wound that already cankered in his heart.

I believed their lies. And then his. Hardly blinking, letting Alasdair guide him down the shadowy path, Deoradhan permitted his thoughts to wander unrestrained into the forest of his past...

The little boy felt afraid. The bright torches shining from the wall combined with the rich tapestries and heavy laughter, overwhelming him like a towering ocean wave. He wanted his papa to come and reach for him, pick him up in his great, strong arms and protect him. Mama should come, too, with her loving hands and laughing smile. Why had Mama given him away to papa's warrior? The lad had cried for her to hold him, but she hadn't listened to him! Fire had burned all around him. Fire was a friend, wasn't it? To keep him warm and safe from wild beasts?

Where was he? Who were these frightful Big People, wearing strange clothing and speaking stranger words? At least, Papa's warrior stayed with him, gripping him in his mighty arms. With all the strength in his chubby fingers, the child clung to the man's forearms.

But wait. The warrior carried him forward toward a great chair, carved with the heads of animals and covered with furs. A man sat in the chair. He was a young Big Person, not as old as Papa, with a beard that matched his yellow hair. The man wore gold things on his head and fingers and around his neck.

"Come here, little one," he spoke and smiled. When the toddler saw the smile, he didn't feel as afraid; the man seemed so kind and gentle. Like Papa.

Deoradhan shook his head defiantly. He would allow no tender thoughts to cloud his attitude toward Arthur. Purposely, he turned to another, more painful memory.

He had always disliked the boy. Now he had a reason and a good one at that. In disbelief, Deoradhan stared at his wrestling partner Modred and wondered if the lad had made his comment only to distract him from glorying in his victory minutes earlier.

"What did you say?" Deoradhan barely forced the question out of his eleven-year-old lips.

His swarthy countenance patient, Modred repeated his remark. "I said that you inherited our father's brute strength. I fear I rather take after my mother in that respect." With a graceful shrug, the slim youth, older than Deoradhan by three or four years, turned and began the stroll from the training grounds back to the fortress walls.

In two bounds, Deoradhan sprang in front of his companion. "Stay," he commanded, grasping Modred's slender shoulders. "What do you mean by 'our father'? Of whom do you speak?" His heart pounded in his chest as with vigorous exercise. "*Your father is unknown. You grew up with your half-brothers in Orkney; you came here to train under your uncle, the high king.*"

Modred shook his shoulders free. "*Others may be ignorant of who fathered me, but I am not. And he is your father as well.*"

At Deoradhan's look of complete confusion, Modred smiled, showing beautiful white teeth. "*Arthur, you fool. I thought you knew.*"

Deoradhan could barely breathe. "*Arthur? Are you sure?*" *he finally choked out.*

Modred sneered. "*Am I sure? Is the sky blue?*" *He resumed walking, and Deoradhan woodenly matched Modred's elegant prowl.* "*My mother, Lady Morgana, told me this. She is a druidess and is never wrong.*"

"*She knows about me, too?*" *Deoradhan could barely believe it. He had never known who he was or whither he had come, except for a few shadowy memories that elusively haunted him. Infrequently, the lad had dreamed of finding his parents to be high-born British Romans or even Irish royalty, who had perhaps set him afloat across the Irish sea to save him from some horrible doom. Like Moses, of whom the Christian priests spoke. Never had he really believed 'twas the high king who had sired him, albeit illegitimately. Pride and shame coursed through every fiber of his lanky body.*

"*No, my mother only told me about myself. I assumed that of you. Think about it, though: your story fits the mold.*" *Modred directed his serene blue eyes to Deoradhan's troubled ones and waited for a response.*

An unknown birth. An upbringing at court fit for a prince's son. The tutoring, the training, the numerous gifts from Arthur. So much that had gone unexplained now made sense.

Deoradhan nodded. "*I believe you,*" *he said to the young man whom he knew to be his half-brother.* "*I must go speak with the king.*"

And he had spoken with Pendragon. Deoradhan gritted his teeth, remembering. Arthur had denied the charge, gently, as a man might break the neck of a favorite bird.

The boy charged into the Great Hall, his chest nearly exploding with conflicting emotions, too weighty for such a youngster to understand or name. His bare feet slapped the brown stones, stinging, as he ran toward the dais, the raised area where the king's throne resided. The cavernous room was vacant, though, except for the few feathery residents in the heavy-beamed ceiling, who greeted Deoradhan with surprised twitters and flutters.

Seeing no one, he slowed, his enthusiasm draining. The boy dropped onto one of the hall's long benches to catch his breath. He could hear female singing from outside, the sweet sounds wafting through the windows, mingling with the cool spring breeze. Without looking, he knew the impulsive young queen must have taken her women outside to sew. He could picture them dappling the grass with their skirts of imported dyed fabric, their laughing smiles glowing beneath locks of chestnut, flax, and truffle.

He swung his legs slowly back and forth. His feet just brushed the floor; at eleven, he could not boast of tall stature like the fierce warrior Gawaine, whom he admired from afar, barely daring to greet the man when he passed him in the yard. Deoradhan's frame promised a more moderate height with a sturdiness that would have spoken of Saxon ancestry, were it not for his rich auburn hair, the color of damp autumn leaves, and his Celtic blue-green eyes. In a way, he felt glad for these obvious traits, for they showed him to be a true Briton, whose roots grew from deep within this loamy soil, not a transplant from other lands. How deep, even he did not know at the time.

Deoradhan breathed the fresh air appreciatively, letting his gaze wander over the long empty tables and benches that filled the hall, toward the dais, until at last they rested with surprise on a lone figure standing silently looking out one of the windows. The sunlight reflected off the man's circlet and long, wavy hair, illuminating the gold of them both before it washed over his straight shoulders and fell to the floor, puddling around his leather-encased feet. He leaned upon a crutch; Deoradhan knew this supported the leg he had injured in the last eastern skirmish against the persistent Saxons.

Heart in his throat, Deoradhan approached the king. At that young age, he did not know yet how to make small-talk before broaching a turbulent subject. Hesitant and eager at once, the boy waited until he was within arm's reach of the dignified man. Then in his childish soprano, he whispered. "Father?"

Arthur froze. He turned slowly, and Deoradhan felt alarm at the relief and confusion written across the king's kind face. Finally, the older man spoke.

"No, I'm not your father, lad."

Hurt ripped into Deoradhan's chest like a northern dagger. "But Modred—"

The king cut in gently. "Don't always listen to Modred. His words are elegant, but like a sinuous adder. he is not to be trusted."

"But—"

Arthur took Deoradhan's small hand in his, and Deoradhan felt how callused and powerful the king's fingers were, how well they must wield the battle-axe and sword. With a hand to the lad's shoulder, Arthur guided him to sit beside him on one of the long benches of the hall. He was silent for long moments, then turned to the vulnerable Deoradhan, smiling compassionately. "You are an orphan, Deoradhan. Your father was one of my best companions, a valiant man. But he is dead now, and so is your mother." He sighed. "I can honor your father most through caring for you as I would my own."

Deoradhan nodded slowly, feeling a bit bereft but relieved as well. Honorable though 'twould be to have the high king for a sire, no boy wished to be illegitimate, without inheriting his father's name or the respect of his fellow countrymen. He opened his mouth to ask the king more about his parents, but Arthur laid a hand on Deoradhan's shoulder.

"Sometimes 'tis best to let the past lie quietly, lad," he stated in his soft, steady voice. "See if you can't get in some more practicing with the sword before the sun sets."

And he had secured more practicing with his sword, and with his spear, arrows, and in wrestling as well. Now, more than eight years after that conversation, Deoradhan could feel his own strength as he rode through the wood. He was a warrior, truly, but without a liege-lord, just as he was a prince without a kingdom to call his own. A scholar as well, thanks to the education Arthur had provided both at his own court and in Gaul. Deoradhan wryly smiled, thinking of how eagerly the king had sent him away to study once Deoradhan learned the truth.

Like an unexpected summer rainstorm, the stranger cantered through the

Pendragon's gates at sundown. He gave his horse, a heavy-boned mare lathered with sweat, to a stableboy's care and moved up the stone steps of the hall with surety of purpose written across his countenance. His clothes showed the dust of travel but were sewn finely. Over his tunic, he wore a polished coat of well-cared-for mail, and an ornamental belt held a well-forged sword to his waist.

Deoradhan and two other boys had been playing a game with knucklebones on the steps of the hall when the stranger's footsteps sounded on the stones. They had heard him ride up but had not paid attention. Many warriors came and went frequently through the gates of Camelot. Only when the newcomer's path to the door disturbed their game did the boys notice his presence.

"Who is that?" Percivale, a scrawny lad of twelve, wondered aloud as the man strode up the steps toward the hall doors. "He's a champion for sure. Look at his belt."

"A gift from his liege for valor, 'tis certain," Alwyn remarked with confidence, his serious brown eyes trained on the stranger's back as the man spoke with the guards at the door.

Deoradhan remained quiet. The warrior seemed familiar to him somehow, like someone he had met in a dream or the dream of a dream. As the guards permitted the man to enter the hall, Deoradhan rose to his feet.

"Where are you going? The game's not finished," Percivale said.

"I want to know who that man is," Deoradhan answered, clambering up the steps on his skinny thirteen-year-old legs.

Alwyn leapt to his feet, nimble as a fay. "I'm coming, too."

"Nobody wants to finish the game?" Percivale asked, disappointment in his pallid face. When neither Deoradhan nor Alwyn sat back down, Percivale stood. "Alright. I may as well come, too. Who knows, the stranger might have a good story to tell."

Deoradhan and Alywn smiled at him and ran up the steps, into the hall, the knucklebones forgotten. The helmeted guards ignored the boys, used to their tireless activity, knowing that their innocent exuberance delighted the childless high king. Indeed, Deoradhan and his fellows were welcome to roam wherever they wished, learning the ways of noble conduct from interaction with the lords and ladies who stopped in Britain's principal citadel.

The evening wall torches did not burn yet. With eyes accustomed to the brilliant afternoon sunlight, Deoradhan could barely discern the figure of the warrior standing before the king's throne. He led the other two boys toward the front of the hall, more composed in Arthur's presence but feeling curiosity prod him toward unusual boldness. Deoradhan moved around the stranger and knelt at the king's feet. Immediately, he felt an affectionate hand rest upon his shoulder and glanced up to see the high king smiling at him. He grinned back, and then they both turned their attention to the sober warrior before them.

"You say you've come from Ireland," Arthur said.

"Aye. I served the king there for ten years. But my heart has longed to come back to this island. Surely you can tell by my speech that I am no native to Ireland."

"Indeed," Arthur paused and leaned forward. Deoradhan saw interest in the king's keen blue eyes. "Your speech tells of a northern birth, rather. Perhaps in Lothian."

The stranger met the king's eyes without flinching. "My lord has guessed it. Only Pict blood flowed through my mother's veins (may the gods keep her). My father relocated to Lothian from Gore during the Saxon invasions."

"What brought you to Ireland, the home of your enemies?"

"Many things. Let it suffice to say, I had fulfilled a duty from which there could be no return to Lothian." The man gazed into the Pendragon's eyes. "Surely, my lord, you know my countenance. This is not the first time I have stood in your presence. A decade ago, I brought a young child here, a princely refugee, for your protection."

Deoradhan felt the hand on his shoulder tense and then grip him. Startled, the boy looked up. The color drained out of Arthur's sun-browned cheeks. "Boys," he finally said, half in a whisper, "leave us."

Deoradhan rose to his feet, trained to obey yet disturbed at the king's agitation. At his movement, the stranger glanced down at him. Sudden interest rose like sunlight across the man's creased face. "Who—?" he began.

"You will be silent!" Arthur interrupted. "Boys, leave us. Now!"

At the king's urgent tone, the three lads scrambled from the hall, their bare feet thudding on the stones. Alwyn led the way into the corridor, followed by Percivale. Deoradhan moved last. He had seen the curious expression on the warrior's face; it appeared only when the man looked at him. Why?

The double doors shut behind the three friends.

"What shall we do now?" said Percivale.

"Let's head out to the stables," Alwyn suggested after a moment. Immediately, he raced down the corridor toward the north side of the fortress.

"Are you coming, Deoradhan?" Percivale called to the boy who remained by the Hall door.

Deoradhan didn't answer. After a moment, Percivale shrugged and followed Alwyn.

Alone, Deoradhan turned toward the crack in the Hall doors, his ear alert to the conversation developing within.

"Surely, that boy possesses the face and eyes of Lord Eion. You cannot deny 'tis he," the stranger's voice said.

Deoradhan heard a heavy sigh. "Aye, 'tis he, the one once called Padruig. I have given him another name now, for another life: Deoradhan."

"Deoradhan. 'Exile.'" A pause. "Why did you keep him here and not send him away to the monks, as you said you would? Are you going to use him as a pawn?"

"As a pawn? Never!"

"What then?"

"I don't know." The king's voice sounded vulnerable to Deoradhan's overwhelmed ears.

After a moment, "What are you going to do with him?"

Deoradhan heard Arthur jump to his feet. "What business is it of yours? You brought him here ten years ago, as your lady charged you. After that, what does it matter to you what I do with an orphan lad?"

"'Tis the son of a Pict chieftain—a king, if you will—you have here. And you know as well as I that he is no orphan. His mother yet lives. As for why I care, my loyalty to my former lord and now to his son should earn your trust, not your anger."

As if the situation had happened a moment ago, Deoradhan saw his thirteen-year-old self fleeing down the corridor, mindless of the astonished guards in his path. Innumerable thoughts filled his mind, shattering the innocent simplicity of his boyhood.

'Twas the day I grew up. The day I found that my hero was a sordid man, indeed, his hands full of blood.

Deoradhan gritted his teeth, his face an anguished stone. *My father's blood.*

CHAPTER ELEVEN

"Winfred, I must have an answer." Bethan surprised herself at her firm tone, but her patience wore thin. "When can we leave for the village?"

The miller from back home continued to tear little pieces from his loaf, tossing them to the sparrows hopping around his feet. He didn't answer her.

"When can we leave?" Bethan repeated. "Tomorrow? The next day? Winfred-"

"Lass," Winfred interrupted, "Lord Drustan has not seen me yet. When he does, and we sort out our contract, I'll let you know."

"How long will that take? Two days? A week?"

He shrugged. "I don't know, Bethan. I don't have an answer. The lord's a busy man."

Bethan felt panic rise within her at her neighbor's nonchalance. "But, Winfred, my family needs me! You said that my mama lies very sick. Who knows what has happened to her in the short time since you've left the village? And what of my sister Enid?"

Winfred looked back at her, lips pressed tightly together, arms folded across his chest. Bethan had never felt so friendless, helpless. Her former neighbor had determined to sort out his own business before giving any mind to hers. She stared into his closed face, realizing that she was truly on her own.

"Thank you for bringing me the news," Bethan whispered. She turned and marched back across the courtyard, her feet feeling the cold, packed earth beneath them. She little expected the miller to call out to her, and so she knew no disappointment when he maintained his silence. After a few steps, Bethan used the adjustment of her shawl to ascertain the man's state. He had already moved from the stone wall; she could see his retreating square back ambling toward the manor's main hall.

Hopelessness paralyzed her limbs. Mama, dear as life-blood to her, lay dying with Papa who-knew-where, and Bethan could do nothing to help. She sank to the ground by the wall, cross-legged, arms limp in her lap, head bowed.

What am I to do, Lord God? Why did you have Winfred bring me this message if I can do nothing? What about Enid? Please help them, Lord. Go in my stead, then, because I am helpless!

Her mind numb with sorrow, her heart sick, Bethan began to cry, indifferent to the curious passersby or to the scolding which Cook surely would give her upon her delayed return.

Have mercy on me, O Lord ...

Something brushed against her knees. Slowly pulling out of her mental turmoil, Bethan heard a familiar voice say, "Oh, lass. I'm sorry. I didn't see you there."

Two boots planted themselves before her, worn and caked with mud but well-oiled. Her eyes rose to the sturdy long legs, clad in gray and wrapped with leather thongs, then climbed up to the heavy brown tunic and woolen cloak. Pushing back the messy hair around her face, Bethan saw Calum standing before her.

Embarrassment crept over her, and she averted her eyes but not quickly enough. The guard had already glimpsed the tears. Bethan felt awkward but strangely solaced as the man crouched down before her. She kept her eyes on the ground and waited for him to speak, wondering what he thought of a girl who wept openly, yet comforted by his protective presence. He smelled like horses and wet wool and sweat, not an unpleasant scent to the loving heart.

"What's wrong, lass?"

Bethan found her tongue disabled. Feeling slightly stupid, she shook her head through more tears.

"Come now, what is it?" Calum prodded. "Did Cook speak harshly to you?"

She shook her head harder.

Calum paused. "Was it another maid, then? I know 'tis hard to fit in as a newcomer-"

"It's not that," Bethan interrupted. At Calum's puzzled look, she forced it out. "My mama is very ill, and I cannot go to her. And I don't know what to do."

Calum nodded, concern teeming in his eyes. "How do you know she's sick?" he asked.

Bethan wiped her eyes on her dress. "The miller from our village came and told me. But he won't bring me until he finishes his business with Lord Drustan." Her eyes felt scratchy from rubbing them on the rough fabric.

The man stayed silent, his gaze to the ground now. Bethan wondered what moved in his mind. Finally, he spoke, smiling. "I think I can bring you home, if you would like. I have to speak with Lord Drustan first, but it should be alright."

She stared at him, astounded. "Do you mean it?" she breathed. *Surely, God sent him as an answer to my prayer.*

"I cannot promise it, but I think 'twill be alright," he affirmed, standing up and offering her a hand.

"Calum, my family and I would be so grateful to you," Bethan said, rising.

He smiled and shook his head. "It will bring me pleasure, Bethan, to know that I can help. I'll talk to the lord right now, if he has time, and will see you again before nightfall."

Bethan nodded and watched him move away. At the thought of his kindness, her heart warmed toward his in friendship.

Thank you, Lord. She moved toward the kitchens, determined to work more strenuously for her long absence.

~ ~ ~

"Ah, Calum, my son." The gangly-limbed potter wiped his clay-caked hands on a damp cloth and rose from his wheel.

Thus welcomed, Calum ducked under the low doorway and into the pottery shed. Cool moisture floated in the air here, and the young guard threw a glance of concern at his friend and mentor. "'Tis cold in here, Bricius. Too cold for your aged knees and hands."

Bricius shrugged. "'Tis my work, Calum. Besides, 'tis very nice in the summertime."

Calum bit his tongue to avoid reminding his friend that 'twas well past the solstice. Instead, he picked up a damp rag and began to clean the soiled table, saying, "It looks like I may be headed for a journey soon."

Bricius stopped his own tidying up. "Aye? Where to, lad?"

Calum hesitated. He knew how Bricius would take his offer to Bethan: as a token of romantic interest. Nevertheless, he plunged forward, knowing 'twould be told sometime to the old man and that 'twould be better coming from him. "Toward the West Lea."

Bricius cocked his head, fingers wandering into his beard, mixing the hair with the clay on his hands as he thought. "The West Lea?" he questioned. "What brings you there, Calum?"

Calum met the man's curious gaze. "I'm helping a friend."

Bricius stayed quiet for a moment. "Isn't that young kitchen girl from that part of the country? The one who came to mass and sat on your cloak?"

"Bethan. Yes, she comes from that village." Calum paused, then guilt drove him to tell the whole truth. "In truth, I go with her."

"With her?"

"Aye."

"Alone?"

"Aye. No one else can bring her. No one else has my flexibility at Oxfield. And her mother is sick." When the potter didn't respond, Calum offered, "You think this is unwise, Bricius?"

Bricius smiled. "You know your own Master, lad. What did He say to you? Did you ask Him?"

"He told me to go with her." Indeed, when he bowed his head before Bethan, he had felt that knowing that had become familiar to him.

I have set the LORD always before me; because he is at my right hand, I shall not be shaken ...

Bricius nodded. "When will you return?"

Calum breathed more easily. "I'm not sure. I must speak with Lord Drustan and see how long I can be spared. I've been working with Marcus, and this would be a good opportunity for him to stretch his legs a bit. Maybe a week or two."

"You'll miss Samhain at Oxfield. I wish I could be so favored," said Bricius.

Calum felt his muscles grow rigid with a fear he thought he had overcome. He swallowed. "Yes, that will be the blessing of this journey."

"Among other blessings," commented the potter.

Calum's brows furrowed. "What do you mean?"

Bricius smiled. "Only that I hope to see you return with not just a servant girl on your horse but a bride-to-be."

Here we go again. Calum stared into his friend's eyes. "I've told you a hundred times over, Bricius. I do not want that life. I must be God's only."

"Marriage wasn't created to rob God, lad, but to give Him more of ourselves through others, to make ourselves more fit for His purposes through love." Bricius paused. "I married, Calum."

"Aye, I know that." The silence waited to be broken. "I must go. 'Twill be dark soon, and I promised Bethan an answer."

"Go then, lad." Bricius followed the younger man to the doorway. Outside, dusk began to coat the buildings and walls with a gray film. Without hesitation, the potter clasped his friend to himself. "Grace and peace to you, Calum."

Calum returned the embrace fervently. "Grace and peace," he replied and moved into the autumn twilight, his spirit perplexed. *I cannot be attracted to this girl. And yet... O God, help me to rest in You.*

May Bricius understand why I cannot do as others may. Why I owe so much to You. I must atone. I must atone.

~ ~ ~

Out-and-in. Out-and-in. Tarian's hands guided the weft with skill that could come only from many years of practice. This loom spanned only a few feet, large enough to make a tunic or cape, but nothing vast like a bed covering. Now, a piece of deep red cloth formed under her fingers.

The noblewoman smiled. 'Twas with a sense of accomplishment that she completed each project, a welcome feeling in such an out-of-the-way place as Oxfield. The finished fabric would suit her husband's tastes well and would keep him warm during any winter campaigns.

And thinking of me alone.

Like a guest that tarried beyond his welcome, a fair-skinned face adorned with large eyes the color of the sea rose within Tarian's thoughts, but she shook off the image. She was resolved to believe Drustan this time; he had said the girl had only stepped into his tent without invitation. Yet why had his clothing smelled like fresh lavender and why had his lips held the lingering taste of mint when he kissed her that day? Tarian had only nineteen years in her hand but knew that men did not perfume themselves nor freshen their breath for one another when on the battlefield. And she knew also the satisfied expression of a camp follower who had just been paid for her services.

You should never have visited the camp that day. Then you would not harbor these suspicions, Tarian. She sighed and began to put away her weaving for the day.

The door squealed open behind her, but she felt no alarm. She knew that Drustan must have entered; he never knocked. Sure enough, she soon felt his beard as he leaned around her to kiss her cheek.

"How are the foals?" she asked.

"Coming on fine. The little bay one surprised me. He's the perkiest of the three now," said Drustan. "My nephew will delight in them when he arrives. He's fond of good horseflesh."

Tarian raised her eyebrows. *And other flesh as well, from what I hear.* Aloud, she said, "And when is he to arrive, Drustan? Has he sent word?"

Drustan shrugged. "Aye, but no specifics. Could be tonight, tomorrow, next week. Surely before Samhain," he added with a little smirk that turned the corners of his fish-like lips upward.

Tarian could not restrain herself. "Drustan, must we sponsor that feast again this year?" She kept her eyes averted, barely breathing as she waited for his reply.

The lord let out a frustrated sigh. "Now what is the problem with the feast? Everyone enjoyed it last year. Even you liked the bard's singing. Indeed," he smiled, "I grew quite jealous when you consented to dance with him afterward."

Tarian ignored his teasing, meant, she knew, to distract her, and made a last attempt to convince him. "The old druids will be back again and—"

"And what?" His tone told her that he had heard enough. "Let the people worship their own gods in their own way. What does it matter to you the name they give the divine?"

"It matters to me that you seem to encourage their wildness," she responded, her anger sparked by his indifference. "Don't you fear God?"

"Ah! Woman, enough!" He slammed his hands against the bedframe. "I little thought that my second wife would be a cursed nun! Stay out of it! It's none of your business, I tell you!"

Tarian stood shocked into silence. He had never burst out at her like this. For a moment, it almost seemed that another shot those words from his lips and twisted his face into a gross convulsion of disgust at her.

After a moment, Drustan composed himself, smoothing his

features with effort. "Now, I am going down to the evening meal. Would you care to join me?"

Tarian shook her head, blinking back the hated tears that forced their way to her eyes. Why did he have such power over her feelings?

"Very well. Good night, then." Drustan raised her hand and kissed it, a bit roughly, and exited with no more ado.

The room settled into silence, broken only by the squeaking of some mice behind the bed. Tarian numbly lowered herself to a chair, mindless that the room darkened and cooled quickly in the autumn twilight. Never had she felt so alone.

O God, help me. Her soul cried out, agonized by the spiritual loneliness that life with her husband had brought. *I cannot go on. I cannot go on.*

After long moments, she rose and made her way to the window through the dimness, her fine skirts dragging across the stones. She gazed out toward the darkening horizon, hurt pulsing through her spirit, unable to think. Unintentionally, she let her eyes drift toward the rooftops nearby. On one of them, a sparrow sat by himself, still and quiet, silhouetted by the residue of the sunset.

Like a lonely sparrow on the housetop... Is this what You see when you look at my soul, O Lord? All the brightness stripped out of me. Nineteen, with my best years behind me, the long dusk of my life before me.

Heavy tears slid from under her lashes as Tarian gazed out on the fading world.

CHAPTER TWELVE

"I don't know how long I'll be gone," Bethan told Cook the next morning. It had dawned bright and crisp, the sky a sheet of deep blue, and Bethan anticipated her journey with excitement tinged with biting concern over her mama. God had provided a protector for her journey, however, and that answer to her prayer bolstered Bethan's confidence.

Be of good courage...

Cook nodded. "Take as long as you need, lass. Your place will be waiting for you when you return." She took a long look at Bethan and then gathered her into her heavy arms. "I'm glad you're going with Calum, lassie. He'll not only guard but be a good companion for your journey as well. Don't be afraid to take his help, lass; he loves to give it."

"Aye, I won't," Bethan promised. She hesitated. "Pray for me, Cook. In truth, I don't know what lies ahead of me at home, and I'm afraid. My mother clings to the pagan ways yet. But my father is a devout man."

Cook smiled. "Keep praying for your mother, then. Few and far between are the women who can withstand the prayers of a man who truly loves his God."

A steady knock interrupted their conversation.

"Come in," Cook called out. The latch lifted, and Calum entered, dressed neatly for the journey in boots, trousers, and a belted tunic. A russet woolen cloak settled around his square shoulders. In addition to the sword hanging from Calum's belt, Bethan knew that probably he had concealed other weapons as well as a chainmail shirt beneath his clothing. Prudence dictated precautions be taken against bandits and worse.

"I'm ready when you are, Bethan. No rush, though," Calum smiled, and once again Bethan realized how his presence soothed her. Letting out her nervous breath, she returned his smile.

Cook picked up a hefty bundle from the shelf. "Now, here you go, Bethan. I've packed up some traveling food for you and Calum, plus a little for when you arrive home. Who knows whether you'll have time to bake when you reach your journey's end."

"Thank you, Cook." Bethan kissed the woman's cheek, ignoring the way her patchy dry skin rubbed against her lips.

The woman let out a sigh, and Bethan noticed troubled shadows flowing into the woman's eyes. "Ah, for a daughter like you, Bethan. I wish Padruig could find such a..." She trailed off, embarrassed. "Pay no mind to me. I'm turning into a silly old woman. Now go. You've a long journey ahead of you. God go with you."

"Aye, and also with you," Calum replied, guiding Bethan through the doorway.

Outside, she felt greatly sheltered as he steered her through the bustling courtyard activity, his strong and gentle hand on her elbow. Glancing up at him, she saw his face held his usual thoughtful, confident expression. *He never hurries yet always is set on some purpose.* As they walked, he greeted many whom they passed with a kind nod and sometimes a word or two. Bethan perceived that other servants saw her with this man, respected almost universally within Oxfield, and felt proud at being considered one of his friends. Her mind flitted ahead to the time when Garan would walk by her side so protectively. So wonderful 'twould be to feel so safe in a nest of peace all the time. *In the spring. I'll be married to Garan in the springtime,* she thought with a smile.

Calum's horse stood tethered by one of the side gates. A boy, perhaps seven years old, held one hand out to the animal, palm flat, offering a carrot. The child's other hand stroked the soft muzzle.

"Brynn, hello," Calum smiled at the boy, whose face grew animated at the man's appearance.

"Are you going somewhere, Calum?" he asked, gazing up with adoring brown eyes.

"Aye, Bethan must go to see her family out in the West Lea, and I want to help her, lad." Calum knelt before the shabbily-dressed child and smiled into his anxious face. "Now, you must do me a favor while I'm away, Brynn. Play with my dogs, aye? See that they get plenty of exercise."

Brynn nodded, trying to smile. "Aye, I will!"

"There's a lad." Calum ruffled the boy's straw hair and rose to his feet. "Lord willing, I'll be seeing you soon. If you need something, make sure that you go to Cook, alright?"

"Alright."

Apparently satisfied, Calum turned to Bethan. "Up you go, lass," he instructed, lifting her onto the horse's sturdy back and then hoisting himself up behind her. He gathered the reins into his hands. "Aidan, open the gate!"

From the doorway of his workshop, the potter watched Calum and Bethan's departure with satisfaction. "Good, very good," he said aloud, smiling. Calum looked pleased, and Bethan appeared equally happy with her lot.

"And what might I ask is so wonderful today, husband?"

Bricius turned, wincing at an arthritic pain in his neck. Lydia, his wife of fifteen years, stood in the archway adjoining his workshop with their living quarters. Despite her relative youth to his sixty-odd years, Lydia had not grown older with ease, slipping from blushing girlhood to mature womanhood with the grace that some woman obtained. Her once-even complexion wore spots from the sun; her skin had leathered beyond her forty-eight years; and her formerly heavy mahogany tresses had thinned and grayed. Yet, 'twas the soul of this woman Bricius loved, and the more her body deteriorated with passing years, the more clearly he could see the unfading beauty of her character.

"Are you going to answer me, Bricius, or do I have to guess?" she teased, coming forward into the work area. Bricius noticed that her hands held a half-loaf of dark bread and some cheese. He had worked the morning away without noticing.

"Why don't we go outside, and you can guess while we eat?" he asked. Knowing his wife, she had probably eaten standing up while preparing his meal, though.

"I've already eaten, Bricius, and I still have much work to do on the mistress' clothing for court."

"'Tis a fine autumn day, love, and 'twill only take minutes for me to eat," he cajoled. He saw her hesitate still and knew she had a long list of things that needed doing running through her mind. As well as doing much of Lady Tarian's sewing, Lydia served as a deaconess of sorts for the Christian community at Oxfield. From early morning to dusk, her hands and mind and heart busied themselves with loving her neighbor and honoring her God. "I know you have much to do, but I would like your company if you can spare the time," he added.

"Well..." Lydia paused, and Bricius waited for her to decide. True, many a Christian man would claim the right to command his wife to do as he wished. Were not wives to submit to their husbands? Yet Bricius wanted a wife, not a worshipper, not a bondwoman. Thus, he strove to love Lydia as he loved himself, not to use her as a tool to indulge his own wishes.

Husbands, love your wives, as Christ loved the church and gave himself up for her...

"I suppose I can use the break, aye," his wife smiled.

Her arm tucked in his, the couple made their way out into the bright October sunlight. Bricius breathed deeply, refreshing himself with the scent of fallen leaves and smoke, his heart delighting in the companionship of his longtime helpmate as they made their way across the sun-dappled earth. Who would settle for the role of king when instead he could have the pleasure of servanthood? Long years ago now, he had offered his wife his life and she had gifted him with her heart in turn, an exchange deemed worthy by the King of Heaven Himself. Looking at the trusting profile beside him, Bricius sighed. It had been worthwhile, indeed.

They settled down on a grassy patch near the well. Bricius marveled at how his wife's inner beauty emanated from her as the fresh perfume of a cultivated rose. The thought passed through his mind also that as their persons had aged, their relationship with their Creator and with one another had come into a second and deeper springtime than when it was new. 'Twas true, then. *God does let the bodies of things fade that we may learn to love the soul of them in truth. When I first loved Lydia, 'twas her bonny face that took me. Now, I see in her another face that will behold eternally the Almighty One, our Redeemer and God.*

"When does Lady Tarian plan to go to court, then?" Bricius asked as he took his first bite of cheese and bread, fine midday fare for any man.

Lydia shrugged. "She says perhaps they will go for the Feast of the Nativity, but the decision really rests with Lord Drustan, of course."

"Of course. But I've no doubt the lord will want to enjoy as much revelry as possible. As is evidenced by the upcoming Samhain feast." Bricius rose to draw water from the well.

"Is it planned again for this year, then? I thought surely after the madness last year..." Lydia's voice held heavy concern.

Bricius snorted, his hand going out to steady the swinging bucket. "Some saw it as harmless pleasure, not madness. And some thought it helped appease the spirits for an easier winter." He drank from the bucket's edge.

"'Twas not harmless, Bricius. That you know."

"No, and we must do as much as we can to counteract its evil influence." He sighed and took Lydia's hand. "That we had a lord who had the true good of his people in mind, not only fleeting pleasure and excitement."

"But we do, love. His name is Jesus."

"Aye. Aye, we do." He drank in the serenity of his wife's smile. "I need you to remind me of it from time to time. We have a heavenly kingdom."

The pair stayed quiet for a time while Bricius continued to eat. As he wiped the last crumbs from his beard, Lydia brought up her earlier question. "And now may I guess why you were so glad?"

"When?"

Lydia's eyes told him not to play the fool. "Standing in the doorway of your shop, Bricius, son of Alain."

"Yes, yes, I remember. I suppose I did look rather happy, didn't I?" Bricius' eyes twinkled. "And can you guess why, Lydia, daughter of Aulus?"

She rose to her feet and, smoothing her work dress, started for the pottery workshop-cum-living-quarters. "I don't need to guess, Bricius. I've known you for too many years not to know."

Bricius leapt to his feet as quickly as his old bones allowed and followed her. "Well, then?"

She stopped and turned toward him with her thick brows raised high. "You were pondering the certain matrimonial bliss of your Timothy. Am I right? Well?"

He shook his head, defeated happily. Lydia had referred to the commander of the guards as his "Timothy" because their relationship felt so like that of the apostle and his young preacher. Now he smiled, thinking again of Calum's protective guidance of the kitchen maid on her journey. "Why not? Bethan's a bonny girl for our Calum. A good Christian wife for him. 'Twill comfort him."

"God should be his comfort, Bricius."

"God uses means."

Lydia changed tactics. "She's young, dear one. No more than sixteen, surely, if that," Lydia reminded him.

Bricius frowned. "Aye. But what of it? Many a girl marries younger and is happy. And Calum is yet a young man, not the old geezer I was when I married you, Lydia."

Lydia smiled sweetly and stopped to brush a kiss on his wrinkled cheek. "No, not a geezer, dearie. More like one of the walking dead. No wonder I met you near Samhain."

"Very funny. Seriously, though, Lydia, I don't know why you hesitate to encourage something that would make Calum a happy man indeed. And think of us, too, love. What a blessing from the Lord his marriage would be. His children would grow up around our feet like the grandchildren we never had," he coaxed. "You know if you encouraged him toward it, he would consider marriage more readily."

His wife remained silent for a moment as they turned their steps homeward once more. Finally, she spoke. "I don't think 'twould make Calum happier in the long run. He's never dealt with his past, Bricius. That you know. Eventually, I think he would feel that by marrying the girl, he had bound her with his own curse." She paused. "But say that it did make him happy, love. Even so, how do you know that marriage is best for Calum? Or for Bethan, for that matter? We don't live by happiness, dear, you know."

"Better to marry than to burn with passion."

Lydia's eyebrows rose. "Calum doesn't seem as if he's exactly burning. I wouldn't even say that he's smoldering, Bricius."

"'He who finds a wife finds a good thing, and obtains favor from the LORD,'" the potter reminded her.

"'Each man should remain in the condition in which he was called,'" Lydia replied.

"'But because of the temptation, each man should have his own wife,'" Bricius countered, taking Lydia's hand.

"Which is a concession, not a command, if they can't exercise self-control," his wife pointed out, pulling away with a smile.

"Are you against Christians marrying, then, my Lydia?" Bricius spouted as they reached the doorway of the workshop. Lydia was as well-learned in Scripture as himself, if not more so, and her prayerful, obedient life strengthened her wisdom, making her a fierce warrior indeed. However, he could not agree with her if she advocated celibacy exclusively; after all, they were married! And he didn't think that state had diminished their closeness to God.

"No," Lydia replied. "It's not that marriage is sin. God made woman as a help for man and said that 'twas good. Besides, marriage triumphs as an example to the dying world of the relationship between Christ and His church. But," she said slowly, "God created individuals for Himself first and foremost, and He may have other plans for each of His creations, plans that they can best accomplish in single devotion to God alone. Others have need of another companion so that they aren't distracted by latent passion. And perhaps for some, even, though they themselves don't require marriage, 'tis a sacrifice of love they can make for another brother or sister. Yet we must never lose sight what matters most."

"And what is that?"

"That God made us not for procreation or for achievement or for personal happiness, but for Himself. I don't want to see Calum trying to find peace in the arms of his wife. Such is for those who have no hope, Bricius," Lydia said gently, laying her work-worn hand on her husband's arm.

He sighed. "It just saddens me to see him sorrow over all that has happened. I think if…"

"Sometimes sorrow heals the heart, dear one," she murmured, catching his face in her hands. "I know 'tis hard. You love him so. But the Man of Sorrows loves him yet more."

"What do you think that I ought to do then, Lydia? You should have seen him so eager to get away from the Samhain celebration."

"Pray, dear one. Pray. There is nothing the evil one fears more than a child crying out to his Father, nothing that so enfeebles his work, you ken."

"Aye." Bricius smiled deeply into his wife's eyes before bestowing a tender kiss on her forehead. "An excellent wife, who can find?" he asked quietly. "One who is willing to fight on behalf of the truth against her husband's ignorance."

"Out of love alone, dear one. And 'tis only an echo of the same love that will one day turn swords into plowshares."

"Aye," said Bricius, settling down at his pottery wheel again. "Amen."

CHAPTER THIRTEEN

As he moved up the wide stone slabs, his heart pounding in his chest, Deoradhan felt as if he had traveled back half a decade. His boyhood called out to him from every familiar corner, every worn step. Was it really so long ago that as a youth on the cusp of manhood, he had strode down these same steps, determined to never cross them again, thoughts of undiscriminating and reckless hatred and revenge rushing through every path his mind took? Now, no longer a child in anyone's eyes, he mounted the way into the king's court again, resolving to remain in this stronghold until he received a final answer to his complaint.

Slowly, he mounted the last few steps, his eyes renewing their memories of this great fortress. Arthur had added more polish to his capitol in everything from the brilliant banners whipping in the breeze to the foreign voices he had heard around him from the moment his foot stepped inside the walls. Camelot had become a modern-day Alexandria for Europe, he thought, a gathering-place for the finest minds of their day. Even while he resided in Gaul, he had heard scholars speak in wistful tones of traveling to Camelot. There, they could confer and debate, share ideas and obtain funding from a king who strove to create a golden age for his people, a tangible hope rising from the ashes of Rome.

He reached the guards standing at the Great Hall's threshold. He didn't recognize them from his days here as a boy; their barely-bristled faces testified that they were new warriors in Arthur's service.

"My name is Deoradhan," he said. "I wish to speak with the High King."

One of the two guards squinted in near-sightedness at him. "Do you come on your liege-lord's behalf?"

"No." Deoradhan knew that they saw that he had no escort or attendant and so surmised that he held the position of an underling rather than being a nobleman himself.

"Then whose business…?"

"I come on my own business," Deoradhan cut him off. "Tell the king my name; he will see me." He stared into the eyes of the guards, his face set like a stone carving.

The two guards exchanged puzzled, uncertain glances. Deoradhan could tell that the young pair had no idea what to do with him. He stood his ground, silently, waiting for them to do his bidding. Finally, the near-sighted one shrugged. "It can't hurt to tell the king your name." He looked to his partner for agreement.

The other one raised his eyebrows. "Alright, but you do it. I don't want to be responsible if…" He trailed off.

The squint-eyed young man huffed. "Thanks a lot." He squared his shoulders and heaved a breath. "Stay here. Keep an eye on this fellow." He shot Deoradhan a warning glance before thrusting open the heavy carved doors and disappearing into the dark.

The guard left outside took the other's orders seriously, fixing his small black eyes on Deoradhan with the stare of a wolf, as if sure that his prey would escape if given half a chance. Deoradhan found the guard's vigilance humorous, seeing that he had no intention of departing before he saw the king. He turned away from his keeper and observed the activity within the fortress' walls, trying to occupy his mind

The time dragged on, and Deoradhan gritted his teeth against the delay. How long did it take to tell Arthur a simple name? A smile rose on his lips when he thought about what the king's expression would say at the moment the guard spoke Deoradhan's name quietly aloud. Would he be surprised that his foster-child had returned after so long? Would any kindness linger toward the one who had so completely rejected his covering? Would those familiar blue eyes warm with reserved affection when the younger man entered the room? Or would his features harden with bitterness, the same bitterness that Deoradhan felt toward him?

Will the king see me at all? Or is this route closed to me as well?

The opening doors sent Deoradhan's thoughts away. He focused his eyes on the returning guard, who had assumed a perplexed but respectful demeanor toward him. "The king requests that you wait for an audience with him until tomorrow, as he has pressing matters to attend to this afternoon." Tensely, the guard waited for Deoradhan's response.

He wanted to brush past this young man, self-important in his chainmail, swing open the doors, and demand justice publicly. *Such a show will do no good, Deoradhan. This you know.* He clenched his callused hands into fists by his sides and then relaxed them. "I will abide by the king's wishes," he said evenly.

The guard's face relaxed. "I'll show you to your quarters, my lord."

~ ~ ~

Later, Deoradhan woke beneath the light silk sheets, his muscles feeling thoroughly rested but his mind ever taut. He took his time in rising, half-opened eyes traveling over the furnishings, feeling lazy in the dim light. Strange, he felt as if an eon had passed since he had last entered these rooms, and yet so little time had gone by their contents remained the same. Even the bedclothes, yellow as an autumn sunset, had not altered.

Shrugging past days from his thoughts, Deoradhan rose. His stomach told him 'twas time for the evening meal, as the twilight filtering in his window testified. The guard had intimated that he would be welcome to take his supper in the Hall with the rest of the residents if he wished.

Do I wish?

Half of him shrank away from interacting, mingling with such shallow people. How could he go along with their insipid conversations about ancient philosophers and current politics when the real grit of life had struck him full in the face?

What is crooked cannot be made straight, and what is lacking cannot be counted...

Yet the social whirl would divert him from the endless bitter tang that his heart tasted continually. And Arthur might be there as well.

Arthur... Something within him, the part that yearned for Aine and tried to recall his mother's face, that regretted that God had turned out to be a cowardly, tyrannical fake, also drew him toward the high king. Deoradhan tamped down the feeling, ignoring it, smothering it by remembering why he had come back. Why he had been sent away. And why he had been brought here in the first place.

Every time he suppressed that tender yet strong part of his spirit, it grew fainter upon its return. But it never entirely died, just as a shoot continues to live underneath a rock, though the rock crushes and tries to smother it. The living thing in every man that mirrors his Creator always survives, though the creature may attempt to deform and distort it. It cannot die and so provides hell's agony with its bite.

Slipping a clean tunic over his head, Deoradhan ran his fingers through his shoulder-length hair, neatening it. He had forgotten to bring his comb. He tugged his soft-soled shoes back onto his feet, clasped his cape around his shoulders, and stood before the polished metal mirror a moment or two.

Who am I? Who am I supposed to be? He looked into his reflected face and silently demanded an answer. His eyes gazed back at him blankly, painfully. No answer came.

~ ~ ~

He woke shortly after dark, glad to come out of the familiar, distasteful vision. Breathing deeply to calm his thundering heartbeat, Calum pulled himself up on his elbows and glanced over at Bethan. Good. She slept still, the firelight flickering on her eyelids, her lips parted, her brow unclouded with worry. They had camped at dusk, near the same stream at which Deoradhan and Bethan had stopped on their way to Oxfield two months ago.

Looking over at Bethan sound asleep, Calum sighed. That he were so childlike, so like a blank sheet of parchment. During the day, he knew his sins were forgiven; he saw his Savior clearly then. But night brought out the thoughts that had slept in daylight. Thoughts of what once had been. Thoughts of Cairine.

Each time he dreamed it, his part in the story changed. Sometimes, he merely stood by, passive eyes taking in the spectacle, hands limp at his sides, feet immobile in the damp, cool morning grass. The sky flushed a radiant blue, the leaves above his head shone like living emeralds, the berries glowing stars against the nearly black oak trunks. His mother's hands rested trembling on his twelve-year-old shoulders, bringing a sense of comfort, of security to his confused mind. But as the dream progressed, her hands would tighten, gripping him, holding him in place when the sight before his eyes became so painful that he struggled to run away, to flee anywhere but here. His heart filled with anguish like new wine in old wineskins, threatening to burst; his limbs turned rigid with cold despite the warming autumn sunlight; his eyes refused to close, could not even blink for some respite. Yet still he stood and did nothing to avert the tragedy before him. As he had in life.

Other times, his dream-self would actually participate in the ritual. He almost preferred this, for then he could flagellate himself emotionally upon waking: *See, you did aid them. You betrayed her ... a Judas.* He would smile grimly in the dark, the cold sweat of a nightmare-come-true soaking his hair and shirt. There was a certain unhealthy pleasure in polishing the manacles that he could not remove.

Yet, despite how he might alter, she remained always the same.

She gazed out from the wicker cage, its crisscrossed weaving shadowing her face. They had bound her hands, small and tough, behind her back and had crowned her earth-colored hair with a wreath of fresh oak leaves. Underneath the greenery, her lovely eyes shimmered with tears.

Blessed are those who mourn, for they shall be comforted...

And, always, she turned those sea-gray orbs toward him. They held no reproach, no anger, no bitterness toward him or Mama or toward those who sacrificed her. Only a soft expression of love. At that moment in the dream, he would always move, tearing away from his mother's terrified grasp and, sobbing, screaming ... awaken.

Sitting up under a tent of branches and stars, he was no longer an adolescent boy unable to cope with the death of his sister. No longer known as the brother of her whose death brought back life to the tribe's fields. Yet he knew that in a sense that boy still lived in him, frightened, guilty, filled with grief. Knew that his past followed him wherever he traveled.

How do you go on living in the present when the past haunts you so?

His heart a lump of rock in his chest, Calum rolled over on his side, closing his eyes to forget the dream again. As he lay there, he thought of Cairine. 'Twas easy to remember her in the days before the harvests failed, before the sheep miscarried, before the old priest had set his eyes on her. 'Twas harder to recall the events and decisions that had led up to the moment when she was not. He would not endure it tonight. He would sleep and forget.

CHAPTER FOURTEEN

Camelot

Arthur was not in attendance.

I knew he was a coward, sending other men to fight his battles, avoiding personal conflict at every turn. Deoradhan lowered the king one more notch in his estimation as he rose from his seat at the common tables. He had chosen to sit far from his old place, spiting his own desire to slip into boyhood nostalgia. Besides, the fewer people who recognized the supposed prodigal, the better.

Gwenhwyfar saw him from her place on the dais. She smiled hesitantly, nodding briefly at him before turning back to her witty flirtation with a young warrior who flashed his strong white teeth in simper after false simper. Deoradhan smirked. The high queen had not changed, then, neither in her behavior toward men nor in her attitude toward him. He half-pitied her in the latter, for her suspicion that Arthur had fathered him missed the mark so badly. He did not think Arthur had misled her deliberately on that score; how could she help believing what half of Camelot delighted to whisper?

Cup of mead in hand, he let his eyes rove over the diners. The divisions among Arthur's followers had grown more obvious with the years. There sat the philosophers, bards, and some of the thinking warriors; he had seen his old friend Percivale among them. They talked quietly with raised brows and pondering eyes. Every once in a while, one of them would burst out at an idea another had suggested. Yonder were those of brute strength, who drank until their heads swam and boasted loudly and sometimes bawdily of their adventures. Pro-Roman dissenters sat by themselves, sulky looks pulling down their faces; they dressed in toga-like garments with not a barbarian trouser to be found on any hairy leg among them. The privileged warriors and honored guests sat with the queen on her raised platform. Deoradhan smiled. He alone had no one with whom he belonged here.

Deoradhan made his way toward the door. Arthur had promised to see him tomorrow, and he had never known the Pendragon to break his word, even to his own hurt. Perhaps, he mused, 'twas this deep-set trustworthiness that cemented the nobles' loyalty to the king, despite all of the political differences that crackled in Logress. For himself, Deoradhan knew 'twas this guilelessness that had allured him.

Still, he could not help asking a gray-haired guard by the door, "Does the king often refuse his supper?"

The guard, who did not know him, frowned. "He takes his supper, alright, but more often than not, in his private chambers. Too much worry over northern rebellions for him to put on a cheerful face every night nowadays, I suppose. Besides, if you ask me, the queen's behavior doesn't do much to encourage a husband to come to supper," he added with a grimace, his eyes resting on the dais.

Deoradhan raised his dark eyebrows and shrugged. "True. Why would he come? To be embarrassed every time the golden bird sings to another?" he stated, using the name for Gwenhwyfar that he'd once heard Arthur call her affectionately.

"Aye." Deoradhan felt the man's eyes on him even as he looked away. "Where are you from, young man?"

"Here and there," Deoradhan replied. "Trying to find my place, you know."

The guard nodded. "Well, Arthur's Camelot is as good a spot as you'll find for doing that. Talk to the king, lad; he's bound to have something for you to put your hand or mind to. Are you a warrior? A scholar? Horseman?"

"A bit of each. Excuse me." Deoradhan moved away from the guard's questions. He no longer desired to lie as Arthur had done about his identity, and yet he could not endanger his chances with a too-soon revelation. Best to be wary and keep his mouth quiet.

Lost in thought, he had gone only a few steps down the long stone corridor when he heard a door whap closed behind him to his left. He gave no heed to it; Arthur's guest chambers appeared full to bursting. Neither did he attend when he heard a buoyant female voice exclaim, "Solas?"

Deoradhan broke out of his reverie when the scurrying feet approached him from behind. He turned just as the speaker caught his elbow in her hand to gain his attention. The surprised look on the girl's face amused him; her beauty and demeanor then charmed him, reminding him of Aine, his Aine.

"Oh, I'm so sorry, m'lord," she gasped, her full cheeks turning pink as she dropped her hand from his elbow. "I thought you were someone that I know."

Smiling, he looked down at the petite young woman. "There's no harm done, m'lady. Whomever you were looking for will be sorry to have missed you, I'm certain."

She shook her head, her heavy blond tresses swinging with the movement. "I wasn't searching for anyone, really. Actually, I thought that you were someone I hadn't expected to see here at all." She peered at him closely. "And truly," she added after a moment, "until I came near to you, I thought you were he. I saw you as you walked by my open door, and I hoped…" She trailed off and gave him a smile that shone from her gray eyes. "Never mind. I'm sorry to have kept you from your business, my lord."

She turned to go, but Deoradhan stopped her on impulse. Her girlish sweetness, her innocence, filled his mind so full of Aine that he wanted to relish the feeling a little longer. "You've not kept me from anything. I'm a newcomer here and thought I'd ramble after supping in the Hall. Would you keep me company awhile? Unless you've something else you must do."

She hesitated, but then Deoradhan saw her eyes linger on his face. Perhaps she, too, wanted to be reminded of him for whom she had hoped. "Alright," she said slowly, "but we must keep to the corridors. The queen doesn't care for her ladies-in-waiting to wander too far after dark."

"Certainly." He smiled. "By the way, I'm Deoradhan."

"Fiona, daughter of Weylin. I'm glad to meet you."

They began walking slowly, their footsteps echoing softly.

"So why have you come to the great Camelot, Deoradhan, if I may ask?"

Deoradhan glanced over at her. She was too young to have lived here many years; he could safely tell her a little truth, he decided. "Camelot was my childhood home, but for some time, I've been abroad."

"Fighting?"

"Learning. I stayed at a great monastery in Gaul, renowned for its library and educated monks."

Her gray eyes glittered with interest. "Truly? I would give much for such an opportunity." She sighed wistfully, her hand running over the stone wall as they walked.

"Aye? You like books, then?"

She gave an enthusiastic nod. "Oh, aye. Well," she checked herself with a smile, "not all books. I'm afraid I draw the line at the really ponderous works. Do you want to know the best passage I ever read, though?" She gave a little skip and then stopped walking, waiting for his agreement.

He nodded. Her eagerness engaged his attention.

"You've probably read it already," she said, "but it's worth hearing again." She paused and then began, her voice drawing the words out like a bee gathering nectar. "*Quia fecisti nos ad te et inquietum est cor nostrum, donec requiescat in te. Da mihi, domine, scire et intellegere, utrum sit prius invocare te au laudare te, et scire te prius sit an invocare te? Sed quis te invocat nesciens te?"* Finished, she looked up at him, waiting for his reaction.

Deoradhan worked to school his features and believed he had succeeded. "I must admit, my lady, I expected Catullus or some other Roman poet. I thought you said you didn't care for ponderous books?"

She laughed. "I don't. Augustine's words feed my soul like a rich dessert, my lord. I cannot get enough of it." She looked at him. "And you, my lord? Do you like the bishop's writings? You must have read them in your monastery."

"I did." He paused, keeping his face composed, reining in the painful desire that rose in his heart at those words. A desire he kept locked away, guarded by lions of anger and bitterness, a desire that disturbed his sleep and drew him relentlessly to beauty.

Quia fecisti nos ad te et inquietum est cor nostrum, donec requiescat in te...
For You created us for Yourself, and our heart is restless, until it rests in You...

"And?" Fiona prompted. "Do you think well of him?"

"Aye and nay," Deoradhan replied. "I appreciate his writing. It's very beautiful. But I cannot believe it to be true."

"Why not?"

"Because if there is a God, He is not the way Augustine describes Him."

She looked up at him, quizzical. "But you said that you find his words beautiful."

He nodded warily.

"Can there be real beauty without truth? Beauty is the child of truth. Even if you disagree with most of what Augustine says, his words must contain some nugget of truth, some way in which he speaks rightly, aye? Or you wouldn't find his writing genuinely beautiful."

Deoradhan raised his chin. What did this court girl know? "Perhaps there is a God, as Augustine says, my lady. But I would rather believe that there is no God, for this world testifies him to be cruel, unjust, and capricious. The worst of men would be more divine than a god like that."

She was quiet for a moment. "I think you have it backwards, my lord. Everything in this world shows man to be capable of the worst atrocities and yet God to be faithful. As the Scriptures say, He is gracious and merciful always."

Deoradhan snorted. He couldn't help himself. "Forgive me, Lady Fiona, but my life has contradicted this. Perhaps I think God unjust because I've found Him to be so."

"What do you mean?" She looked at him with steady eyes, holding no anger toward him despite his rudeness.

"I've seen great suffering, my lady, in my own life and in that of others. Suffering that had no reason preceding it nor any following after." His lips turned up in contempt. "And much of it carried out in the name of your God."

She had her head tilted to one side, listening hard. Good. She would see he spoke judiciously. He continued, laying out the case before her. "My father was a good man, loving, who treated the ancient gods with respect and cared for the poor at his own expense. Yet, an enemy struck him down while he was a young man, an enemy who claimed to follow your God. According to your beliefs, my father, the innocent one, will suffer—is suffering—eternal death at the hands of a merciful God." He paused to let his words sink in. "Is that fair?"

The golden-haired girl remained silent for a few moments. *She doesn't know how to answer that one.* Finally, she stopped and turned toward him. When she spoke, it was in a quiet voice, gentle as a spring breeze touching his cheek. "My lord, may I tell you a story?" she asked, and they turned a corner in the corridor. At Deoradhan's nod, she continued, "Not far from here there is a bog where, many years ago now, the druid priests tossed a body."

Deoradhan waited, not seeing how this connected to his question. "The druids often engage in ritual human sacrifice, even for celebrations. They revive the earth."

"Yes, but this was no ordinary sacrifice. 'Twas the body of a prince, strangled, throat cut, skull crushed. His years numbered only a few more than yours, my lord, and yet he went to his death willingly, believing that he would enter life again and more than that, bring life to all his people. You see, the Romans were invading the island, and this young man's father feared for his tribe. So the chief asked his only son to give his life in the place of others. And his son endured a gruesome death, glad to do his father's will, glad to redeem many lives with his own." She looked intently at him, seeing if he understood.

Deoradhan could not resist. He raised his eyebrows and said, "But it was for nothing. The Romans came and conquered the land, destroyed it, and ravaged it anyway. The prince's sacrifice was for nothing."

She shook her head. "No sacrifice passes without meaning. His father watched, Lord Deoradhan. He saw the priests cut his son's throat, garrot him, crush his skull, toss out his body like refuse in the wet bog."

"That the father had been compassionate to his son as well as to his people," Deoradhan muttered.

"There was no other way. A sacrifice had to be made of the highest and noblest, the most worthy."

Deoradhan raised his eyebrows. "My guess is that you're drawing a comparison between the Roman God and this chief-father. And so you call what this man did to his son merciful?"

He watched as she bit her lip. "'Twas a hard mercy, to be sure. How the prince's death must have killed the father as well. Yet, remember, too, that the druids believed that the prince would be reborn someday, remade into something more glorious for his sacrifice."

Deoradhan nodded reluctantly. The theme of rebirth wove its way into all druid practices, giving hope to the sacrificial victim. The natural cycle of life and death, summer and winter affirmed this belief as well. *Still...*

"My lord," Fiona said in earnest, "there is another Father who also gave His Son, not for His friends but for His enemies. I think you know of whom I speak."

Deoradhan raised his head. He would not soften toward this invading, cowardly Roman God. *He took from me everything I had, everyone I could have loved...*

"Stiffen all you like, my lord, but it's true. You wouldn't be angry unless there was some truth in it or some wrong in you."

Red rose to Deoradhan's cheeks, and he determined to hear the girl out. "No, my lady. I'm listening."

"I'm not a learned girl, Lord Deoradhan. I don't have all the logical answers for you. But when the Living God at last captures your heart, I believe that you will have all your answers."

He met her gaze coolly, feeling the anger burning up in his chest. "Your God will never capture my heart, Lady Fiona. He forfeited His rights to it a long time ago."

She looked back at him without a trace of anger, and he felt like he addressed this almighty God Himself through her. "You see, I don't want a god who is unjust, a god who damns a man because he's seen through that god's hypocritical cruelty. I would rather suffer in that god's hell eternally than serve him," Deoradhan stated.

Lady Fiona was silent for a moment. Finally, she spoke quietly, "God does not need to justify Himself to you, my lord. My whole life has been a lesson in that, I think. And you know," she added, "when I come up against something I don't understand, there's a Scripture that always comes to my mind." Her eyes gazed simply into his. "'Shall not the Judge of all the earth do what is just?' I must bow before His wisdom then, aye?"

Deoradhan could not reply. The pressure to run built up within him, to flee from this idea as well as to flee toward it. Everything that had been settled and clear suddenly appeared a dark upheaval to him. *I cannot see to step forward or to hold back.* Finally, he said, "My friend Calum believes as you do."

"Oh?"

"Aye. He lives at Oxfield in the south, where he is commander of the guards. He often tries to convince me to follow him in his beliefs, but..."

"But...?" she prompted after he paused.

"Maybe I need time to think."

"Don't procrastinate, my lord. 'Tis the one duty in life for which 'twill not do to put it off," Fiona cautioned.

They continued walking silently for a time before he said, trying to lighten the mood, lessen the tension that hung heavy as a coat of mail on them, "So who did you think I was when you first called out to me, Lady Fiona?"

He saw a smile grow on her lips. "Solas. I thought you were Solas."

"Solas? Is he a sweetheart, my lady?"

She shook her head. "Nay, nothing like that. Solas is my younger brother. Well, half-brother," she corrected herself.

"You have the same father then?"

"Aye. Unfortunately, it seems at times." She gave a little laugh.

"Your father is unkind," Deoradhan stated.

"To put it mildly, aye, he is unkind." She bit her lip. "Poor Solas. He tolerates such abuse toward himself. He is not the brutish warrior my father would wish for in a son; he lacks vengefulness, pride, callousness—everything my father believes is needful for the next king of Lothian."

King of Lothian. The words spun into Deoradhan's brain with the power of an axe. "Lothian, you say? Your father is king of Lothian?" he asked, unable to swallow.

"Aye, for many years now."

"Then he was not always Lothian's king?"

"Nay, he was not. But how he came to be, 'tis a story I would rather not tell. 'Tis too sad an account to speak of," Fiona said. "I do not know all the details anyway; I was so young at the time it occurred, only a babe in my nurse's arms, really. Solas knows more, but he doesn't want to burden me."

"How did Solas come to know of this, if he was born after you?"

"His mother, the queen, told him, my lord. But again, I think it best not to speak of what has gone before and can't be changed. Better to look ahead and do rightly now."

With a thundering heart, Deoradhan nodded his assent and brought their walk to as swift a close as politeness would permit. He had much thinking to do before the next morning dawned and his audience with the Pendragon commenced.

CHAPTER FIFTEEN

West Lea

Calum's horse moved forward with relentless smooth swiftness. Already, Bethan glimpsed her childhood home, its thatched roof rising humbly against the fields behind it. The wide road ran right past the hut's door, and a traveling stranger would have taken the abode for a place of peace, of homey country existence between the late autumn fields and the golden wood beyond.

Bethan closed her eyes, taking a lung-filling breath. Her heart leaped ahead of her, toward the cottage, rushing down its dirt path into the shadowy doorway. The entrance to her home gaped wide; it seemed to her a toothless mouth in a disheartened countenance. In that darkness, she knew her mama lay ill.

Maybe to death, or I would never have been summoned from Oxfield.

Yet, while her deep love for Mama drew her on, moved her to rush to her side, a visceral fear loomed over her as well. Like a night owl descends on its prey, it threatened to engulf her. That part of her urged her to hold back, to run away, even. To save herself from the fear and sorrow that surely awaited her within that doorway.

God is our refuge and strength, a very present help in trouble. Therefore we will not fear...

Bethan felt Calum riding behind her, a sturdy and unwavering presence. An unexpected sense of security, tinged with joy, filled her. *Lord, You have provided a fortress of Your strength for me in this friend.*

"We're here, lass," Calum murmured, reining his horse to a halt. He handed her the thick leather straps and dismounted, then reached up to help her to the ground.

He must have sensed her hesitation because he smiled and said, "Don't be afraid. God is with you, Bethan." The gentle tone smoothed the rough texture of his voice and replenished her courage. With a steadying breath, she set her hands on his shoulders and let him lift her down to the ground.

Hand on her arm, Calum guided her forward, his nearness assuring her that he would support her regardless of what they faced within the cottage. Side by side, they walked down the rocky little path to the door. It stood open, despite the biting late October chill. A few steps away from the door, Bethan saw a pair of blue eyes staring at her from within. They belonged to a little girl dressed carelessly, her hair wild and her face uncommonly dirty and frightened.

"Enid!" Bethan exclaimed. The child hesitated just a moment before rushing forward, landing with a thump against Bethan's skirt. She hid her face and clung to Bethan with a grip from her tiny hands so strong it almost hurt. Pained to see her little sister so terrified, Bethan gathered Enid in her arms, soothing her with words and long strokes on the child's hair.

After her sister seemed a little reassured, Bethan asked, "Where is Mama, Enid-love?"

The little girl stayed silent, head buried against Bethan's legs. Bethan looked up at Calum who encouraged her with a nod. Crouching down, she pulled Enid up into her arms, feeling the bony pressure of her arms and knees as she clung like lichen to a tree trunk. Holding the child thus, she pushed her wayward hair out of her eyes and willed her feet to move through the doorway and into the cottage.

He had entered many houses of hardship, had put swords through men's guts, had bound numerous open wounds, so the stench and sights could not frighten him. Indeed, 'twas very like what Calum had expected to find, right down to the neighbor woman tending to Bethan's sick mother, bathing her head with a rag dipped in brackish water. 'Twas Bethan that would need acclimating, not he. He glanced at her, still clutching her sister to her, eyes wide with dread. Bethan stood motionless in front of the doorway, silhouetted by the bright afternoon sunlight. Calum knew he must be the one to act right now, not she.

The nurse had stood when they entered, her gruff face tired. Calum stepped forward toward her. "Ma'am, I'm a guard from Oxfield. Bethan and I have come to tend her mama."

The woman sighed, her weariness a little lifted at the news. "Well, that's good. Me, I'm bone-tired, what with caring for my own home and these ones as well. Good. Well, then, I'll leave you both to it." She moved toward the doorway, evidently eager to shift the mantle of responsibility onto someone else's shoulders.

The woman paused when she reached Bethan's side and laid a forefinger on Enid's cheek. "Sweet one, this," she remarked. "Poor thing, so young to be motherless."

Calum saw the fear run across Bethan's eyes at the woman's words. Quickly, he said, "Thank you for your help here, ma'am. Bethan and I can manage now, I think, and you'll want to be getting back to the village before dark."

The woman nodded and stepped outside, her shawl-draped figure dissolving into the twilight. Calum shut the door and turned toward the bed, one of the few pieces of furniture in the cottage. There Lowri lay, her face rash-red with fever, covered to her chin with woolen bedclothes. Knowing that the village woman had been caring for her, he felt easy to take the time to stoke the fire in the hearth before tending to her.

By the time he had finished adding more peat to the fire, Bethan had begun to pick up where the nurse had left off. She bathed her mama's arms and face, tenderly drawing the rag over her cheeks and eyelids. Enid stayed closely beside her all the while, her huge brown eyes trained unblinkingly on her immobile mother. How long the child had been left without real care, Calum did not even desire to question. He knew only that she needed distraction from sorrow and Bethan needed his help.

"Little lassie," he said, coming down on one knee before her, his eyes on level with hers, if she would turn them toward him, "little lassie, I must fetch some fresh water from the river. Will you come to show me the way I must go?"

The child glanced toward him with troubled eyes, her thoughts evidently still on the woman lying on the bed, then she looked up at her sister. Calum saw Bethan force a smile despite her concern. "Enid, this is my friend Calum. He's come to help me take care of Mama." The child turned her eyes back to Calum. "Can you show him the way, lass?" Bethan prodded.

Enid nodded and picked up one of the buckets by the door. Bethan turned to Calum. "Thank you," she said.

Gladdened to help her, Calum grasped the other bucket's handle and opened the door. "We'll return shortly, lass," he said, his hand guiding the little girl before him.

CHAPTER SIXTEEN

Oxfield

"Have you seen him?"

The unexpected exclamation behind her made Aine stab her finger with the bone needle. "Ouch! Winter, don't do that!" she said and put her finger in her mouth to staunch the bleeding.

The tall girl flounced into the room, slamming the door behind her. The kitchen was nearly empty. The morning work had been completed; Aine sewed by the light of a candle stub. Only Cook sat snoozing in the corner by the great hearth, her feet propped up on another stool. With her eyebrows raised, Winter dropped onto the bench beside Aine.

"Someone's peevish, aren't they?" she said, and Aine blushed, uncomfortable. She never spoke a word contrary to Winter. Her outburst resulted from her anxiety over Deoradhan's absence, she knew.

"I'm sorry, Winter," she apologized. "Forget that I said that." She hoped the older girl wouldn't hold the little incident against her. She needed all the friends she could get.

Winter shrugged, obviously still put out. "Perhaps I needn't tell you about him after all. Maybe you've already seen him. Or maybe you don't care anyway."

"Seen whom? What are you talking about? Is Deoradhan back?" The question slipped out before she thought. For the second time since Winter entered, she flushed berry-red. No one knew of her pledge to Deoradhan yet.

Winter's mouth turned up at the corners. "Oh, is that it, Aine? Marcus mentioned he had seen the two of you kissing on the night of the dance. And are you promised to him?"

Aine blushed a deeper shade at being found out. She nodded, helpless to lie to Winter.

The girl leaned back, a satisfied smile on her lips. "Well, that explains it, then. I don't know why I didn't guess."

"Explains what?" asked Aine, desperate to get onto a different conversation track.

"Explains why you are uninterested in our very interesting visitor."

Aine frowned. "Whom are you speaking of? I've not seen any new visitor to the kitchens. For certain, not a boy."

Winter's laugh became unbridled at this. "No, he's not a visitor to the kitchens. To the great house, my lass! And he's no lad like your Deoradhan, but a hearty warrior of thirty years or so. A cousin to the lord or something like that, on his way to Camelot." She sighed and rested her chin on her hands. "So handsome he is! Hair as black as the raven's feather, eyes the color of a moonless sky. Confident, dashing, everything you could wish for, I'm telling you."

"Aye, and what good does it do you, Winter? Or any of us? He'll not care one bit for a common girl with no family or money, not give a second glance."

Winter's head came off her hands. "Oh, won't he? We'll see about that." She rose to her feet and began to loosen her blond hair from its double braids.

Worry crept into Aine's heart as she watched her friend. "Winter, what are you doing?"

Her hair falling in a wavy cloak down to her waist, Winter smirked. "You'll see." She moved toward the shelf where Aine knew she kept her personal articles and extra clothing. The older girl rummaged among her own things a little, then pulled out a clean shift. Quickly shedding her clothing, she slid the new garment over her head. Aine expected her to finish by putting on her everyday tunic over it, but Winter turned to another shelf.

"Winter..." Aine trailed off as Winter snatched a green linen tunic from Riach's belongings.

"She won't mind," Winter said. "She never wears it anyway. See, doesn't it fit me well?" She tied the brown girdle around her small waist and turned to let Aine behold the moment's full glory.

Aine looked back at her, uneasy. "What are you planning to do?"

Winter raised her chin. "I'm going to prove that he'll give me a second glance, dear Aine. Care to come along?" she asked, moving toward the door.

Aine hesitated, torn. Part of her wanted to join in on the lively fun Winter had planned for herself; but another part of her desired to stay here, sewing this new tunic for Deoradhan, happily dwelling on the remembrance of his face and their affection for one another. "Well..."

"Come on," Winter commanded. "You can see for yourself."

Aine obeyed, reluctantly following the determined footsteps of her leader.

~ ~ ~

Winter tossed to the other side. Her feelings of anger and humiliation wrestled her, preventing her from sleep as surely as if they guarded a holy city from an intruder. If asked, she wouldn't have been able to say whether she hated the young man or Aine more. In the dimly-lit room, she stared at the back of Aine's head. *I hate her more*, she realized and felt bitter satisfaction as the admittance settled in her heart.

It's your own fault. The thought pushed forward, a symptom of her lingering conscience. *If you hadn't paraded before him...*

No. I just shouldn't have brought her with me. She always spoils everything. Winter rolled onto her back and gazed unblinking up at the ceiling, remembering.

She had rushed into the courtyard, her hair streaming behind her like a palomino horse's tail. Riach's fine green dress hung perfectly on her, she knew. Riach always had a little more than everyone else; her father served as a personal attendant to Lord Drustan. Eagerly, Winter looked for the visitor. She had seen him talking with some guards near the stables just a little while ago. With any luck, he would still be there.

Aware of wide-eyed Aine trailing behind her, Winter tried to think of a way to surely attract the man's attention if her appearance alone didn't accomplish the feat. She couldn't fail before Aine. She just couldn't. How would she ever regain her authority among the girls?

Ah. She stopped. There, among a group of gabbing men, he sat, occupying a stone bench like a king on his throne. My, wasn't he handsome, like a god? His raven hair fell to his shoulders, slightly unruly, as became a man of action. His molded face held a pair of flashing black eyes, framed by eyelashes which any maiden would crave for her own countenance. His teeth (and none were missing) were as white as newly-washed sheep when he laughed, which he often did.

Studying him, Winter wondered how she would make her approach. Then she saw her friend Owen among the cluster. Perhaps the best way would be indirect, to catch his attention without seeming to try. With a smile, she raised an eyebrow to Aine and plowed forward, making sure to put an extra bounce to her steps and a come-hither expression to her eyes.

"Owen!" she exclaimed when she was still far enough from the group to see how many of the men looked up. To her satisfaction, they all did, including the man with the shiny black eyes. She was aware of how his gaze traveled over her from her golden tresses down to her delicate bare feet, which wore an anklet bracelet with bells, a gift from a former admirer.

Owen flushed with pleasure at being singled out by her. He had always wanted her attentions. "Winter," he greeted her.

"Why haven't you come to see me lately?" she asked, giving him the most inviting smile she could conjure. She would show this young noble visitor a temptation he could not resist. Already, she sensed the man's eyes sliding over her

curvaceous form, and she reacted to the feeling with a shiver of gratification.

Owen grinned back, and Winter forced herself not to grimace at his filthy teeth, knowing that appearance counted for all at this moment. "I didn't know I would be welcome, but now that you've invited me..." he trailed off, his eyes telling her things she would rather not hear. Not from Owen, at any rate.

"Of course. Come any time you like," she hastily assured him. "Now, aren't you going to introduce me to your new friend?" She turned her eyes, letting the lids droop slightly, toward the man in question. "Or shall I do the honors myself? My lord, my name is Winter, daughter of Aden. And you are..."

"Lancelot, son of Bors," he answered her, standing up with a polished smile, "A lord without land or money, my lady."

"Winter is a common girl, my lord," inserted one of the guards present.

"Do you have eyes in your head, man?" rejoined the god. "Is such beauty ever common?"

Winter flashed him a shy smile, and he grinned back. The other men snickered and whistled, teasing and goading on their flirtation.

"If you think Winter is pretty, look to her friend, my lord," piped up another young man, that awful Peter, who had always thought that Winter was too vain for her own good. Her heart skidded to a halt as the whole group of men turned like buyers at the village market to compare cuts of meat. Now 'twas too late for Winter to prevent Lord Lancelot from looking at this friend. Aine still stood closely behind her, and with one step, he could see her.

He audibly inhaled at the sight of what Winter knew was an ethereal, fairy-like loveliness. If he was a warrior god, Aine was a goddess who combined the double draw of innocence and desire in her every look, every line.

And Aine had the nerve to blush at his open admiration. Though only a trained harlot could have withstood such a stare without coloring. His eyes undressed her with their dark, heavy gaze. He might as well as run his fingers through her hair, pulled her garment from her back.

At that moment, he forgot all about me in his lusting after her.

Aine's beauty of form and face had fascinated him, like the scent of a mare intrigues a stallion. Aine knew it, too. Winter was certain of that. The younger girl had remained quiet, even more so than usual, on their way back to the kitchen. That despite Winter having tried to converse with Aine, showing her that the man's behavior had not affected her in the least.

Stupid girl! Not only had she captured Deoradhan, Oxfield's prize, Aine now continued her heart-hunting. *She always has to be the one everyone admires. And innocent as she is, she probably doesn't even know why men look at her.* Winter flopped over onto her other side, no closer to sleep than she had been an hour before. *And I'm stuck with foul-breathed Owen!* Who would now be coming to call, thanks to her open invitation this evening.

Innocent as she is...

A smile crept onto Winter's lips. Perhaps Lancelot was just the man to show Aine the dangers of having that oh-so-pretty face. The daisy would be no worse for the wear with a few petals plucked. Better for Deoradhan, too, in the long run. If Lancelot despoiled her just a bit, maybe Aine wouldn't be so eager for men's attention, would she? Of course, Winter wouldn't encourage the girl toward too much folly; just enough to make her a little embarrassed when Deoradhan returned. What pleasure it would give Winter to see the little goddess try to hide her romantic intrigue then!

Really, I'm doing both Aine and Deoradhan a favor if I push her toward a little foolishness now. How will she ever become wise to the ways of men if she doesn't learn to navigate their tricks?

Her heart eased by the incubating plot, Winter pulled her scratchy blanket up to her chin and sighed. Recompense drew near; she was sure of it.

CHAPTER SEVENTEEN

The moon still tenuously held its silver sway over the sky when Tarian slipped from her elaborately-carved bed. She hurried with curled feet over the stone floor, trying to not feel its frigidity while also making her footsteps silent. Her clothing hung on pegs by the door, which seemed at least three stades away.

Reaching them, Tarian gave a mighty shiver that ran through her whole body before she pulled down her simplest dress. She didn't want to appear lofty before her fellow brothers and sisters, gathered together on this Lord's Day. Clutching the dress to her, she raced back toward the hearth near her bed. The fire burned low, anticipating the coming daylight to help to heat the room, but 'twas still warmer here than near the drafty door. As quickly as her numb fingers could accomplish the task, she struggled into the russet garment, lacing up the sides. No need to change her woolen stockings; she pushed her feet into the cold leather shoes.

God, give me courage.

The moon began to lose its power, black giving way to an ash-gray as Tarian brushed her thick auburn hair with deft strokes. She wove it quickly into a braid, finishing the end with a leather cord. A splash of freezing water from the basin finished her preparations.

There. She was ready. Taking a deep breath to steady herself, Tarian crossed to the door once more. Hesitation would be the death of her actions. She plucked her cloak from its peg and wrapped it around her, drawing the hood over her head to conceal her white face. She stood there for just a second, welcoming the warmth of the wool. Then she moved, out into the dark corridor, lit only by torches sparsely placed in brackets on the walls.

As mistress of the estate, Tarian knew where the guards patrolled, knew who was watchful, who was less cautious and more eager to stay near the warm main hall. Eyes alert, she darted through the shadows, keeping her face well-hidden from the flickering torchlight and her dark cloak concealing her presence.

She moved less fearfully once she had passed Drustan's door. The first Saturday evening, she had needed to make an excuse for leaving his room in the night. As a result, she had spent this past week worrying about what she could say to him to once again excuse herself from his bed. Much to her relief, he had not summoned her last night. 'Twas unusual, for Drustan always wanted her available in his chamber when he stayed at home.

Thank you, Lord. You know I would never have been able to get out this morning. Tarian breathed a sigh as she reached one of the fortress' side doors, meant for servants to exit and enter. With both hands, she guided the latch so that the door hinges would not creak. A moment more and she stood outside.

Tarian closed her eyes as the wind brushed her hair and clothing. Here, in this undefiled air, with the distant horizon slowly turning from soft gray to palest yellow, she felt redeemed. She knew it at other times, aye, but now she felt most keenly that she belonged to another kingdom. In this dawn, with no one else around her, the sense of another Presence grew and surrounded her. The sense filled her so strongly that Tarian felt that One walked beside her, One more real than the stone that made up the fortress behind her.

She breathed in the bitterly crisp air, and unexpected tears sprang to her eyes. *I have heard Your voice, Lord. Why has Drustan not? He says he knows You, but how can he, living as he does, thinking as he does?*

Walking forward, she bit her lip, her heart agonized. *Why did I marry him? Why did I go against my parents' wishes? I was a fool.* Though 'twas four years past, she could still see her mother's worried face amid the wedding splendor, her father's reluctant blessing. And her priest-uncle's smiling face encouraging her to go through with the marriage, despite all the warning signs.

'Tis in the past now. I can't go back. Tarian sniffed back her tears, wiped her eyes with her hands, and wiped her hands on her cloak. She quickened her pace across the courtyard. One of the kitchen maids, Deirdre, had offered to accompany her to the mass this week, and regardless of her confident air, Tarian eagerly had accepted.

Lord, I do want a friend, she had entreated silently afterward, almost embarrassed at her vulnerability. *Don't let Deirdre think that I'm not worthwhile.*

Well, time would tell what the servant thought of Tarian. Now, she waited for Deirdre by the kitchen door, rubbing one foot then the other against her legs to keep warm.

~ ~ ~

Calum awoke from a deep sleep. Lifting his head from his hands, he sucked in his breath from the ache in his back and looked toward the house's single window. Dawn had begun to barely touch the night sky. All night, he had dozed in and out of sleep sitting up by the bed of Bethan's mother. In her fevered illness, Bethan's mother thrashed from time to time, her eyes sometimes open but not seeing. Her skinny face looked gaunt and deeply lined from the disease that ravaged her body, yet her disquieted, anguished expression brought him more distress to see. *How different from Cairine...* 'Twas an inexplicable peace that had guarded his sister, even as the flames licked her bare feet. *So must Enoch have looked, and Moses, Samuel, and John the Baptist...who walked with God.* Gazing into the firelight, Calum felt an unnamable longing.

So might you look. The thought came suddenly and not from his own mind, he knew. Tears rising to his eyes, he responded. *But how, Lord? I am not like these men. My heart is not like theirs.* Feeling the sorrow in every crevice of his spirit, Calum let his tears drip one by one down his cheeks, watched them spot the knees of his trousers. In this darkened house, where one woman slept in aged sickness and two others in youthful exhaustion, he knew that no one saw his tears but One.

Cannot You give me a new heart, Lord, that I may think and do only right and walk purely before You? With few words, he poured out his aching heart before his God, knowing that he was heard, yet unsure whether his words would be considered worthy.

After a time, Calum wiped away his tears and stood. The dawn had lightened the cottage but had brought little warmth with its arrival. Taking his flint, he quietly started a fire in the hearth, coaxing it to vibrant life with dry leaves and twigs.

"Thank you, Calum."

The softly-spoken words caused him to turn his head. Just awake, Bethan sat up next to her slumbering sister. Her sweet, pale face held a smile of simple gratitude.

"'Tis my pleasure, lass," he answered, smiling back with an effort. "Your mother still sleeps. I thought we could get breakfast going before the little one wakes up."

Bethan pushed back her blankets and rose. "Nay, Calum. I'll get breakfast. You've not had any sleep."

He shook his head. "I have, Bethan. I dozed all night, if the truth be told."

Her eyes questioned him.

"I'm fine, lass," he said firmly. "If I want some sleep, I'll take a nap later."

"Alright, if you're sure, but I'm still preparing breakfast," she said, her hands going to her unbound hair. She began to smooth and braid it, and Calum turned away.

"I'll fetch some water," he said and grabbed the buckets.

~ ~ ~

Feeling more like a child than she had ever, Tarian picked up the skirt of her dress and ran after Deirdre. Her feet pounded the ground beneath her as quickly as her heart beat within her chest. Rushing through the dewy, late-autumn grass, she caught up with her gasping friend as they neared the manor's walls. With a glance at the gate, Tarian grasped Deirdre's hand.

"Come," she said. "I don't want to go back just yet." She pulled Deirdre down into a little dip in the ground. Here, sitting down, they were invisible to those guards on the manor walls.

Deirdre fell on her back, breathing heavily and laughing. "Oh," she panted, "I thought you would never run after me."

Tarian fell back on the grass, too. "Why not?" she demanded.

Deirdre smiled. "No reason."

"Come, now. Why did you think I wouldn't chase you?"

Deirdre shook her head.

"Deirdre, tell me! I must know."

"Well…" Deirdre glanced up at the sky, her distant smile still pulling up her wide mouth. "'Tis beneath your dignity and all, you know, my lady. And 'tis not what the master expects of his wife, I'm sure."

Tarian sobered. "No, it's not." She plucked a few pieces of grass and twisted them together. "But neither is attending mass."

Deirdre turned on her side, propping her head up on her long hand, so thin that Tarian could see the blue veins running through it. "Will he be very angry if he finds out you came today?"

Tarian tamped down the fear that rose in her at the thought of facing Drustan. "I don't know. I hope not." She forced a smile. "Probably, he won't find out. He was still sleeping when I left. His nephew is visiting, and they stayed up past midnight. I'm sure that a cask of ale couldn't have bested him for drunkenness last night."

Deirdre smiled back, sympathy in her dark eyes. Tarian felt relief that 'twas not pity lurking there.

With a sigh, the kitchen maid rolled up and stood, brushing the bits of grass off her skirt. "Well, I must get back. Cook will be waiting for me to start the bread with the younger girls." She offered a hand to Tarian, who accepted it and rose to her feet. "'Tis too bad you can't meet Cook; you'd like her, I think, my lady."

"Why does she not come to mass?"

Deirdre started walking toward the manor walls. The sun had fully risen now, but the air still held a deep chill, and mist clouded their (and Tarian hoped, the guards') vision. "She can't move too far from the kitchens nowadays. Her legs have been badly swollen for some time. She spends much of her time with them propped up, delegating tasks rather than being able to do them herself."

"Has a physician seen her?"

Deirdre shrugged. "Bricius has some medical knowledge, but Cook prefers the old remedies, she says. God works best through nature, she says. She takes potions and such."

Tarian nodded. Her mother would agree with the old servant, probably. "I would like to meet her."

Deirdre smiled. "Well, maybe you will, my lady, if God heals her legs and the master doesn't stop you from coming to meetings."

And maybe sooner, if I keep my courage. "We must part ways," Tarian said as they approached the side gate. She pulled her hood up to conceal her face again. "Farewell. And thank you, Deirdre."

"For what?"

Tarian's heart felt full, perhaps for the first time since she'd left home. "You don't know…"

She trailed off and dropped her gaze. The kitchen maid hesitated a moment, then pulled her into a gentle embrace. After a moment, Deirdre released her with a kiss to her cheek. "Grace and peace in our Lord, sister," she murmured.

"Grace and peace," Tarian said, not minding the tears that flooded her eyes.

CHAPTER EIGHTEEN

Camelot

He walked with a measured, steady step, remembering times gone by. Days and weeks, months and years, when he had sprinted down this same corridor, his heart as light as his feet, his laughter echoing across the stone walls.

That time has vanished. He raised his chin and quickened his pace. But the memories of the past persisted; the pictures rose to his mind unbidden...

He was eight years old again, his feet bare as they slapped the stone. Halfway down the hall, he stubbed his toe on an uneven flag. Oh, it hurt! Wincing, he grabbed his offended member and bent curious eyes toward it. Already red. And it looked like the toenail might blacken at that. But never mind! The child dropped his foot and set off again at a limping trot. He must hurry. The high king waited for him.

Arthur had said they would go riding today, just he and Deoradhan. Of course, some guards would come along for safety's sake, but other than that, 'twould be just the two of them. Deoradhan would have the fine little sorrel pony, and the king would ride his favorite black mare. He couldn't stop the smile from nearly splitting his face in two, showing the gaps where his last baby teeth had fallen out. How magnificent! He would get to spend a whole day with his favorite person in all of the world.

Suddenly, from behind him, someone grasped his shoulder, making him whirl around. 'Twas the king! The man's blue eyes laughed along with his pleasant mouth at having surprised canny Deoradhan. Good. He was dressed in riding clothes, ready for their day. He hadn't forgotten. Arthur never forgot, never went back on his word.

"Ready, my lad?"

Deoradhan nodded. "Aye! I've brought provisions for us," he added, lifting up a hefty sack filled with bread, cheese, and oatcakes.

"Good. And shall we bring the dogs with us?" asked the king.

Deoradhan shook his head. "No."

"Why not?"

"They always scare away the rabbits and thrushes. And I like to watch them."

Arthur smiled, that golden smile that lit up his whole countenance, and Deoradhan felt the blessing of the king's approval. "Most boys your age and older only like to kill the little animals. I'm glad you're not like that, lad." He took Deoradhan's small hand in his large, battle-callused one. "Be a protector, lad. 'Tis easy to destroy."

And he should know. *He destroyed my father's kingdom and nearly wiped his lineage from the earth.* Deoradhan set his jaw and strode the last few steps to the king's private chambers. *I will take what is rightfully mine.* No more trickery. No more empty words to stave off a legitimate hunger.

Once again, two guards stood before the door, alert to his approach.

"Name?" one of them asked.

"Deoradhan."

The two guards exchanged looks. "Deoradhan of...?"

Deoradhan looked the man straight in the eyes. "Deoradhan only," he stated. "The king expects me. Please tell him I've arrived." He would stand for none of their self-important bustling this morning.

The authoritative tone worked. "Aye, my lord," one of the guards murmured and disappeared into the king's chambers.

He returned almost immediately, his manner respectful. "The king awaits you, my lord."

The guard held the smooth wooden door open, but Deoradhan hesitated for just a moment. He would enter this chamber as a penniless wanderer, dependent on his conquerors for his livelihood. He would exit either unchanged or much changed, a commoner, forever deprived of his legitimate inheritance, or a king himself, possessing a dominion in fact. With a deep breath and his head held upright, he moved through the familiar doors.

Bearskin rugs carpeted the floor, their rich color coordinating with that of the gold-threaded tapestries covering most of the walls. Deoradhan remembered how often as a boy he had run his finger over the threads, tracing the stories told in those tapestries. He had also liked to lift the heavy wall coverings to see the Roman-style frescoes behind them, fading remnants of a unifying and civilized culture. *The kind of state which my hero Arthur wanted to create once more.*

And failed. The image of the intensely-divided great hall flashed into Deoradhan's mind, and a strange mixture of sadness and satisfaction filled his heart. Scholars, warriors, druids, Christians, Romans, British. Logress might hold against intruders, Saxons, Jutes, Angles, Irish; but could it stand the pressure to collapse from within? Deoradhan guessed not.

He strode forward, between the wall torches that always held a flame within this secluded chamber. The room was large, holding several recesses, and Deoradhan was unsure where Arthur would be waiting for him. *Will anyone be listening to our conversation?* Deoradhan smiled. *Or shall I call it, our confrontation?*

"Deoradhan?"

The familiar voice called from one of the recesses on the far side of the chamber. Something within Deoradhan stirred to hear that sweet tone again.

"My lord Arthur," he responded and stepped to the alcove, his footsteps soft on the rugs. He held his breath inwardly as he peered in at the once-beloved man he'd not set eyes upon for years.

Arthur sat at his carved writing table, companioned by two shelves holding a few dozen volumes. Deoradhan remembered that the king had valued highly the wise works of the ancients and knew that he must have spent a great deal to procure his little library, which had grown since the young man left the court. Even now, the king had a volume laid open before him as he worked.

As soon as Deoradhan entered the king's view, the older man put aside his reed pen and stood. "Deoradhan, welcome."

"Lord Arthur," Deoradhan acknowledged, noting that Arthur didn't offer his hand in friendship. *How far our relationship has gone from where 'twas once.* "I'm disturbing your work, I think," he stated.

Arthur smiled, weariness hanging around his mouth. "Nay, I'm just making notes on a few things. My memory isn't what it once was." He shook his head, and Deoradhan noticed gray lacing the gold in the king's hair. His cheeks, too, appeared lean and colorless.

"Have you been ill, my lord?" Deoradhan found himself asking. *What do you care if he is ill?* But tenderness for the man took him by force.

Arthur shook his head. "I have many concerns." He sighed. "I suppose they have worn me down a little. But I'm glad to see your face again, Deoradhan. Come, share a cup of wine and some cakes with me. 'Tis early yet, and I've not breakfasted."

With a nod, Deoradhan acquiesced, and the king moved out of the alcove toward a few cushioned chairs. Deoradhan felt the heat rising from beneath the floor and remembered that Camelot still used its Roman heating system. He tried to ignore the pleasant warmth. *I prefer the peat fires of the north to this conqueror's borrowed luxuries.*

"How is your old nurse, Meghyn? Still at Oxfield's kitchens, aye?" Arthur asked as he walked, his movements as always like that of a steady war-horse.

"Aye. She's well, as far as I know." Deoradhan felt a bit guilty that the woman who had encompassed his whole maternal world now entered his thoughts so rarely.

"A good woman, she is," commented the high king.

"Aye," agreed Deoradhan. *A little small-minded when it comes to religion, but a good woman overall.*

They seated themselves, Deoradhan sitting very straight, and Arthur poured two silver cups of deep red wine. Deoradhan accepted his cup, the rich fruity scent filling his nostrils as he sipped it. A plate on the low table held some oatcakes, but neither he nor the king touched them.

"Why have you returned, my son?"

The question came so suddenly, so simply. Taken aback by the king's directness, Deoradhan couldn't find the words to reply at first. Finally, he answered, "Because you have taken what is mine, Lord Arthur."

A look of pain passed over the king's face and he stayed silent for a moment. Deoradhan tensed, readying himself to answer what defense the man would give. But the words that fell from Arthur's lips surprised him.

"I ... cannot tell you how much I regret some of my early decisions as high king," he said softly. "I was young, but youth doesn't excuse sin. I wronged you, Deoradhan. I should never have authorized Weylin to do many of the things he did in the north. I am sorry, lad."

Arthur's eyes testified to his sincerity, and Deoradhan couldn't stop the old affection from rising in his spirit. He knew how hard 'twas for a ruler to admit he had done wrong. Perhaps then the man had prepared himself to offer Deoradhan his rightful reparation. He waited, sure that the king had more to say.

But Arthur stayed silent. Tensely silent, his kind eyes holding Deoradhan's own. Finally Deoradhan commanded quietly, "Give me my father's land, my lord. Return what you have stolen by force."

Arthur shook his head. "Nay."

"Why? You said you were in the wrong. Do now what is right by me!" he pleaded.

The tired shadows around the king's eyes were pronounced as he leaned back in his chair. "What is done has been done, lad. Let it rest."

Deoradhan snorted. "Let it rest! It has rested for too long. For half my life, I thought I was your misbegotten son, for three years that I was orphaned, dependent upon your benevolence. When I finally learned the truth from someone else's lips, you exiled me to Gaul!"

"I never exiled you, lad. We both agreed 'twas for the best that you spend time away."

"And who benefited from that?"

The king furrowed his eyebrows questioningly. "I sent you to the best schools to be found abroad. I paid for the best tutors, the best education for you, Deoradhan."

Deoradhan set his jaw. "Aye, you bought yourself time, my lord. You paid for my education, I'll admit that." He leaned forward, staring into the king's eyes. "And tell me, O king, what have you decided to do with me now? I'm not giving up my rights as the son of Eion, king of Lothian, no matter how much you pay out of your treasuries."

Arthur's eyes became kind iron. "I cannot give you what you desire, Deoradhan. Ask for something else, almost anything else, but Lothian I cannot give you."

Deoradhan's anger flared. He jumped up from his seat, glaring down at the king. "Cannot, or will not? Sometimes I think you enjoy torturing me."

"My son—"

"I am not your son!"

"I know that." Sorrow occupied the king's face. *I hope he's as miserable as he's made me*, thought Deoradhan. Suddenly, he remembered another grievance.

"You never even told me about the son Weylin begot upon my mother," Deoradhan burst out. "Is that why you hesitate? Because you would rather see that brute's spawn on Lothian's throne?"

The king looked surprised. "Who told you about Solas?"

Deoradhan smirked. "Who do you think? His sister, Lady

Fiona. She mistook me for her brother from faraway."

Arthur nodded. "He rarely comes to court, but you do look very similar. Solas, however, is beside the point. He has nothing to do with my decision." He looked straight into Deoradhan's eyes. "And it is a decision, Deoradhan, not a hesitation. For the good of all Logress, I must stand firm. How can I possibly put you on Lothian's throne? Years ago, I gave Weylin leave to conquer Dunpeledyr because your father would not submit to the unification. Now you think I can replace my representative with the son of my former opponent?" He shook his head. "Nay. As long as he stays loyal to me and abides by the laws of Camelot, Weylin remains on Lothian's throne."

"But it is my rightful place!" Deoradhan exclaimed, tears of anger rising to his eyes. "Lothian was not yours to take."

Arthur stood. "I am high king, Deoradhan. And I decide what is your rightful place."

Deoradhan faced that unyielding wall, resentment rising. After a moment, Arthur sat back down. The king continued softly, "I cannot change what Weylin has done. He will have to answer to God for that."

Deoradhan gave a hard laugh. "Your God judges even less fairly than you do."

Arthur paused, then said, "There are several regions across Logress in need of leadership. If you wish, I will name you lord over whichever land you choose—"

Deoradhan turned his back to the king, purposely disrespecting him. "Keep your lands. I don't want them."

"Then I have nothing else to offer you, Deoradhan. There is nothing else I can give." The king's voice held tired authority.

Without glancing back, Deoradhan moved toward the door. "Then this interview has finished," he said.

"What..."

Arthur's question trailed away, and Deoradhan felt compelled to turn around. "I knew you would deny me before I came. I thought I would give you an opportunity to do right. I showed you mercy, though you've given none to me. But now I know what I have to do."

With a grim smile, he turned on his heel and swept through the doorway, into the bleak corridor. He let the door slam behind him, glad to see the guards' astonished faces as he disrespected the king.

Their king, he reminded himself, moving down the hallway. *Not mine. I have no lord but myself. I will have no master but my own spirit.*

CHAPTER NINETEEN

Oxfield

The cold wind whirled the dry leaves into a dance at Bricius' feet. He stood from his work and limping a little with stiffness, moved toward the open doorway. Once there, the crisp air intoxicated him, and he stood, letting the wind brush through his graying hair, caress his wrinkled cheeks, and cause him to shiver. A mystery existed in the changing of the seasons, 'twas certain.

But the LORD was not in the wind...

Bricius smiled. "Aye, Lord, but sometimes I can hear Your voice in the wind," he spoke aloud.

"Talking to yourself, old man?"

He turned to find Lydia smiling at him, a basket of unspun wool in her arms. He held out his hand, and she came to his side, smiling up at him. His arm gently circled her shoulder, and he felt her relax in his protection.

"Meghyn's poorly," murmured Lydia after they had stood thus for long moments.

"Aye?"

She nodded. "I visited her today. Her ankles have turned blue and swelled up like a blown-up bladder-ball."

Bricius raised his brows. "I've tried to give her my medicines, but she insists on those pagan potions." Of course the woman wouldn't get well if she refused the aid of modern science, given by

God.

"Oh, Bricius, I see your commonsense, but where's your compassion? So your pride's hurt because she won't take your help." Lydia sighed and turned imploring eyes up to her husband. "She covets your prayers, you know."

"Very well. I'll go see her in the morning, if you've time to come along." *And you can help me try to talk some sense into her.*

Lydia smiled her thanks. "I knew you would, love." With a peck on his cheek, she moved out into the courtyard with her basket of wool.

Bricius shook his head. He had a sermon to prepare.

~ ~ ~

Tarian hummed as she buckled the bridle of her favorite mare, Archer. True, she could have the stable lads tack up the small chestnut horse, but she preferred to do it herself. She took pleasure in the glossy red-brown coat, soft under her fingers as she moved on to saddle the mare. She felt a nuzzle against her arm and playfully pushed the mare's nose away. Such a gentle horse Archer was.

"Is all ready for the feast?" Tarian heard her husband ask as he entered the stable. At his question, her heart thundered so hard that it hurt her chest. She tried to breathe evenly, tried to avoid betrayal by her swiftly rising and falling shoulders. She felt fear clutch at her lungs, freeze her limbs.

"I said, is everything prepared for the feast, wife?"

His tone demanded an answer. *Be my help, O Lord. Give me courage.* She turned to face her husband. *My enemy,* she realized, looking up at his hard face and wintry eyes.

"Well? Is it?"

"Nay," she finally replied and felt relief. She had done it.

Drustan smiled, his eyebrows lowered as if he didn't understand. He gently took the bridle reins from her hand and began stroking the mare's nose. "Well, hadn't you better get started with the planning, my dear? Samhain draws near, you know. Tomorrow night."

Tarian heard the familiar, lecherous excitement trickle into his voice. She shook her head. "I will not plan that feast," she answered.

"What do you mean? Don't you know I can't wait to see you all dressed up, dancing and laughing by the bonfires? We must have a feast, Tarian."

She looked him straight in the eyes. "You may have a feast to indulge your lusts in the name of religion, Drustan, but I will not. I will have no part of it."

He stayed silent for a moment. Perhaps he would let it pass. Perhaps the only outcome would be additional coldness to their already numb marriage. Tarian turned and began to fasten the saddle cinch around the mare's girth.

With a lurch of his muscled arm, Drustan suddenly yanked the bridle reins down. The horse gave a squeal of pain and pulled its head up toward the ceiling. Tarian watched immobile as Drustan jerked the reins down once more, bringing a more frenzied reaction from the animal. Then her mind and body moved, and she flew at the man, trying to grab the leather straps from him.

Drustan was ready for her and shoved her away with a push so hard it propelled her into the stone wall. Tarian fell to the straw bedding and quaked as her husband, finished with tormenting the mare, turned toward her. Bending down, he wrenched her to her feet by her elbow and gave a heavy blow to her cheek.

"Let's understand one another, Tarian," he said, pulling her close to his face. She couldn't breathe for fear. "If you go against me, I will go against you. If you hurt me, I will hurt you. I hope I've been plain."

She nodded, unable to speak.

"Good. You're going to regret not participating in this feast. I give you my word on that, my lady. I give you my word." He dropped his hands from her elbows, by all appearances calm, except for the florid coloring of his countenance. He smiled at her. "Now get cleaned up. I won't be embarrassed by a wife of mine looking like she demeaned herself in the stables."

Tarian's face turned white with insult. "You are a...a depraved man," she choked out as he strolled toward the stable door.

Drustan paused and turned. The same slight smile decorated his lips, making his thick cheeks puff a little. "Depraved?" he questioned. "You haven't seen me depraved yet, wife. Watch and wonder, my dear. Watch and wonder."

~ ~ ~

Set your house in order, for you shall die...

Meghyn struggled to open her eyes. They were heavy, so heavy...

Set your house in order...

Even before full consciousness came, the throbbing pain pushed through her legs.

Will I die, Lord? Blurry-eyed with sleep, Meghyn gazed down at her calves, raised up on a stool. No matter how long she kept them up now, the swelling only increased.

She turned her eyes toward the busy gaggle of kitchen maidservants, chattering as they prepared for the evening meal. *I was once young, too. How fast the days fly. Have I redeemed my time?*

Meghyn watched Deirdre helping one of the younger girls with a stew bubbling over the fire. Sweet she was, that one. *You cut her and Bethan from the same cloth, Lord.* Reluctantly, her eyes traveled over toward Aine, whose rapt face turned up toward that troublemaker Winter.

What of when Deoradhan returns? Will he marry Aine? Lord, help my headstrong boy if you take me home.

Meghyn was just closing her eyes again when she heard a flurry of whispering and then abrupt silence. Her eyes snapped open to see a young woman entering the kitchen through the interior door. After a moment of confusion, Meghyn realized 'twas the mistress of the estate herself. The kitchen girls had already recognized someone significant had entered and stayed mute, bobbing a curtsy or two.

Meghyn struggled to her feet and stood, bent a little with pain. "Lady Tarian," she greeted the noblewoman. "Welcome."

Lady Tarian seemed relieved to hear herself well-received but kept her poise in place as she stepped across the warm kitchen to Meghyn. "Meghyn, aye?"

"Aye, my lady, I'm head of the kitchen," replied Meghyn. As was her place, she waited for her mistress to tell her why she had come. She hoped 'twould not take long, for the pressure in her painful legs increased with each moment.

"I'm very glad to meet you, Meghyn. Please, sit and put your legs up. Deirdre told me about them."

The woman's smile seemed sincere. Meghyn breathed a sigh as she sat back down and heaved her club-like calves up one-by-one. "Thank you, my lady," she murmured.

Lady Tarian pulled up a stool and sat across from her, almost as if she planned to stay for awhile. She sat up very straight but her long, slim fingers played with the wool fabric of her dress. "Have you had a doctor look at your legs, Meghyn?" she asked suddenly, as if her occupied thoughts had been invaded suddenly with the question.

Meghyn smiled. "Aye, my lady. Bricius the potter has given me his opinion."

The noblewoman's eyebrows shot up. "He is a medical man as well, then? Is there nothing the man doesn't do?"

Meghyn chuckled. "He learned something of the medical art when in the monastery, and 'tis helpful to others from time to time."

The woman looked thoughtful, her auburn hair wisping around her serious eyes.

Meghyn paused. Would the lady take a question without offense? She decided to start small. "Deirdre tells me you've been coming to the Lord's Day meeting under the oak, my lady."

Lady Tarian's lips turned up. "Aye, I have. I overheard one of the servants talking about it and when I asked, Bricius told me I would be welcome."

"And do you enjoy it, my lady?"

"My heart hasn't felt so light for a long time."

Meghyn's smile grew. "'I was glad when they said to me, "Let us go to the house of the LORD,"' aye, my lady?"

The noblewoman looked at her questioningly.

"'Tis from the Scriptures, my lady," explained Meghyn. "The psalms of David."

"Oh."

Meghyn took courage at the woman's vulnerability. "May I ask a question, my lady?"

"Aye, please feel at liberty, Meghyn."

"Would you call yourself a Christian, Lady Tarian?"

A thoughtfulness grew on the countenance of the young woman sitting across from Meghyn. She stayed quiet for a few moments, then murmured, "When I was a young girl, I asked Jesus to purify me from my sin, and I determined to follow him. But now I don't know, Meghyn."

"Why do you say that, Lady Tarian, if you permit my boldness in asking?"

The noblewoman looked at her, and Meghyn thought she detected a settled sadness in her eyes. "Because much of the time I don't feel that I belong to Christ. A true Christian is one who is holy, set apart for God's use, whose thoughts are only full of God."

"And what are your thoughts full of, my lady?"

A heavy sigh escaped from Lady Tarian's chest, as if her heart groaned in its prison. "My own happiness, Meghyn. I want to be happy." She grimaced a smile. "'Tis why I married my lord."

"I think we all want to be happy, my lady. 'Tis not an evil," smiled Meghyn.

"Then I sought my happiness in the wrong things, I suppose." Meghyn cocked her head, listening, as the lady continued. "This all goes back a long time. I grew up in Cantia, near the southeastern coast. Though not wealthy, my father held a position of influence as one of the lord's advisors. His brother, my uncle, served as a priest of the Church for the lord's household. My mother came from one of the oldest tribes in Cantia; she was born a princess, the daughter of a chieftain, subjugated by Uther Pendragon.

"As I grew older, I realized 'twas expected that I marry well, to bring the family wealth and honor, as any daughter should. When I was thirteen, my uncle undertook the task of betrothal; the lord of Cantia himself contributed generously to my dowry as a thank-you to my father for his years of service. My parents left the matter entirely in my uncle's deft hands, stipulating only that the man chosen be an honorable man of the Christian faith, not holding to the old ways.

"After a year and a half of negotiations and bartering, my uncle announced that he had purchased a bridegroom for me and thereby a favorable alliance with a neighboring lord. That lord was Drustan of Oxfield, an older man, aye, but favorable in every worldly respect."

Lady Tarian looked Meghyn straight in the eyes, as if to make her understand through her earnestness. "My parents opposed the match from the start. Initially, aye, they felt flattered that their daughter would become lady of Oxfield, a great and rich estate. But then my mother remembered hearing of Drustan's ambivalence toward religious matters. He acted a Christian when 'twas convenient and a pagan when not. Not to be trusted, my father said when he met him, and he knew the look of deceit from his many years of dealing with such ones."

"Why didn't you listen to them, my lady?"

Lady Tarian shook her head and smiled. "It goes back to what I said earlier, Meghyn. I felt discontent in Cantia, as the carefully-guarded daughter of the lord's advisor. I thought I would be happy as the mistress of Oxfield, having my own way, spending my time as I saw fit, doing as I pleased, the petted wife of a rich nobleman."

Meghyn nodded. She had known the feeling too at one time. "So…"

Lady Tarian shrugged. "So I married him with my uncle the

priest's blessing, the lord of Cantia's blessing, the people's blessing. But not God's blessing. And I have paid for it. Dearly."

She smiled and turned her gaze toward the floor, and Meghyn noticed for the first time that the young woman's right cheekbone looked dark bluish. *Perhaps 'tis only the shadows from the firelight.* "My lady," she said, reaching across and grasping Lady Tarian's hands in her own heavy rough ones, "Have you asked the Lord's pardon for going against your parents' judgment like that? For doing what you sensed 'twas wrong?"

Lady Tarian raised her eyes, brimming brightly with tears. She nodded. "Aye, and I've tried to follow Him again. Meghyn, do you think that God gives second chances? Or am I condemned for life to..." The tears spilled over, running down her pale cheeks.

"The Lord's compassions fail not; they are new every morning, my lady."

"But Drustan..."

Meghyn rubbed the girl's hands. "Don't you worry about him. God will take care of that man. Do you think he can stand in the Almighty's way for a moment?"

The noblewoman shook her head. "Nay."

"Nay is right."

"But I got myself into this," Lady Tarian burst out. "I'm not suffering because I did rightly."

"Then pray the prayer of David, my lady: 'Remember not the sins of my youth or my transgressions; according to your steadfast love remember me, for the sake of your goodness, O LORD!'" Meghyn paused to let the words sink into the young woman's soul like rain on dry moss. "'Tis not my place to say whether your early conversion to Christ was real, my lady. That's between you and your Lord. But whether 'twas or 'twas not, you can begin this moment to obey. As David says in that same psalm, 'The friendship of the LORD is for those who fear him, and he makes known to them his covenant.' The Lord may have a hard lesson for you to learn, but 'tis from the hand of a loving Father, not a punishing judge."

The lady turned her face toward the fire so that the kitchen maids couldn't see her rapid tears. Meghyn watched as the young woman pushed back the flowing emotions and wiped her eyes. After a few moments, Lady Tarian turned back to Meghyn.

"'Tis late. I must be going."

Meghyn nodded. "My prayers go with you, my lady."

A smile blossomed on the lady's face. "Thank you, Meghyn. For everything you've said. You don't know..." She stopped. "Thank you."

She rose to her feet, and Meghyn began to struggle up herself. "Nay, don't trouble yourself," Lady Tarian pressed a hand to her shoulder. "Rest your legs, dear woman."

"Thank you, my lady," said Meghyn. She watched the young woman move across the kitchen toward the exit.

In wrath remember mercy, O Lord...

CHAPTER TWENTY

West Lea

"She looks very ill," Bethan heard her own words spill from her lips without emotion. "You think so, aye?" She glanced up at Calum. He stood by her shoulder, silent but his eyes filled with thought.

She wiped her mother's face again. *It does no good.* Over and over, she had cooled the red face with water, but the heat rising from the skin would not decrease. A rash covered her mother's body like leprosy. Mama had not recovered real consciousness since Bethan and Calum had arrived several days past.

"Where's Enid?" she suddenly remembered.

"She's gone to the neighbors' to play," Calum replied. He gently took the bowl of water from her hands. "Why don't you heat some gruel? I'll take over here."

Bethan felt reluctant to leave her mother's side but relieved as well. 'Twas well-past noon, and she'd been sitting at her mother's side since daybreak. Her back felt as if a knife had split it in two. She rose from the three-legged stool, giving place to Calum, who folded his tall frame onto the low seat.

As she prepared the light food, Bethan found her eyes moving toward the guard again and again. How patient he was as he wiped Mama's face, running the cloth over her taut skin with the tenderness of a doe toward its fawn. Grace flowed through the scars on his face, making what would have been disfigurement, beauty. He bent himself to the task single-mindedly, not eager to rush off or impatient for Bethan to resume her place.

Whatever happens, Lord, Bethan prayed as she stirred the watery mixture over the hearth, *thank you for Calum.*

She felt her heart constrict as she realized what she had prayed. *Whatever happens…*

Camelot

"Lord Deoradhan! You're not leaving us already?" About to mount, Deoradhan turned at the sound of Lady Fiona's voice. She stood at the stable door, a heavy shawl wrapped around her shoulders. Deoradhan smiled, despite the storm raging within his heart. Or perhaps because her appearance proved to be a soothing influence.

"Aye," he replied. "I'm going."

"You've an estate to get back to?"

Deoradhan gave a twisted smile. "Nay. Not yet, anyway."

Lady Fiona tilted her head to the side. "You stand to inherit your domain, then?"

"Let's just say someone is holding it for me," he answered. "And you, Lady Fiona? Where do you make your home?" he asked, not really caring but wanting to be kind to this friendly girl. *She can't help who her father is, after all.*

She moved toward his mount Alasdair and began to stroke the horse's neck, her pale fingers running over the gray mane. "Here mostly," she said without smiling, yet with peace in her eyes. "My father has determined it best that I remain as a lady-in-waiting to the queen. He and I do not see eye-to-eye on many things."

"So you are not often at…what is the name of your father's estate?" he asked.

"Dunpeledyr," she supplied. "Nay, very seldom. I go there perhaps once a year, if that. 'Tis in beautiful country, though."

"You must miss your brother."

"Solas? Aye, very much. He and I have the same heart, though different ways of expressing our feelings." She ran her hand over the horse's nose and smiled up at Deoradhan. "Which is why he can remain at Dunpeledyr and I am sent away."

Deoradhan smiled. The young lady had spirit, a sense of freed individuality. Aine came to his mind then. *She can be forgiven a few faults, Deoradhan. She is young yet and a more innocently perfect girl never breathed.*

"A beautiful horse, this," she commented. "My father raises horses. My lord king himself has purchased some for his stables." She shook her head. "Father never thinks anyone can care for his horses well enough. There's always a new horsemaster at Dunpeledyr, every time I visit. Last time I heard, he had let the latest one go as well."

Her words caught Deoradhan's interest. "Indeed, my lady?" He paused, knitting his plot quickly. "Would your father take me on, do you think? I am well-experienced with horses, you know."

Lady Fiona raised her eyebrows. "You, my lord? Why would you want to be horsemaster at Dunpeledyr? I'm sure you have more lofty things to occupy you. Why not go abroad to study some more? Or become a court intriguer. Arthur can always use another," she smiled.

"Nay, I've studied and entertained myself to my heart's content. All I can do now is wait for my inheritance. And there's no better place to wait than in Lothian."

"Why do you say that?" Her eyes narrowed, puzzled.

Deoradhan caught his breath. *I've said too much. This one is quick.* "You said yourself that Lothian is beautiful. Who wouldn't wish to wait out the years in beauty?" *Though not many years now.*

Lady Fiona smiled. "Well, you can try, my lord. If you like, I'll write to my father about you, asking him to consider it."

"I beg your pardon for saying this, my lady, but if relations are strained between the two of you, would that do more harm than good?"

She shook her head. "Nay. My father and I disagree on many

things, but even I must admit that he conducts his business affairs well and he must admit that I give good counsel on such issues. So, you're not to fear, my lord. My recommendation will do you good. Trust me."

Deoradhan nodded slowly. For some reason, he found it easy to believe this pleasant but fiery girl. "Alright," he replied. "Thank you."

She nodded.

"Until we meet again, then," he said, mounting.

"Aye, my lord. And see that you do my recommendation good, as well."

'Twas meant lightly, he knew from her sparkling eyes, but the uneasy guilt in his heart choked any answer he would have given her.

CHAPTER TWENTY-ONE

Oxfield

"Aine, someone wants to speak with you." Deirdre's voice brought Aine's head up from her sweeping. At Aine's questioning look, Deirdre added, "She's waiting at the door."

Strange. In her three years at Oxfield, she never had received visitors. Aine laid her broom aside. "I'll be right back," she promised, and Deirdre nodded. The older girl had become an unofficial stand-in manager since Cook had become so immobile in the past few weeks, and Aine felt obligated to let her know her whereabouts.

It's not Deoradhan, returned from Camelot, because Deirdre said 'twas a "she." Her heart fluttered like a butterfly caught in the hand. *Though I wish 'twas he.*

She frowned as she made her way toward the passageway leading out to the exterior door. Deoradhan had not written to her since leaving almost two weeks ago. Soon, their promise of a speedy marriage would be null. 'Twas nearly a month since he pledged to marry her. *And a month can bring many changes. I hope he has not changed.* Then Aine bit her smiling lips as another thought stole into her mind. *Though if he has, my prospects have brightened for sure and certain with Lord Lancelot's attentions to me lately.* Since yesterday, Lord Drustan's nephew had spoken to her twice as she went about her work in the courtyard. Interesting, to say the least. Aine's step took on a bounce.

Her hand lifted the latch. The heavy door wasn't bolted during the day, and she pulled it open easily. As the squeak of its hinges died away, the cloaked visitor turned to meet Aine's curious gaze.

Eyes as dark as her own lifted to Aine's face. Though just a few short years had lent gray to the midnight hair and more creases to the once-plump cheeks, Aine recognized the woman immediately. With dismay.

Her hand dropped from the latch. "Mama," she whispered.

~ ~ ~

He noticed her from across the wide hall. Indeed, 'twas hard for a man to ignore such drooping eyelids and musical laughter. Lancelot smiled. *Especially a man like me*, he thought, *who knows his women.*

And well 'twas for him that he did. *When it comes time to woo and win a lady of means, I'll know what I want, in addition to the gold.*

And land.

And horses.

And a warrior force.

Come to think of it, a woman with all of that attached might not be so attractive…visually. And might be a good deal older than he as well.

Lancelot chuckled. 'Twas a good thing, then, that he enjoyed himself now. Later, he might have to suffer to obtain the satisfaction of his material needs. Taking out one of his charming smiles—not his best, mind you; that was reserved for special occasions—the nobleman strode across the hall toward the hearth, where the object of his eyes basted the several chickens roasting on a single spit.

"Winter, isn't it?" he called out as he neared her. The pretty girl looked up, seemingly surprised, and dropped a curtsy.

Lancelot smiled. *I know this game, little fool, and I'm better at it than you. Your eyes have been darting toward me for half the morning, since you entered the hall.* "Sorry if I startled you," he said, imbuing his tone with sincerity. He took the spit handle from her. "Here, let me help."

"Oh, my lord…" she breathed. Her mouth gaped open and closed. Rather like a pretty blond fish. *One I'm about to land.*

He knew she was scrambling for things to say, ways to amuse him, captivate him. "Are these for the feast tonight?" he asked, knowing full well that they were.

"Aye."

"Are you going?"

"To the Samhain feast? I wouldn't miss it, my lord!" she exclaimed, pink flushing into her cheeks. "And you, my lord? Will you attend? Or is Lord Drustan planning something more sedate for his own household?" she asked, teasing creeping into her voice.

"Not to worry, I'm attending. Arthur himself couldn't keep me away. We must appease the ancient spirits after all." He looked down into her cool blue eyes, frosted with fluttery lashes. "Especially when such beauty promises to be present."

A shameless flush rose to the maid's cheeks. Lancelot liked her well for it. *She will be mine after the bonfires tonight without hesitation.* The realization didn't give him the supreme, biting pleasure he so enjoyed, however; that intense pleasure never came without having emerged the victor from a struggle, a battle of wills in which he triumphed, forcing the conquered to enjoy his pleasures.

"The priests have already arrived," he continued, brushing her hand with his as he shifted to avoid the flames' heat.

"I saw them coming in with the peddlers." The girl shook her head. "Funny how they seem like ordinary men in ordinary clothes."

"Until they put on the white robes. They will do that for the ceremony tonight."

"To purify the people and animals," Winter added.

"Aye, to purify." He gave her a half-smile. "Though I must admit I enjoy the possible excitement afterward more than the mysterious ceremony."

Audacious girl, she smiled back! "Isn't it all a ceremony, my lord? And doesn't it all please the gods and the spirits?"

"True," he replied, inwardly laughing at what his oh-so-prudish mother would think of this trollop. "Though, of course, you know, the fertility rites are not so important to Samhain as to Beltane," his logical tongue put in.

She looked at him, eyes narrowed in fun. "Aren't they, my lord? Isn't it necessary that the earth be prepared during the long darkness for a fruitful spring?"

"Aye, aye, indeed," he agreed. The maid's predictable mind wearied him. He gave the spit another twist. He could enjoy all he wanted of her this evening; this interaction had assured him of her willingness. "So I hope to see you in the courtyard tonight?"

"Aye," she said and paused. He waited a moment to see if she had anything worthwhile to say and was glad that he had done so. "Though I doubt you'll notice me with Aine present," she added.

"Aine?" he frowned. Who was the girl talking about?

She gazed into his eyes. "You remember her, my lord. A kitchen girl. You met her near the stables yesterday."

"Oh, aye." Now he remembered! He'd spoken to her again, too, just this morning in the courtyard, but hadn't remembered her name. So that was it: Aine, the pretty sprite.

"I'm surprised you'd forgotten her," Winter chided. "She hasn't forgotten you, my lord."

"Oh?"

"Aye." Winter shook her head and lowered her voice. "In truth, my lord, she hasn't forgotten you for a moment since she met you. She praises your bonny face and even murmured your name in her sleep last night."

Lancelot felt intrigued.

"She's shy, though, my lord," confided Winter. "That's probably why her passion for you wasn't clear."

Lancelot couldn't resist asking. "And has she a lover?"

"Aine?" Winter laughed. "Nay, men must be bold with her, and most find themselves weak at the sight of her beauty. Though I suppose you wouldn't be, my lord."

Another servant girl came up as Winter finished her comment. The newcomer dropped a curtsy to Lancelot and turned to Winter. "Deirdre sent me to replace you here for the midday meal preparations."

"Alright." Winter gave place to the girl. She smiled at Lancelot before exiting. "I don't blame you, my lord, if you pursue Aine for the evening. It will give me pleasure just to see if you can catch her."

Lancelot watched the girl saunter away before heading off toward his uncle's chambers and smiled. Tonight would provide great amusement for the one who mattered: namely, himself.

West Lea

Her soul had departed. As she stared into her mother's cold face, Bethan's chest felt as if her heart and lungs had been torn out. The tears bubbled over the rims of her eyes and spilled down her cheeks. The numb sorrow pervaded her being too much for her to wipe the tears away.

She is in hell.

The thought ran repeatedly through her mind like a dog on a short chain.

She is in hell, and no one can save her now.

The tears soaked a dark circle on her skirt as they flew down her cheeks, dripped off her chin. A great sob wrenched free from her throat. "Why?" she moaned. "Why couldn't You save her?" Her head fell to her knees, and she slid off the stool onto the ice-cold dirt next to her mama's bed.

Oxfield

Aine hated the way her mother made her feel. Restrained. Boxed in. As if she stood in a windowless room with no lamp. *I didn't always feel this way,* she realized, looking into her mother's dark eyes. *Something is different from when I was little.*

"Aren't you going to ask me in?" her mother said quietly.

Aine glanced behind her. "They're busy preparing for the feast tonight, Mama."

Her mother nodded. "Maybe we could sit out here in the courtyard, then—"

"I'm expected to help, Mama," Aine cut in. Seeing the startled look on her mother's face, she added, "'Tis Samhain, you know. There's much to prepare."

"Aye, I ken. The feast of the dead." Her mama gave a soft sigh. "I wish you had nothing to do with such things, daughter."

Aine pursed her lips. Mama had no right to tell her what to do anymore. Didn't Aine provide her own bread? "'Tis just a little fun, Mama. Dancing and singing, that's all."

"'Tis of the evil one. You know that, Aine." Her mama's eyes sought her own, and Aine dropped her gaze to the ground, defiant. The rebellious feelings surged up within her heart even as part of her yearned to embrace her mama.

I will not be told what to do. She stood in the doorway, her arms clasped around her for warmth in the late autumn wind. What had Mama come for, anyway? Surely not to reprimand her. She waited.

"Daughter, I've come to ask you to go home with me." Her mama's voice grew soft, gentle as a robin's laughter. "Surely you've had enough of your rambling away. Come home with me. You've already missed so much, what with your brothers and sisters growing up."

Aine shook her head. "I have a good place here, Mama. Besides, I want to be free."

"Free from what, Aine? Free from those who love you?"

"I don't know, Mama! I don't want everyone telling me what to do. Here, I'm my own mistress. Besides," she continued, "I have someone who loves me here."

"What do you mean?"

"What I said. I've promised myself to Deoradhan, Lord Drustan's messenger. I expect to marry him any day now."

Her mother stayed silent for a moment. "May I meet him?" she finally asked in the tense quiet.

Aine shook her head. "Nay, he's away from Oxfield right now." She gave her mother a mirthless smile. "You wouldn't care for him anyway, Mama. He's a pagan to his very heart. If he were here, I'm sure he would join in the Samhain feast happily."

"Oh. I see."

"So I guess 'tis good he isn't here to meet you." Aine grew uncomfortable in the quiet strain. "I have to be going, Mama." She hesitated, then pecked her mama's cheek. "Good-bye."

Feeling like a hunted doe, Aine ducked inside the kitchen doorway and shut the door without waiting to hear her mother's reply. In the darkness, she leaned against the heavy door, heart galloping, feeling she had escaped narrowly from the snare.

~ ~ ~

Twilight came rapidly tonight.

"Quickly, now, girls. We'll bring the bread upstairs, then off to bed you go," Deirdre instructed the very youngest three kitchen servants. Watching their unruly heads bobbing together in childish chatter at the table, she sighed. May the Lord be thanked, these at least would not be subjected to the festivities to honor the dead.

But whoever causes one of these little ones to sin ...

The three small girls finished rolling the fresh loaves into towels. Deirdre quickly packed the bundles into manageable baskets, giving each child one to carry.

"Now, be sure not to wander. Hand the baskets over to the servants at the top of the stair and then come right back down." She crouched down in front of the threesome. "And I'll have a story and a treat for you tonight, you've worked so hard today."

With smiles and giggles, the children gaggled out of the kitchen. Deirdre turned to the two girls who tended the stew bubbling over the huge hearth. "One of you fetch a boy to bring out the pot for you, then you are free for the evening."

She watched as they exchanged excited glances. Both of them

rushed out of the kitchen to obey the order. Feeling lonely, Deirdre moved toward Cook, who held her usual propped-up position near the hearth.

Cook's eyes drooped closed, and Deirdre gently took her hand, mottled blue. The older woman blinked her eyes open, pain ever-present in them now.

"How do you feel?" Deirdre asked.

Cook smiled. "Like my soul's flying up toward heaven with the weight of my legs to hold it down."

Deirdre nodded. She and Cook understood that the older woman's time had come. 'Twould not be a time of heathen sorrowing but of solemn rejoicing. She leaned over and kissed her motherly friend's cheek.

"My part in Samhain is finished for the year," she commented. "I'm glad of it."

Cook nodded, then rasped, "But don't be frightened, Deirdre. Who can separate us from the love..."

A surge of pain cut her off, and Deirdre gently finished, "From the love of God in Christ Jesus our Lord. Aye, 'tis true." She smiled. "I will not be afraid, even of the feast of the dead, then. Does that please you, Cook?"

Cook's eyes stayed closed, but her lips bowed upward. "Aye, it does. Whatever pleases my heavenly Father does please me as well."

For some moments, Deirdre stayed holding Cook's hand in the comfortable silence. She was just about to rise when Cook tightened her grasp just a little on her hand. Deirdre waited to hear whatever the woman must want to tell her.

"Deirdre, will you do something for me?"

"Aye, of course."

"When Deoradhan comes back here, tell him that I loved him despite everything. Tell him I know I shall meet him again in the kingdom that never ends." Cook opened her eyes and beseeched Deirdre with them. "Will you tell him, lass?"

Deirdre felt timid at the thought of telling such things to the unbending Deoradhan but pushed the feeling away. The woman was dying. 'Twas no time to shirk her duty of love because of fear. "Aye, if you wish it, Cook."

"Thank you." Her eyelids slid shut, and she let out a shaking sigh.

Deirdre leaned forward and kissed the woman's cheek again. "I'll let you rest," she murmured and moved away.

CHAPTER TWENTY-TWO

Deoradhan could see the double bonfires from his camp beneath the large oak tree on the forest's edge. The fire's smoke billowed up; they must have put wet wood on it. A perfect night for Samhain: crisp enough to cause shiver after shiver to run through his body, clear enough to see every droplet of starry light in the liquid sky, and already so dark that the veil between the living and the dead could be lifted. Tonight, Deoradhan would not participate, only observe. *Next year, when I am king by the gods' pleasure, I will sacrifice one hundred sheep in my father's honor.*

After glancing over at his grazing horse, he leaned back against the trunk to watch the pageant unfold before him, the unseen audience member. Even two stades away, he saw several men enrobed in white wool glowing among the bonfires, set side-by-side atop the hill. Silhouetted against the sunken, bloodshot sun, the shapes of villagers moved, made grotesque by the masks and animal skins they had donned for the occasion. Excitement shuddered through Deoradhan's limbs as he realized how close the supernatural world drew this night.

Oxfield

Hidden by a thick silk curtain, Tarian stood at a second-story window, her eyes roving over the milling crowd below. The druids had entered the courtyard, their robes distinguishing them as priests of the native gods. All wore crowns of mistletoe around their brows;

Tarian could see the pale berries glistening through the twilight. All were assembled, then.

Drustan has not arrived yet. Perhaps he abides by my wishes yet.

His appearance at that moment squashed her hopes. Her husband wore a white mantle, similar to that of the pagan priests, and entered the courtyard to a drumbeat.

That was orchestrated. She closed her eyes. *God forgive me, I feel such bitterness toward that man, mixed with love. Love for who he could have been.* She was glad now that their marriage had borne no children. *At least I don't have to concern myself with him poisoning the little ones' spirits.*

The several priests opened their arms toward the lord of the estate. Tarian watched as one held out a mistletoe crown like their own and decked his gray hair with it.

So it has come to this, then, with my husband hobnobbing with demonic priests at a festival of the dead.

My God, my God, help me in this hour.

West Lea

She hadn't heard him enter the darkening cottage. 'Twas only when Calum rested his hand on her shoulder that she became aware of his presence.

"When did she pass?" he asked after a moment.

Bethan drew a shuddering breath. "While you were caring for the animals. There was nothing more we could do." She turned her eyes toward him, seeking affirmation. "Was there?"

He shook his head. "Nay."

She felt only sorrow. Not guilt, not relief. Only tearless grief. *Lord God, could not You have saved her?* Suddenly, she thought of something. "Where's my sister?"

"Still in the animal shed. It's warm there." He was quiet for a moment; Bethan could see him trying to decide what had best be done. "Is there a priest of God nearby?"

"Aye, in the next village over, three miles away."

"So far?" Calum paused, then said, "Then I think 'twould be

best to do nothing tonight, Bethan. 'Tis Samhain," he explained, "and better if no one knows your mother died tonight."

She had forgotten how late in the month 'twas. "Aye. And we'll say nothing to Enid when she comes in. She'll sorrow soon enough," she murmured.

He nodded and drew her into the selfless embrace of a brother, which she did not reject.

Oxfield

> *"The LORD is my light and my salvation*
> *Whom shall I fear?*
> *The LORD is the stronghold of my life;*
> *Of whom shall I be afraid?"*

The stableboy's voice carried through the small room to each listener. True, Bricius noted, some did not attend very well, their hands picking at their fingernails, eyes darting toward the open doorway whenever a shadow passed by. The potter sympathized with their nervousness, though he himself knew none this year. Strange things happened on Samhain, and some without natural explanation.

Yet this is my Father's world…

As the young man continued to read, Bricius heard the beat of skin drums begin. They would be leading the stock between the bonfires to cleanse the beasts soon. This, he knew, would be followed by some kind of blood sacrifice, hopefully animal.

The reader faltered, and Bricius saw that he was looking toward the open door, out into the twilight. The potter turned to see what had caused the young man to hesitate. Past the door, a procession of half-naked, costumed revelers passed, their faces painted black for their role as impersonators of the dead. One looked in on the little gathering and began laughing wildly, his red tongue hanging half-out.

Drunk. And 'twas only dusk. Bricius felt apprehension for the rest of this night for Oxfield.

"Lydia, shut the door," he said.

Solemnly, his wife nodded and rose, moving toward the door. He saw Lydia stare into the darkness, unflinchingly. Then she pushed shut the portal opening.

'Twas night.

The priest had slaughtered the bull, and Lord Drustan himself, decked in festal robes, had been given the honor of throwing the bones into the fires. All the stock had passed between the bonfires and thus had been cleansed for this darker half of the year. The servants, too, had walked between the fires. They had observed the necessary rituals to placate roaming spirits, dark and otherwise. They had satisfied the requirements.

Now the real excitement could begin.

The music swiftly altered its course from ponderous drums and mournful whistles to a side-stream of lilting though still-mysterious melodies. The large group composed of many house and yard servants, as well as herds, stableboys, and guards, separated as dancers came forward to participate in an intricate circle dance, whose ancient meaning had now been lost.

Lancelot positioned himself where he could gain the best view of the dancers. He held a silver cup half-full of very good wine in his right hand. He never drank the diluted stuff if he could avoid it. With a swig, he feasted his eyes on the flesh moving before him. Lovely how strong drink made these women so uninhibited. His fine uncle could be thanked for the abundance of wine and mead flowing from the casks on the feasting tables yonder. He smiled. Religion be blessed for the provision of this entertainment.

Now there's a river of life! His smile grew wider when he realized a very pretty girl stood a few steps away to his right, eyeing him every few moments. *By the gods that are not, she's a ripe one for picking.* His own gaze met hers, and he grinned an invitation. He stopped in the middle of another gulp when he realized that the servant girl timidly moved toward him.

She looked familiar to him, but he couldn't place her face. His brain felt a little fogged. He took another gulp to clear it. There. 'Twas better. Lancelot squinted at her, thinking hard.

Aine.

How could he have forgotten? He had thought he would have to seek her out. Evidently, the lass was not as shy as Winter intimated. A little disappointment seeped into his spirit. He had been looking forward to a challenge.

She looked up at him, her eyes dark and restless "My lord, you wanted to see me?"

He smiled. So this was her game: playing innocent. Though maybe she was. And if so, who knew but that he would be the one to show this little bird the ways of men? And who better to do so than he, Lancelot, man of the world, who knew how to charm maidens and how to guild guilt with virtue?

"Are you going to dance, Aine? 'Twould be a delight to see," he answered.

"Aye, perhaps later, my lord." She looked confused and turned her eyes to watch the torch-lit dancing.

"I see longing in your eyes, Aine," spoke Lancelot very quietly after a few moments.

The girl turned toward him, wearing her surprise across her face. "Aye, I do. And for whom do you long?"

Her eyes flitted down. "For one whom I love, my lord." Her cheeks flushed dark in the moonlight.

"I didn't know you loved one other than me, Aine." Lancelot smiled. He stared at her cream-smooth face, graced by lush black eyelashes and apple-red lips, cheeks blushing at his words. "I thought you liked me as well I do you," he added, trying for a verbal reaction.

"I...That is, my lord...I like you well," the girl stammered, looking down.

"I'm glad to hear that, Aine, for I may as well tell you," he paused for effect, "that you are my desire."

Her eyes shot upward, soaking in the unexpected tenderness.

This one thrives on smooth words of affection. He would play that way, then.

"Indeed," he continued, "from the moment I saw you, I knew I must have more of your company. Much more."

He let his eyes travel over this little goddess, reveling in her delicate proportions. Aye, she would be luscious as a dainty honey cake, the fitting finale to an evening of revelry. "Please, Aine, give me a word of hope."

She stared at him, obviously tongue-tied.

He leaned down and put his lips to her ear. "Let me know that I may love you," he whispered and finished with a kiss to her temple.

"Love me?"

"Aye, I want to love you, sweetest of all maidens," he coaxed. "Dance with me, Aine."

Slowly, she nodded, and he pulled her into the dance. Lancelot felt his heart thundering as they came to a halt, and he pulled her against him in an embrace. She clung to him, rather than pulling away. He grinned, the world swaying around him.

Eager though she seemed to be, 'twould be an odd maid to give herself fully without more wooing. And if he was to have her, he would have her fully. *No idle kisses in a courtyard for Lancelot, son of Bors.* He would drink freely of this cup of desire, as much as he wished. And such freedom on his part sometimes required more…liberation on the part of the maiden in question.

"Come, let's get a drink, Aine," he said and reached for her hand to guide her over to the feasting table. Without hesitation, she trusted her little hand to him.

As he poured a cup of wine for the girl, he glanced up to see a few couples already making their way toward the courtyard gates, the stables, the shadowed doorways. 'Twas a night to indulge and then to forget by the morning light. 'Twas a night of shadows, a time to make unchaste vows and false commitments. For this evening, most of Britain would forget their Roman God and return to the pagan ways of their ancestors, unfettered by moral fears. *'Twas when men were truly free.*

He looked sideways at Aine. She had turned her back to him, shivering arms across her chest, staring into the darkness. After a moment of thought, he slipped a hand into the little pouch hanging at his waist. With a deft motion, he had broken a tiny vial open and poured it into the cup, swirling it with experience.

"Here, Aine."

She turned with surprise, as if she had forgotten he stood there. "Oh, thank you, my lord." Aine took the cup and drank. Lancelot admired the way her hair mantled her shoulders, a thick black river that his fingers would soon run through uninhibited.

Why did she feel so dizzy? And where was Lord Lancelot taking her? Suddenly, she couldn't recall. And it didn't matter too much, did it? She was safe with Lord Lancelot. He loved her.

With blurry eyes, Aine gazed at the profile of the man leading her onward, onward endlessly it seemed, through these shadowy corridors. He reminded her of Deoradhan, tall and dark-haired. Wait, Deoradhan had auburn hair, didn't he? She shook her head. Everything seemed hazy, unreal. Her feet felt like sponges. Unsteady, she grabbed the elbow of her companion.

"Feeling tired?" he murmured, low and comfortingly. "Here, 'tis only a few steps away now."

His arms went around her back and under her knees. Aine felt herself floating up in the air. He must be carrying her; or had she sprouted wings? Deoradhan had called her a fairy. She let her eyes sink closed. Was she a fairy? If so, was this man a prince from fairyland? "I can't recall," she mumbled, resting her head against something soft that smelled like evergreen trees and leather. How peaceful everything seemed.

"You don't need to remember anything, Aine, my love," whispered the lord. His words soothed her, drove away any thoughts of worry away. "I'll take care of you tonight."

"Alright," she sighed. "Where did you say we're going?"

"I'm taking you to a kind of paradise, my lass," he answered.

"Avalon...Isle of Apples..."

She heard him laugh. "Aye, We'll call it Avalon."

"Why...why are we going?" she yawned.

"I want to show you something that you will enjoy, I promise."

"Alright," she heard herself reply as if from faraway. She knew now. She had turned into a fairy, and he carried her to paradise.

She felt the long strides beneath her pause. When the forward motion stopped, her mind cleared just a little, enough for her to remember she was no part of the immortal race. Her eyes drifted open, and she saw Lord Lancelot's hand lift the latch on the door before them and push the door open. It led into a dark chamber. Inexplicably, the sight wrought terror and helplessness deep into Aine's heart. Some bad thing waited for her in that room, she knew it. She began to wriggle in his arms, desperate to get away.

"Nay, not in there, not in there," she mumbled through heavy lips.

He chuckled and held her tightly, stepping into the darkness. "You'll not get away so soon, Aine. You must spend some time here with me, in Avalon. Then I'll bring you back to earth." She felt his smooth cheeks brush her hair as he bent his head to kiss her mouth. "There's nothing to fear, I promise. You'll like it here very much."

His kiss brought back some awareness back to her. Faintly, she heard the door close behind them. Never had Deoradhan kissed her so intensely. *Deoradhan...* She began to squirm again, her limbs gaining back a little strength.

"Stop, stop it, Aine. I just want to kiss you. Just let me kiss you, my love," Lord Lancelot implored, gripping her until she stopped moving.

Her mind moved slowly but clearly now. *I'm in far over my head. Stupid, stupid girl! What was I thinking earlier?* His arms wrapped around her like a sea serpent, threatening to drown her.

He is Lord Drustan's nephew. She stiffened but didn't pull away when he lowered his face to kiss her again. And again. *I can do nothing now. He is Lord Drustan's nephew.* Perhaps he only wanted her to give her kisses, like he had said.

"Come, we'll be more comfortable here," he said after long moments. Holding her in his arms, Lord Lancelot stepped through the room, toward the deepest shadows.

Breathe. Keep breathing. Aine let out a shattered breath as he lowered her onto a bed in the darkness. She clutched the fur covers with both hands as the blood pounded in her ears against the pillows. Lord Lancelot sat on the edge of the bed, blocking out the moonlight entering from the one window.

Finally, she whimpered, "Please, my lord, I am promised to another man. You haven't the right to…"

"Is he a nobleman?" he asked, his hand stroking her hair as he would pet a lamb he was about to slaughter.

Aine shook her head, tears blinding her.

"Then I have the right," Lord Lancelot assured her kindly. "Don't be afraid."

Feeling how powerless she was, Aine closed her eyes as she felt his fingers moving down her neck.

"How I love you," the lord whispered.

Deoradhan, where are you?

CHAPTER TWENTY-THREE

Oxfield

For some time now, light had streamed through the one window. Morning had fully come; Aine could hear the bustle of work beginning in the courtyard below. She shivered and realized without emotion that her entire body shook beyond her control. The heavy furs lay within reach, but she cared little whether she froze to death.

I wish I were dead. Never before had that thought entered her mind. Always, Aine wished for more enjoyment, more indulgence, more, more, more. But in the space of a night, she had realized how dreadful life really could be. And she wished to die.

If he had left the door unlocked, I would have gone out by now, into the woods, never to return.

Her chest felt like someone had hung a millstone in it. Lifting her hands and turning them over, she examined them. *It's like they're someone else's hands.* She let them drop to her lap and looked numbly over at the man sleeping soundly beside her. His stubbly cheek rested on the pillow, his profile still perfect, yet so disgusting to her now.

I am utterly disgraced. How will Deoradhan think of me if he knows? Her eyes filled, and she watched through a blur as the droplets spilled onto the woolen blanket. A hope trickled into her thoughts. *He need never know. I will conceal it forever. He will believe me virtuous still.*

The thoughts helped her to sniffle back her tears, clear a little of the numbness, and lift her spirits from despair to quiet misery. Aine pulled one of the furs up over her shoulders. She wore only her linen under-tunic, and the warmth soothed her. Drowsy, she closed her eyes, promising herself not to sleep.

Dunpeledyr, Lothian

Seonaid glanced out the upper-story window along the corridor. Her feet paused in their quick steps for just a moment as her eyes caught sight of a stranger riding through the ancient stronghold's iron gates. Probably the new horsemaster about whom Weylin had told her. Lingering for a moment at the window, the lady's eyes rambled up to the sun. Already high in the sky, and so many things left to do before the noon meal! Weylin would also expect her to receive the new horsemaster. She sighed. *Solas is more than capable of doing that work if only Weylin would entrust him with it.*

Her bare feet moved down the hall even more quickly now, making a slapping noise against the smooth flags. *I must talk to the laundress before receiving him.* Seonaid grimaced. *Hopefully, he'll work out better than the last three horsemasters did.*

West Lea

Working side by side with two other village women, Bethan washed her mother's body. They would bury her in the village cemetery late this morning. Calum had begun to dig the grave with other men from the village.

She glanced at her mama's still face. Strange, she had been a woman of such varied emotions, each flickering constantly across her countenance; 'twas sad to see the empty expression chiseled there now. And to know that Mama had been hers to know and love only for this life, that Mama had already stood before the Judge of all the earth...

The pain became too much for her to linger on the thought for long. Sniffling, she raised her mama's hand to her lips and kissed the cold, spiritless flesh. She saw her own tears sliding between the hand's fingers. *Can God's sorrow be any less for such a one?*

Bethan became aware of a touch on her shoulder. Lifting her head, she saw 'twas Garan's mother, the priest's wife, her eyes aloof as always. "Aye?" asked Bethan, wiping away her tears.

"We've done all that needs doing, child. You must get your little sister now and come along to the burial. The men will be here soon to carry her out." She said it all in so matter-of-fact a way that Bethan felt compelled to push back her tears. The woman acted as if she proposed a stroll through the countryside and not the burial of Bethan's unconverted mother. Anger toward her betrothed's mother sprang up in her spirit, as well as quick words to her tongue, but she bit them back before they could escape. She knew that the woman must mean well, though she did badly.

"Aye, I will," Bethan finally replied and moved toward the door to fetch her sister.

Oxfield

A lurching movement awakened Aine, startling her from a dreamless oblivion. Her eyelids felt as if rope tied them shut, and she struggled to open them. With sleep-blurred vision, she saw Lord Lancelot standing next to the bed, his back to her. The same cold grief she had woken with earlier that morning returned and brought fear as well. She didn't move, not wanting to know what would happen to her now.

With care, he finished dressing, straightening his tunic across his shoulders, running his hands through his sumptuous black hair and sweeping it away from his ears, smoothing his knee-length pants. Yawning melodiously, he reached to the ground. From half-closed eyes, Aine saw that he'd picked up his sandals. He sat down on the edge of the mattress and began to lace the straps up his calves, his elegant profile turned slightly toward her.

She must have fluttered her eyelids a little because the nobleman knew she was awake.

"'Tis late in the morning, my fair maiden." The man paused and then smiled. He reached over with one of his well-formed hands and carelessly ran a finger down Aine's cheek. "Or should I say, maiden-no-more. But still very fair." He turned his attention back to tying on his sandals.

Lying there rigidly, Aine realized her striking beauty no longer mattered to her. *I wish I had been born plain, even deformed.* Tears stung her eyes. *I wish I had never been born.* She drew a deep breath to stop the tears from running down face.

"Hadn't you better rise and dress, little fairy? Your mistress in the kitchen will wonder what keeps you." Finished, Lord Lancelot stood and stretched. "And I doubt you'd want to tell her the truth."

"I...I..." Stunned, Aine could not push the words out. *I don't even know what I want to say.* She scuttled up, sitting with her arms clutched tightly around her knees.

"Aye?" The lord smiled, showing his straight teeth.

He's amused. The thought made her ill. *This man has known me more intimately than any a man I've known. Even Deoradhan. And he's laughing at me.* She felt lower than any clean, crawling insect roaming the earth. *So this is what a prostitute feels like after she has provided her service, like an ugly piece of trash, like a dirty cup with its contents all drained.*

And the thought suddenly came to her, pouring horror into her. "What if there is a child?" she whispered, her eyes on her knees.

"What do you mean?" His smile contained iron now. She saw it when she glanced up. "If there is a child, I think you'll know what to do. Do it before it causes trouble for you. 'Tis no concern of mine."

Aine looked at him in numb silence. *He means I must do away with it...*

"But I wouldn't worry. Most of the time, that isn't the case." He dropped a kiss on her brow. "Now, I must be off. I promised my uncle that we would go hunting this morning, and I'm sure to be late. Naughty girl, you've kept me here talking to you." The lord grinned. "'Twas a wonderful night, Aine. A true Avalon, aye?" With a wink, he moved over to the door and lifted the bar.

How can I face the world?

Dunpeledyr

"Pardon me, my lady, but the new horsemaster has arrived. Shall I show him into the hall?"

Seonaid turned from her conversation with the laundress and smiled at the servant boy. "Aye, show him in, but let him know I will not receive him immediately. Make him comfortable before the fire."

The boy gave a short bow. "Aye, my lady." He hurried from the room.

Seonaid concluded her conversation with the laundress regarding the washing of some new fabrics she'd bought from traders and then moved toward the hall. The great room functioned as the center of Dunpeledyr's existence and was the proper place for her to receive new employees.

Though not physically, her inward steps slowed as she approached the hall. Sometimes, it seemed to Seonaid that if she walked into that room, so unchanged by the passage of decades, she would see Eion about to take his throne on the dais. Odd, despite the years, he never changed in her imagination. Always, his wide smile greeted her; his eyes shimmered with delight as he saw her coming.

No one sat in the throne in Dunpeledyr's great hall now, not even the lord of Dunpeledyr. Weylin kept it empty as a reminder that Arthur ruled Britain and, Seonaid suspected, to reinforce his own power as Arthur's representative.

Somehow, I doubt that Arthur meant for Weylin to use his authority thus. She shrugged mentally. The high king had never desired to visit Lothian. *Or he does not dare to.* Commanding her thoughts into orderly control, Seonaid paused under the heavy-beamed archway and took stock of the new employee before making her presence known to him.

He stood around middle height for a man, perhaps a hand or two above Seonaid, and dressed in a decidedly Britonic manner with a hooded cloak draping his shoulders, a woolen tunic covering his form, and bare feet. The lady smiled to see thick auburn hair waving down to his shoulders, much the texture and color of her own. *He must come from the north.* She already had a kindly feeling toward this new horsemaster.

She entered the room, and he turned fully toward her. In the few steps between herself and him, she took stock of him. Restless blue-green eyes gazed from an inquisitive sun-browned face. He held himself upright, shoulders squarely back, hands loose at his sides. Determination set his chin with more than natural firmness, and she noticed he watched her very closely.

There is something so familiar about him…

"I am Lady Seonaid," she said, holding out her hand to him.

He took the offering, kissing it quickly. "I am glad to come into your husband's employ, my lady. I am called Deoradhan, lately of Oxfield in Arthur's southern dominion."

"Deoradhan? That means 'exile,' aye?" Seonaid looked at him sharply.

"It is what I am called," he acquiesced.

"And are you an exile, then?" Her eyes held his gaze. *We want no troublemakers at Dunpeledyr. The Lord knows, we've had our share of trouble here. And may yet have in the future.*

The young man looked back at her without flinching. "Nay, no longer, my lady. And never through fault of my own."

She nodded, studying him. Finally, Seonaid replied, "Your eyes are honest, Deoradhan. I believe you." With a hand, she gestured toward the great hearth. "Come, sit with me and refresh yourself. We must discuss the terms of your contract with Dunpeledyr. Then I will have someone show you to your quarters."

She moved toward a low stool near the fire, close enough to warm her in the chilly cavernous hall. He followed her slowly, taking a seat on another stool facing her.

"You seem unsure about something, Deoradhan. May I ask what it is?"

His eyes darted up to meet hers. "I thought, my lady…that I would discuss these matters with my lord. Weylin is his name, aye?"

Seonaid smiled. "Aye, the lord is called Weylin. But my husband entrusts these estate matters to my judgment. Should any trouble arise, you will see me first. Is that understood?"

"Aye, my lady."

"That's well." She folded her hands across the green wool of her skirt. "Now, you will have charge of the horse training, feeding, pasturing, and breeding at Dunpeledyr. Many seek horses from us, including the stables of the Pendragon himself. 'Tis a difficult job you set out to master, Deoradhan." She peered at his face. "And by your countenance, 'tis easy to tell you've no more than twenty-five winters behind you. Aye?"

The young man did not smile but looked at her intently. "I am twenty years old this past summer, my lady. I was born the year Arthur ascended the throne."

'Tis almost as if he is trying to imply something, but I can't understand what 'tis. Seonaid frowned. *Something here is odd, very odd.*

She stood. "You realize that you will stay without leave for this entire winter, that you may not quit Dunpeledyr's territory until spring."

The young man furrowed his eyebrows, worried. "Why not, my lady?"

"My husband keeps this policy with all his servants. He believes that it tries their loyalty. In the spring, you may request and receive leave by me," she explained. She paused. "Is there a problem with this, Deoradhan?"

He hesitated. "I left my promised wife at Oxfield and told her I would return for her soon. She is a kitchen servant there."

Seonaid thought he flushed a little red at this last bit, and she smiled inwardly. *How interesting the differences in class even among servants!* "Well," she spoke aloud, "You may send word to your young woman and let her know you will fetch her in the spring."

"That would be acceptable, for me to have a wife at Dunpeledyr?"

"Aye, of course. There may even be work here for her."

He smiled, his first since he'd met her. "Then I agree to your terms, Lady Seonaid."

Oxfield

Wearily, Deirdre lifted the bucket and poured water into the wooden bowl. She rolled up her tunic sleeves and splashed the cold water over her arms, rubbing them to remove the caked flour. Then she shook the water from her hands and wiped them on her skirt. With a sigh, Deirdre picked up the small clay lamp and willed her feet toward the fireplace to see if Cook needed anything.

Deirdre moved quietly toward the woman, hoping to not awaken her if she already slept. As she neared the fire, however, she could see by Cook's profile that she was still awake.

"Cook, do you want water or anything else?" Deirdre asked. "I'm going to bed now."

Cook didn't reply. Knowing the older woman was a little deaf, Deirdre took a seat across from her to try again. "Cook—"

Her words died as she realized Cook stared blankly, her head slumped back against the pillow behind her. Fear touched Deirdre, and she reached to lay her hand on Cook's.

'Twas cold as snow, stiff as wood. Deirdre retracted her hand and sat still, her eyes gazing across at the ugly shell that had housed such an exquisite person. Her love for the woman filled her more than it ever had during Cook's life.

CHAPTER TWENTY-FOUR

West Lea

"I'll return in a few weeks," Calum promised. The late morning had seen Lowri's burial, and now Bethan walked beside him as he led his horse toward the road. Exhausted from weeping, Enid slept inside the cottage. "You have enough food to get by until then?" he inquired.

"Aye. Thank you, Calum," Bethan answered quietly. "I cannot thank you enough for every way you've helped us." Her voice soothed him as a mother bird with its hatchlings. Even in sorrow, serenity accompanied her. *Could she transmit such peace to me?*

At the road's edge, Calum stopped and turned to look at her. After a moment, she asked, "What is it, Calum?"

He paused. *Lord, help me to see Your way for me. This is opposed to everything I thought I would do. But my feelings...*

"Have I done something wrong, Calum?" Her face grew serious and pale. She stood there like a child about to be chastened for some error.

He shook his head. "Nay."

She reached a hand to his forearm, her eyes beseeching him. "Tell me, Calum, please. Whatever 'tis, it can't be any worse than these past days have been."

He inhaled deeply. "I hesitate to say it, lass, because you're grieving over your mama, and I don't want to take or seem to take advantage of that. But what I must say...that is, I don't think 'twill come as a shock to you. At least, I hope it won't."

Calum observed her carefully. She stood silent, waiting. *Speak, lad, while she's listening.* "I care about you, Bethan. Very much." He sighed. "I never thought I would say that to any lass. But, truth upon my lips, I admire you more than any lass I've ever met."

She sucked in her breath audibly and turned away from him. Calum felt his insides cave.

"I have spoiled our friendship, aye?" he whispered, laying a hand on his horse's neck. *That I had kept my feelings to myself!*

After a moment, he saw Bethan shake her head. When she turned toward him, he thought she blinked away tears. *She, too, cares!*

"I am promised to another man." Her words sent the arrow of providence to kill his hopes. "One of the women you met at the burial...'tis her son I'm to wed."

"Who is he?" He couldn't stop the words.

She cradled the muzzle of his horse in her hands. Calum watched as the animal lipped her fingers in play. "Garan, son of the priest from the next village. I'm to marry him in the spring."

The son of a priest. "Is he a good man, this Garan?" He kept his eyes on the horse.

She swallowed. "Aye, very good. I couldn't ask for better."

Calum nodded. He couldn't speak. There was nothing worthwhile to say, and he wouldn't make it worse for them both by vocalizing regrets.

"'Twas arranged a year ago." She met his eyes. "I'm sorry, Calum," she whispered.

They stood silent for a moment. Then Calum mounted his horse, handling the reins gently. "I'll return in a few weeks," he restated. "Grace and peace."

He saw the sadness in her eyes. "Grace and peace," she replied, and he nudged his horse into a trot.

Looking back a few moments later, he saw that she'd already returned to the cottage, not waiting to see him disappear.

Dunpeledyr

His lips turned up in pleasure. For as long as he could remember, the boy-turning-man had loved sitting by the burn, trying to mimic its childlike laughter in his mind, thinking of songs as he soaked in the warm sunlight. Now Solas moved his hand over the grass and suddenly felt a moist, hot tongue run across his palm.

"Giant! You came!" The dog rarely obeyed his commands immediately, so 'twas a surprise to have him come at only a whistle or two. "Good dog. Good dog." Solas delighted in feeling the rough heavy fur between his fingers.

"Lad!"

At the unexpected call, Solas alerted. He felt Giant's fur rise beneath his fingers and a soft growl begin deep within the dog's chest. "Easy, boy. Easy." Solas rose to his feet and turned toward the voice. "Who is it?" he asked, not at all nervous. The fields were his keep, as Dunpeledyr was his father's.

"My name's Deoradhan," the man said.

He is on foot; I can tell by the level of his voice.

"I've come from Dunpeledyr, but I think I've lost my way. Can you help me with directions?"

Solas smiled. *The new horsemaster. Mother liked him well.* "I can do better than that. I'm headed back now and will take you myself. Does that suit you?"

"Aye, it does," answered the man. "And you are...?"

"Solas," he supplied, "Lord Weylin and Lady Seonaid's son."

The man was silent for so long that Solas wondered if he'd decided to try to make it back to the fortress on his own. "Are you still there, Deoradhan?"

The horsemaster found his voice. "Aye, aye, I am. And you will lead me back, Solas?"

Solas couldn't help but laugh at this. "A blind lad, lead you? Nay, man, Giant will lead both of us and see us safely home. Come, Giant."

The dog moved forward, and Solas picked up his walking staff.

"He'll bark for me to know where to go," he explained to his new acquaintance, "but there's little need of that for you."

Solas knew that the man must be nodding, and he began walking toward the barking ahead. "Mother has been pleased with your work these few days, Deoradhan."

"I'm glad she's satisfied, lad," answered the man.

Solas paused. "You met my sister at court, did you not?"

"Aye, I met her."

"She spoke of you highly and said you'd studied abroad."

"Aye, I did."

"But grew up in Camelot, at the high king's table? How did that come to be?" asked Solas.

"Through a difficult circumstance," the horsemaster answered. "And you, Solas. Lady Fiona told me that you come to court but rarely."

"Aye, 'tis a far distance for a blind lad. And my mother never goes. I don't care to go with my father alone. You'll see the fortress just over these hills, I'm told," Solas said as he felt the ground rise under his feet.

Oxfield

The young nobleman turned in his polished saddle and raised one hand in a wave. From her place on the steps beside Drustan, Tarian saw that Lancelot's mouth carried his perpetual half-smile and that his eyes gleamed even more brightly than usual. *He anticipates court life eagerly.* She glanced over at Drustan, who held his hand up in send-off.

"So departs Apollo," commented the lord, his eyes following his nephew as the horse and rider cantered through the gate. The hooves sounded sharp as lightning on the cold stones. "Ah, well, I'm sorry to see him go," he sighed.

Tarian stayed silent, watching him. *He looks as if he would go with Lancelot if he could. I am a noose around his neck.* She swiveled her gaze back to Lancelot's retreating back and heaved her own sigh of relief, not yearning. *Never have I been so glad to see someone leave. What a bad influence. Though I don't know how much worse Drustan can get.*

With a shiver, Tarian turned toward the hall entrance. Her husband's voice stopped her. "Do you want to begin seeing candidates for a new head cook this week?"

Tarian spun in surprise. "What do you mean? Meghyn is our head cook." Surely the older woman hadn't quit. Not at the beginning of winter.

Drustan furrowed his eyebrows. "Meghyn's dead, Tarian. I thought you would have heard."

Dizzy with sudden distress, she shook her head, clutching her thick shawl around her shoulders. "When did she die?" she managed.

"The day after Samhain," replied the lord.

I spoke to her only days before. "And where have they buried her?"

"In the cemetery outside the gates." He shrugged. "At any rate, we need a head cook as soon as possible. You'll take care of it right away?"

Of course. You wouldn't want your meals disturbed, Tarian thought bitterly, feeling guilty and justified at once. *God forgive me, but he cares for no one but himself. I know that now.* Forcefully, she turned her thoughts to the present. "Aye, but I don't think I need to see anyone. I have a person in mind already."

"Who?" Drustan frowned. "I hope 'tisn't one of your upstart religious friends, Tarian. The head of the kitchen needs to know what she's doing. And don't try to deny you have such friends."

Anger mingled with her sadness over Meghyn's death. "I won't deny it, Drustan." She raised her chin. "And I think you know me well enough to believe that I will choose someone competent, my lord."

Drustan nodded. "See that you do, then. I'll leave it in your hands."

Dunpeledyr

"Deoradhan, Lord Weylin has returned from the south and wishes to see you."

Deoradhan paused with the soft brush half-way down the length of the bay horse. Finally. Heart thundering, he turned to the young stable lad. "Jamie, you'll finish—"

"Aye, I'll finish him!" the boy snatched the brush from Deoradhan and began to draw it over the horse with long, gentle strokes.

Not bothering to thank the boy, Deoradhan rushed from the stable, slipping on the straw under his leather shoes. The sun blinded him as he came into the light, and he suddenly realized that he hadn't asked where Weylin would meet with him.

Never mind. I'll find him. And one day, not today, but one day I'll... He let his thoughts trail off, not daring to complete them yet. When he had allowed his mind to travel down that path in the past, the idea had paralyzed him with desire. *I will have what is mine by right. And he will be no more. No more a torment to my mother, no more an obstacle in my path.*

But for the first time, one corner of his mind played the traitor. *But what of Solas? And what of Fiona?*

The questions tore him in two without warning, freezing his will with an indecision he'd not known before.

Oxfield

"Her mother is dead, my lord," Calum informed Lord Drustan. The two men sat in the lord's private chambers. Having traveled all day from the West Lea, Calum wished he could have retired immediately, but he knew that business came first at Oxfield. After handing over his horse to a stable boy, Calum had reported to his lord without delay.

"And her father?" Drustan asked, sipping his wine. His slippered feet stretched out toward the hearth, and he had wrapped a heavy robe around his shoulders against the early winter's chill.

"Away working at another farm. No one knows where. He told some of the neighbors that he planned to return after the harvest."

"And he hasn't come back yet? And no word from him?"

"Nay, no word."

The lord raised his eyebrows. "Either he's dead or a deserter."

"I'm sure he's no deserter, my lord," Calum asserted.

Lord Drustan smiled. "Nay? Well, then, he's dead, aye?"

Calum stayed silent. *Lord, let him be alive, for Bethan's sake.*

"And if he's dead, he died with a debt on his land. His daughter realizes what that means, aye?" asked Drustan.

"The land will revert to you, my lord." Calum shook his head. "Nay, I'm sure the girl hasn't thought of that. But I'll tell her."

Lord Drustan nodded and stood. "So I'll see you in a week or so?"

"Aye." Calum rose to his feet. "My lord, Bethan has no relatives nearby that I know of, and she has a little sister in her care now. Would you retain both of them in your service, my lord?"

The nobleman thought for just a moment. "Aye, aye, bring them back with you. You've said the girl is a fine worker in the kitchen?"

"Aye, the finest I've seen."

"Good."

~ ~ ~

Tarian accepted the cup from Deirdre with a smile of thanks. A cup of warm mead in her own hands, the kitchen maid sat across from her. Deirdre's eyes roamed over the other servants in the kitchen, silently supervising them as she talked with her mistress.

"I was very sorry to hear about Meghyn, Deirdre," Tarian spoke. "Did she have any family nearby?"

Deirdre shook her head, then paused. "Well...aye, I suppose Deoradhan could count himself her family. She raised him from a small lad, I understand, as his nurse. You ken, Deoradhan, the lord's messenger."

Recognition came to Tarian. "Aye, I do. I hadn't realized that he and Meghyn were connected."

"Aye, but he knows naught of her death, I think. He's away who knows where."

The two young women sat silent before the hearth for a few moments before Tarian spoke again, "Were you the one who found her?"

"Aye, 'twas I." Deirdre smiled. "But she's with the Lord now, my lady. And we press on here."

"Aye, I can see that you do. You run this kitchen very efficiently, Deirdre," Tarian commented.

"Thank you, my lady. We all work hard."

Tarian paused. Would the girl accept? "I wonder if you would take Meghyn's place as head of the kitchen, Deirdre."

She heard the girl suck in her breath. Deirdre leaned back in thought, the chair creaking as her back pressed against its frame. "I don't know if I could do it, my lady," she finally said. "You don't realize how much Cook actually did in the kitchens."

"But I thought you'd taken her place as she became more and more ill," put in Tarian.

Deirdre shrugged. "I did, somewhat. But always under her supervision and guidance, my lady. It's not the work, don't mistake me. I'm not afraid of hard work."

"I know that, Deirdre. But I've seen you with the younger maids, managing them, instructing them. You have an eye for detail and getting things done well. I believe that you are very suited to this position," Tarian urged.

Deirdre stayed silent for a moment, staring into the glowing fire. Tarian held her breath when the servant turned back toward her. "Give me a few days, my lady. I need to pray about this. If I take the job, I want to do it well and that will take commitment on my part," she explained.

Tarian nodded a little reluctantly. *I wish she'd agreed right away.*

Twould have made my heart rest a little more easily. "Alright," she said aloud. "May I return in a few days' time for your answer?"

"Aye, a few days, my lady."

Tarian smiled and rose to go. Suddenly, she decided to act upon something she'd desired but been afraid to do. *Tis only fear that holds you back. A fear of man that is sin.* "Deirdre," she spoke, "would you mind meeting with me to pray every now and then? Maybe every week?"

Deirdre's eyes opened wide. "You don't have to," Tarian added, feeling her embarrassment growing. *Twas foolish to believe she thinks of you as a friend...*

"Nay, I'd like to," Deirdre answered, "You caught me by surprise, 'twas all."

Tarian wanted to hug Deirdre but kept her composure. "Fine. When shall we start, then?"

Deirdre thought. "May I decide about this position you've offered me first, my lady? We could begin after we've settled that."

"Good," Tarian replied as calmly as she could. "I'll send for your reply in a few days, then."

"Aye, in a few days."

CHAPTER TWENTY-FIVE

Oxfield

Bricius wrapped the heavy robe more closely around his shoulders. His steps matched, though feebly, those of the younger man walking beside him. Their feet crushed the last autumn leaves, sending up a wild, earthy odor to their nostrils.

"Her mother died on Samhain," Bricius' companion suddenly spoke. For a long while, they had been striding along silently through the wood outside Oxfield's walls. "The feast day of the dead. Do you think there's anything in that?"

Bricius cocked his head and looked into Calum's eyes. *They always hold that secret sorrow.* "What do you mean, lad?"

Calum ran a hand through his hair. "I know it sounds pagan, Bricius. I just wondered if there could be any significance in the day a person dies and is born."

The waters run deep in this man. Bricius paused. "I would have to say, lad, offhand, that the days themselves hold no power over us, have no significance in and of themselves."

Calum nodded.

"But," Bricius added, "the Scriptures tell us that God appoints every man a day to be born and to die. And some days have taken on significance, and He surely knows that."

"Like the solstice."

"Aye, and we celebrate the Christ's birthday, then. A light to shine during the darkest time of year."

Calum stayed silent for a moment, then said, "Forgive me, Bricius, but you didn't answer my question directly."

Bricius smiled. "Nay, for I don't have an answer from my brain for you. But my heart answers, 'aye,' and I think some truths have an expression there that they cannot find in words."

Calum nodded, and the two meandered on, plucking leaves from the bushes they passed every now and again. Finally, Calum spoke, "The time has come, Bricius, you know."

Bricius stopped walking. "What do you mean, lad?" *Oh, God, I thought you would deliver him before it came to this.*

Calum turned to look at him, arms held loosely at his sides. "I'm bringing Bethan and her sister back to Oxfield." Calum set his jaw. "Marcus has learned all I can teach him. He can take over the command of the guard for me. And then I'll go as I said I would."

Bricius had never known such frustration with the younger man as he felt at that moment. "And what of the church here at Oxfield? You are one of its leaders."

Calum shook his head. "You are their pastor, Bricius. Not me. I've never been able to put it all…" He shut his eyes for a brief moment, and Bricius saw the inner suffering of years pass over his face.

Oh, Lord, give me wisdom. "You've never returned to the village, have you, my son?" Bricius asked quietly.

"Nay, not since that day."

"Don't you think 'twould help you to face it, Calum? To look at it squarely in faith and dare it to do its worst?"

"What, exactly? To look at what?" The younger man's voice had grown brittle.

"The past."

Calum was silent.

Bricius tried again. "Don't you think, my lad, 'tis cowardly to run away from your fears, aye?"

The bitterness emergent in Calum's smile startled Bricius.

"Don't you know by now, Bricius, that I can't run away from what I really fear?"

The potter furrowed his brows and waited for an explanation.

"I fear what lies within myself. And I can never get away from that."

The eyes of the two men met briefly. Bricius' gaze continued to follow his friend long after Calum had continued on the path, pushing aside the brambles that barred his way.

Dunpeledyr

Deoradhan relished the hatred that he felt rising within his chest. *This is the man who killed my father.* He kept his gaze respectfully lowered as Lord Weylin gushed praises over his favorite mares. The nobleman's finger moved over the pedigrees, inked on squares of parchment. Deoradhan despised the pale flesh covering that bony finger.

"Arthur himself buys from us, and that's an honor," Lord Weylin boasted, ignorant of his companion's thoughts. Then he added, smirking, "Weakling though he is."

He rolled up the parchments carefully and handed them over to a servant standing at his elbow. "The world knows Dunpeledyr's horses as the swiftest and strongest Britain can breed."

"And was it always so, my lord?" The words fell out of Deoradhan's mouth. He stood still, trying to appear unknowledgeable. *He must never suspect.*

The lord met his gaze with heavy-lidded eyes, half-hidden under a thatch of gray hair. "What do you mean, young man?"

"Well, Lady Fiona told me that you won Dunpeledyr in battle. I only wondered if your predecessor also bred fine horseflesh."

Lord Weylin chuckled. "Nay, nay. The wild Lothian tribe that dwelt here knew nothing of such civilized pursuits. Wine and women were all old chief Eion cared for, I'm sure."

"Do any of his descendants survive, or did you deal judiciously with all of his kind?" Deoradhan kept his voice only moderately interested.

The man shrugged. "Nay, no direct descendants live. His wife's only child is also mine. These people put some stock in maternal descent as well as in mastery, so 'twas useful to have her as wife in two ways."

"Well," replied Deoradhan, "all to the glory of Logress. All for Arthur's kingdom." He offered a grin, knowing the lord would agree wholeheartedly.

But Lord Weylin stared at him a moment, then smiled. "Aye and nay. I think I see that sentiment in your eyes as well, my lad, aye? There are some who think another would do a better job at leading these confederate kingdoms. And confederate they are. That's what Arthur doesn't understand."

What?

His employer laid an arm around Deoradhan's shoulders. "But enough political talk. We must go look at those horses. I'll tell you of my plans for spring breeding. And then, I wish you to join my family for dinner. My daughter Fiona has arrived, and both she and Solas requested your presence."

Surprised but intrigued, Deoradhan nodded. "Aye, my lord. I'll certainly attend with pleasure."

West Lea

A rapping knock startled Bethan from her sewing. Putting aside the needle and cloth, she eased Enid's sleeping frame off her lap to the fur rug and tiptoed to the door.

'Twas late for visitors. "Who is it?" she called softly through the wooden barrier.

"'Tis I, Garan, Bethan."

At the voice of the priest's son, Bethan felt her heart speed up in nervousness. *'Tis never love I feel for him, nor affection. 'Tis admiration and awe.* She opened the door, pulling on it slowly so the hinges wouldn't creak.

Outlined by the half-moon, Garan stood, tall, thin as a blade of wheat. She couldn't see his eyes in the darkness but knew from experience that the pale orbs would be carefully curious, articulate. Pious and yet…

"Come in," she said. "Only quietly. Enid is already asleep." Bethan stepped to the side to let the young man pass.

He moved with short, quick steps. His hands continually played with the edge of his belted tunic. Bethan had not noticed before what large hands he had. *Almost too large for his person. As if he has yet to grow into them…*

Garan positioned himself near the dim hearth. "It's cold in here," he remarked, more to himself than to Bethan, and drew his cloak around him.

"Aye," she agreed and stood still, waiting for the reason he'd come. *What if he wishes to break the engagement? My dowry no longer exists; there is no reason for him to keep it.*

His pallid eyes kept darting from the fire to her face, illuminated by the ruddy glow. After a long silence, he spoke, "You no doubt know why I have come, Bethan."

Her heart quaked. *Lord, give me strength to push forward.* The vision of life without a protector for her and Enid rose before her mind, but she pushed it away. "Aye," she managed. "I understand that you cannot keep our commitment. I do not hold you to it."

His eyes widened with surprise. "Nay," he said. "On the contrary, I wish to reiterate our promise. Despite my parents' (and mostly my mother's) reservations, I chose you because I saw much to admire in you, not because of your dowry, Bethan. I see in you strength of character, determination, a willingness to deny your natural feelings, a holy innocence of worldly things." He turned his gaze back toward the fire. The light danced into his eyes, warming the blue. "I have a passion to reach the lost, to go where the gospel has not been heard, but I cannot do it alone. You, you, Bethan, are the one who can aid me, be my helpmate, my joy. An example to the heathen."

Bethan stood stunned. Always, Garan had seemed self-sufficient, strong, burning with an internal flame. *Not as if he needed me. And yet he says he does. To go on this holy mission.* She thought of her yearning for Calum and realized how paltry it must be in the eyes of the Lord in comparison with this calling. With trembling steps, she crossed the small space between them and took his cold hands in hers. They shook with emotion. She lifted her eyes up to search his face and found the words came to her lips, as if the moment had been predetermined:

"Here is your maidservant."

CHAPTER TWENTY-SIX

Dunpeledyr

"Deoradhan, if you will take the lead, I will follow with Solas," Lady Fiona spoke, her smile reflecting the brilliance of the early winter sun. Her furry pony plodded along beneath her along the rocky path toward the coast. Deoradhan nudged his own wooly animal to the front of the threesome and led the way up the winding path.

"I remember when 'twas dangerous to move from the fortress and even more dangerous to ride to the coast," remarked Solas, who straddled the same pony as his half-sister. His eyes looked calmly toward the sunlight, unseeing.

Fiona smiled. "For fear of the Saxons, aye."

Deoradhan couldn't resist. "And for fear of the Britons."

"What do you mean? We are Britons." Fiona's face grew quizzical. "Lothian is part of Logress."

"Now 'tis. But don't you know your history, my lady? You yourself told me that another once ruled in Dunpeledyr."

"Aye," answered the girl, "and I wish you would call me Fiona, without that formal title. Anyone who grows up in the high king's household cannot be common-birthed." She raised her eyebrows.

Deoradhan smiled. What they didn't know! Strange, though, he had wanted to despise them because of what he knew he must do. But he couldn't.

"Is your father a nobleman, Deoradhan?" Solas spoke up, his

voice a little muffled by the wind and the clopping hooves.

"Aye, he was."

"He's dead, then?"

"Aye, for seventeen years."

"The year I was born," Solas said quietly. "And your mother? Is she also gone?"

Deoradhan paused. "Nay, but she doesn't know I'm alive."

"Is there any danger in her knowing, Deoradhan?" This came from Fiona. "I know if my son lived, I would want—"

"Aye, there is danger in it," replied Deoradhan. "I don't wish to speak of it anymore," he said suddenly, wishing he'd not delved into the subject. "I see the coast ahead."

Oxfield

The messenger arrived shortly after sunset. His horse wore a film of dirty sweat, and his clothes displayed the mud of a multiple-days' ride. Calum stopped as the man reined to a halt and dismounted in front of the guard tower.

"Messages from the Pendragon and Camelot," he sighed, patting his horse's neck.

Calum nodded. "Bring them into Lord Drustan at once. Is there more talk of trouble in the north?"

The messenger's face grew grim. "Aye. Aye, there is." He lowered his voice. "More than one lord has spoken openly against the high king. After years of peace…"

Calum shook his head.

"Oh, speaking of the north, I've a message from Dunpeledyr. It came to Camelot, and so I've brought it on." The man pulled a rolled parchment from the saddle pouch. "For a person named Aine, daughter of Llewellyn. Do you know her?"

"Aye," answered Calum, "I can get this to her. From Dunpeledyr, you say?" He took the sealed scroll from the man's hands.

"Aye," agreed the messenger. "Funny place, 'tis, with a stranger lord. I wouldn't live there if I could help it."

From Deoradhan. At last.

"My thanks," he said aloud and turned his feet toward the kitchen.

Aine herself answered. "Oh, hello," she said. "Do you need to see Deirdre?"

The girl's voice sounded as though she'd been hollowed out, like the pipe Calum had heard her play at gatherings. He knew her only by name and had never conversed with her, but even so, Aine seemed so much quieter, less lighthearted than he'd ever seen her. Her hair looked oily as well and her usually rosy face was paler than he'd ever seen it. *Something must be bothering her. Perhaps she's ill. Winter's coming, after all.*

"Nay, I've brought a message for you, lass. 'Tis from Deoradhan, I think."

He watched her face brighten, then cloud over. *What is it?* "I can read it for you, if you'd like," he offered, knowing 'twas likely she couldn't read.

The lovely young woman hesitated, then nodded. "Aye, would you? Calum, 'tis, aye?"

"Aye. May I enter?" he asked. She hadn't moved from her place in the doorway.

At his question, Aine jumped to the side. "Aye, come in."

She shrunk away from him as Calum moved through the narrow doorway. *Odd.* Aine had not flinched from any male presence in the past.

The kitchen was nearly empty; 'twas after supper, and most of the maids busied themselves with handiwork in the adjoining large room. Aine and Calum sat on a fur rug by the hearth.

Aine kept a careful distance from him. Her cheeks showed bony in the firelight and her beautiful dark eyes had sunken back, as if she hadn't eaten much for a long while. As Calum broke the seal and unrolled the parchment, he glanced up to see Aine closing her eyes.

"Are you well, lass?" he felt compelled to ask, reaching a hand to her arm.

Her eyes shot open like an arrow from the bow, and she drew her arm away from him. "I'm alright," she whispered. "Please read the letter, Calum."

He studied her for a moment and then lowered his gaze to the message. "'Deoradhan, to Aine, daughter of Llewellyn,'" he read, "'I trust this finds you well, beloved of my heart. While I travel this dangerous path, my love, 'tis your face I see both in my waking and sleeping dreams.'"

Calum paused. He knew the emotional currents ran deeply in Deoradhan, but he hadn't thought his friend's affection for this girl had grown so strong. "'I hold to our promise and cannot wait to have you again in my arms, and you alone, as I did the night we parted. And now, my love, I must beg for your forgiveness. I cannot keep the pledge to marry you so soon as we wished. I rest knowing that you are faithful to me as I am to you, in spirit, body, and heart. May the gods of our ancestors keep you.'"

Aine's sob caused Calum to set aside the letter. Tears coursed down her cheeks, despite how much she wiped them away. Calum sat silently, not knowing what to say to this weeping young woman, whose grief seemed deeper than that of a maid for her absent lover.

Finally, she whimpered, "Tell me something, Calum. You are Deoradhan's friend, aye?" The tears kept spilling over the rims of her eyes without a sign of ceasing.

"Aye, I am, lass."

"Does he easily forgive a trespass against himself?"

Calum felt dread surround his heart, press upon his lungs, as he looked at the terrified girl. *Oh, dear God, may she not have betrayed him!* "Nay," he murmured finally, knowing lies would not help her. "Nay, he forgives little and forgets nothing."

"I thought so," she whispered, her head dropping. Her stringy hair shadowed her face, and Calum felt more pure pity for her than he had ever felt for himself.

I dare not ask her what troubles her. He sighed. *That I could bear others' burdens. But I've a burden of my own to bear.*

West Lea

The robin woke her, its joyful laugh penetrating the stiff, timeless predawn hour, forcing the day to move forward, heralding the sun. Bethan stretched her limbs, feeling the joints pop into place. Opening her eyes, she stared into the dim living quarters for a few moments. But ease of heart fled from Bethan as her gaze rested on the shadowy chair by the still-glowing fire.

Where Mama used to sit. Tears blurred her vision. She shook her head quickly to shoo them away. Her eyes dropped to her sister, slumbering beside her. Poor Enid. To lose Mama so young.

I must be her mama, then. Surely, Garan will take her in when we marry. How many times had Papa quoted that Scripture passage about those who didn't care for their families being worse than unbelievers? If Papa put stock in that, how much more so a priest's son must?

Bethan stroked her sister's hair, love filling her heart. *I will be her mama, and Garan will be as a father to her until Papa returns and finds us.*

Unless Papa is…

She closed her eyes, refusing to finish the idea. Hardly thinking, Bethan pushed back the thick woolen cover and rose to her feet. 'Twas only November; no need for shoes yet. Plucking her shawl from the chair, she wrapped herself and hurried outside.

Specks of snow drifted around her as Bethan made her way down the path toward the stream, made familiar by so many trips there in the past. *I shall never walk this path again to fetch water for Mama,* she realized. The grief trickled through her spirit, reaching all its recesses.

Bethan stopped at the edge of the stiffening stream and sank onto the cold dirt. She looked around her. Every tree, every rock, bush, and stone seemed alien, foreboding. *Never did it seem so to me. Always, I felt God's presence all around me, He in His heaven watching over me, as I walked the good Christian road.*

The tears overflowed her eyes. *Why are You so far from me in my grief and so near to me when I'm happy? When I need You, it feels like the door has been shut in my face.*

"I don't mean to be disrespectful, Lord. 'Tis only how I feel," she whispered into the silence. "And I know...You know what You're doing. But couldn't my mama have been spared?"

And the impenetrable silence spoke back, *Shall not the Judge of all the earth do what is just?*

Dunpeledyr

Seonaid took the now-frozen woodland path, her feet following its familiar way without hesitation. *How many times have I traveled this path over the past fifteen years?* She smiled, the dappling sunlight making her eyes squint. *Too many times to remember.* She first had trodden it as a young woman despairing of her life. And God had sent a minister of mercy to meet her there.

The trees grew steadily sparser until a clearing became visible just before her. The noblewoman hurried her steps when she noticed smoke emerging from the chimney. Caratacos was at home.

A few chickens pecked in the dirt in front of the plain one-room cottage. They may have been scavenging, but Seonaid knew how well-fed they were. *The fattest and most petted chickens in all of Lothian and most likely of Logress as well.* She shook her head and patted the she-goat tethered by the door as she came up to the cottage's front stoop.

"Caratacos," she called out, rapping on the doorframe. The door stood open a crack, and the smell of vegetable stew wafted out. "Caratacos, are you at home?"

"Aye, aye, lassie, I hear you. Come in, come in," a thin voice scratched out from within.

Seonaid stepped into the warm, dark room, lit by a peat fire in the hearth and a few shafts of light from the window and door. In front of the hearth, seated on a three-legged stool, a bowed, elderly man crouched, holding something in his hands. Wordlessly, Seonaid moved toward him and knelt beside him. She peered into his cupped hands.

'Twas a sparrow, its wings destroyed by some trivial accident. The blood from its wounds stained Caratacos' fingers. Seonaid turned her eyes away instinctively, then looked up into the old man's face. Grief and love mingled there with a settled peace. 'Twas not surprising to see that harmony on the hermit's face, but to observe it when such a fragile creature sighed out its life in his hands!

"It's dying," she whispered.

"Aye," he murmured, his eyes pitying the bird embraced by his arthritic fingers. "'And he will swallow up on this mountain the covering that is cast over all peoples, the veil that is spread over all nations. He will swallow up death forever; and the Lord GOD will wipe away tears from all faces.'" He turned cloudy eyes toward her. "Thus says the Father of our Lord Jesus Christ, aye, Seonaid?"

His gaze traveled back toward the little winged animal, now shuddering in death's last pain-filled moments, and Seonaid saw that his lips trembled as he lowered a kiss to the creature's head. "Somehow, even this must be a mercy, though we cannot see it," he whispered.

The tears slipped down Seonaid's cheeks, and the image of dying Eion flashed through her heart. "Aye," she replied finally. "Even this."

CHAPTER TWENTY-SEVEN

Dunpeledyr

"She is my favorite among Father's mares." Deoradhan heard the cheerful voice from the other side of the roan horse. Pausing in his brushing, he peered over the animal's sleek back and saw Lady Fiona smiling back at him. She clutched a thick shawl around her shoulders and head. Frosty breath wafted from her mouth when she smiled.

"My lady," he greeted and went on with his work. Weylin's daughter had a fondness for horses and often came to the stable while he worked. Her summery presence brightened the chilly air of the stalls as well as his gloomy thoughts.

"I wish you would call me Fiona, as I've asked, Deoradhan," replied the young woman. Deoradhan smiled and nodded, enjoying her feisty forthrightness, but her next words surprised him. "After all, we are almost brother and sister, aren't we?"

He froze, his brush mid-air. *Act normally, you fool, and she won't suspect anything.* The breath caught in his lungs, but he held his composure. "What do you mean, Fiona?" he asked, as if he was nothing more than a horsemaster and she only his employer's daughter.

He glanced up to find her gray eyes fixed on his face. They held a calm blunt steadiness. "I know that you are Lady Seonaid's firstborn son, Deoradhan."

He couldn't deny it. Her honest gaze trapped him. Tearing his eyes away, he said nothing and continued brushing the mare.

"Why are you here?" she asked quietly, coming toward him.

Deoradhan stayed silent, unsure of what he should say.

"Are you here to harm us?"

He shook his head. "Nay, not you, Fiona. You've no part in this."

"Who, then? My father? And Solas?"

The blind boy's face rushed to his mind, and Deoradhan shook his head again. "Nay, I'll not harm Solas, rest assured. Perhaps before I met him, I would have, but not now."

"But how can you avoid that, Deoradhan? If you seek vengeance, and I assume that you do, 'tis Solas who stands in your way. 'Tis Solas who hinders your inheritance, once my father is disposed of, one way or the other." The young woman spoke without drama.

She states the truth, Deoradhan admitted. *I've not seen Solas for what he is: an obstacle barring me from my rightful place on Dunpeledyr's throne.* Even if he did away with Lord Weylin, Solas stood to inherit the kingdom, blind though he was. *And Arthur will support his claim.*

Solas would have to die.

There is no other way. The thought of killing the sweet-natured, glad-hearted youth revolted him. And his mother loved Solas, he could tell. *What am I going to do?*

"Whom have you told about me?" he swallowed.

"No one." Fiona stared at him.

As if she reads my thoughts.

"So what do you plan to do?" Her voice jolted him.

With a sense of sick emptiness, Deoradhan realized that he did not even know his heart's desire anymore. "I don't know," he answered. "I need time to think."

She nodded. "Deoradhan, my family has done yours great harm. For what 'tis worth to you, I ask your forgiveness for the wrongs we've committed." She lowered her eyes. "I can't atone for what my father has done to yours...or for anything else. But I ask for your mercy."

Her words puzzled and angered him. *Why doesn't she stand her ground and act as if her father did rightly?* Her humble attitude made him feel like he ought to forgive her and all she represented. Deoradhan stared at her for a moment, then turned and left the stall without answering.

She ran to catch up with him. "Deoradhan, God works in strange ways, and I know that He has brought you here for a purpose." She grabbed his arm and forced him to stop walking toward the tack area. "But I ask one thing of you: that you tell me when you have decided to act. And that you spare my Solas."

Anger filling him, he shoved her aside. "Your Solas should never have been born."

"How can you say that?" she cried and grasped his arm, pulling on him to face her. He resisted and continued on his way. "How can you say that of Solas?"

Enough. Deoradhan held her by her shoulders and pinned her against the wall. "Listen. Your beloved Solas is the product of your father raping my mother after he put my father through a gruesome death. Your father would have killed me also if my mother hadn't sent me into exile." He saw that he had frightened her and released his hold on her, a little guilty. He continued in a softer tone. "Perhaps you can understand why my heart is not as tender as yours toward your brother."

"But he is your brother, too," she whispered.

"He is not my brother!"

"He is not like my father. Surely you know that. He has the living Christ within him, Deoradhan, as do I."

Deoradhan smirked. "This living Christ headed your father's army as well, Fiona. Forgive me if I don't think of Him with affection or trust."

The girl stayed silent, her eyes on her feet. "So you will not spare Solas, then?"

"I will do whatever I must." Deoradhan ground his teeth. "But no harm will befall your brother by my hand, if I can help it, Fiona."

Her face relaxed. "Thank you, Deoradhan." She kissed his hand. "I pray that mercy will be shown you, as you've shown it to others. Now I must leave you. Lady Seonaid will be wondering where I've gone."

She moved toward the entryway, but near the door, she turned curious eyes to him. "What is your birth name, Deoradhan?"

He hesitated, feeling the intense anger draining from his spirit. Clearing his throat, he answered, "Padruig. I am Padruig." The name felt strange on his tongue, like an unfamiliar food.

"Padruig," Fiona repeated, nodding.

Deoradhan felt compelled to ask. "And Fiona, answer my question. How did you know my secret?"

She smiled wearily. "Have you forgotten our first meeting in Camelot, Deoradhan, when I mistook you for Solas? Seeing you here, hearing a little of your story…I put the pieces together, Deoradhan." Fiona gave a faint laugh. "You are not as complex as you think, my lord."

She curtsied to him and exited. Deoradhan watched her retreat toward the main hall. For the first time in long years, he realized, bitterness had to struggle with other emotions for kingship in his heart.

West Lea

"I will come for you in the spring," Garan assured her. His pale eyes shone. "I have to find a party with whom to travel north. Then we'll go, together. And we'll be married in the land where we'll serve our God."

Awed at his passion for Christ, Bethan nodded. She hardly noticed when Calum took her sack of belongings from her hands and strapped it across his horse's back.

"God go with you, Bethan," Garan stared into her eyes.

"And with you," Bethan replied. She wanted to add some term of affection, but Garan had never used such toward her, so she felt awkward to do so now.

Garan turned to Calum. "I am glad you've come to take her back to Oxfield. Bethan speaks well of you."

Calum responded only with a nod. Pained at what she knew he might feel, seeing her new regard for the priest's son, Bethan hurried toward the horse. Her sister Enid already sat on its back, secure among the sacks.

'Twas Calum who assisted her with mounting, not Garan, who stood white in the icy sunlight. With a quick motion, the guard swung himself onto his own horse, and they trotted off. Bethan felt that she must say something, anything, to break the tension she felt within herself.

"Calum, I'm sorry—" she began.

He cut her off softly. "Nay, Bethan. 'Twas meant to be. We have our own paths to tread, ones that have been cut out from eternity past, aye?"

"Aye." Bethan stayed quiet for a moment, then tried again. "I am glad you are my brother at Oxfield, Calum, though."

She saw his face grow taut with…pain? Grief? Glancing at him, she saw a deep-set agony surface in his countenance. *This cannot have resulted from what has passed between us.* Aloud, she said, "What is it, Calum?"

"I will not be remaining at Oxfield."

Fear rose in her heart. "What do you mean?"

"When we arrive there, I will resign from the command of the guard. I've been training a young guard, Marcus, to take my place for some time."

"So this has been long-planned?"

"Aye. Something I've thought and prayed over for years now."

"Years?"

"Aye. Since…"

"Since what?"

Calum's glance went over to Enid, sitting in front of Bethan. The little girl dozed in the twilight, her head falling back against

Bethan's chest. "'Tis alright. She's asleep," Bethan said, feeling afraid of what Calum would reveal.

Calum guided his horse gently forward. The hooves made a heavy, dull thud on the packed dirt. "I have an atonement to make, Bethan. For something I did many years ago."

"What did you do, Calum?" she nearly whispered, her mind running.

He looked over at her, as if judging how much to tell and how much to conceal. "My sister Cairine was older than me by six years. When I had only passed twelve winters, she took part in the solstice rituals. I'm sure you know what that entails, especially in the wilder parts of the country."

Bethan nodded and waited for him to go on.

"She carried a child as a result. But while the child was yet forming within her, a man came through the village, preaching the gospel. God used that to turn my sister to Christ for salvation, as He did for me and a few others in our village."

Bethan watched as he sighed and sought the words to tell the history. "The pagan leaders of the village were enraged at this but did nothing immediately. That summer, Cairine lost the child in a fever. Many of the animals also aborted in that season. In the fall, the harvest failed. For all of it, the druids blamed unfaithfulness to the gods."

He stayed silent for so long that Bethan prompted him, "And then?"

"They killed her. They sacrificed one who had carried death within her so that the crops might live. They burned her alive." His words were toneless, stilted, unable to convey the horror she knew he still must feel.

"But, Calum," Bethan spoke after a time, "you said that you had to atone. Why? What did you do?"

He glanced over. "I watched and did nothing. I should have done something to prevent it. Anything. Or at least not been ashamed."

"But you were only a boy, Calum. What could you have done?"

He shook his head. "I don't know. Something. It haunts me worse than any Samhain spirit, Bethan. The memory hangs over me like a shroud. And I cannot rid myself of it." He cleared his throat. "After that day, I ran away and have not returned to my home village since."

After a long and quiet moment, Bethan asked, "So where are you going to live, if not to Oxfield?"

"In the wilderness. God must provide some door of hope for me, though I don't deserve it. Otherwise," he swallowed, "otherwise, I feel I cannot endure this life anymore."

She wanted to say something, anything, to persuade him that his sins were atoned for. 'Twas so clear to her that Jesus' blood had covered all Calum's sin, that he was a new creature in Christ. That there was no condemnation for him. But his feelings were too real. Only a fool would ignore them. And Calum was no fool, that she knew. The words died in her throat.

"We've a long way to ride before we camp for the night. Let's quicken our pace," Calum said after a few moments. His horse moved from a trot to a slow canter and Bethan followed suit, her spinning mind able only to pray with a simplicity her Father loved to hear.

Dunpeledyr

"You will remain with us this winter." Lord Weylin's voice threaded its way across the table to his daughter.

Deoradhan saw her eyebrows rise. "Here? At Dunpeledyr?"

"Aye. Did you have other plans, Fiona?"

"Nay," she said hastily. "I only thought that I would spend the winter with the queen, as I usually do. May I ask why—?"

"Plans change," her father cut her off, smiling. "I would like to have my family here at Dunpeledyr this winter, especially as the Feast of the Nativity approaches."

"Alright, Father," Fiona agreed slowly, casting Deoradhan a

questioning glance.

Why does she think I know what her father is about? I'm trying to get rid of him!

"Now," Weylin said, rising from his chair, "I'm off to see to my kennels. Deoradhan, will you come along?"

"Gladly, my lord, as soon as I finish my bread," Deoradhan agreed, reaching for another piece, even though he didn't want it.

Weylin nodded his satisfaction at Deoradhan's hearty appetite before throwing a scornful glance at his own son. When Deoradhan's eyes turned to the youth, he saw Solas quietly nibbling at a piece of roast pheasant. His heart felt a desire to love this half-brother, though his mind hated the thought.

The lord exited, followed soon after by Lady Seonaid and Solas together. Fiona and Deoradhan sat alone at the table, exactly as the two wished.

"What is my father up to?" her immediate question came.

Deoradhan shrugged, a little irritated. "Why would I know, Fiona? Remember my place here."

She glanced toward the door. "But you are in my father's confidence. Or soon will be. He does not trust me as he does you."

"And what is that to me?"

"To me 'tis much. My father has never kept me here for a winter. 'Twas odd for him to pull me away from court as he did. He's scheming something, Deoradhan." She paused. "You know that Arthur's situation is precarious now, aye?"

How precarious? "Explain yourself, Fiona. What have you seen at Camelot to make you think that?" Deoradhan demanded.

Fiona bit her lip. "There are pockets of opponents who send letters to the king regularly. I hear this from the queen. And Lothian has been a nest of trouble in the past."

Deoradhan snorted. "There are always adversaries to the throne. That means little."

She shook her head. "Nay, I know that. But there has been an attempt on the king's life. His cupbearer was poisoned."

Deoradhan frowned. "A cowardly thing to do." *I would use a knife and let him see my face.*

"Aye." She hesitated, then leaned forward earnestly. "I tell you this, Deoradhan, because my father may... may be part of the growing conspiracy. And because he trusts you, he may ask you to take part. He may ask for your help in overthrowing the king."

"I bear no fondness for Arthur."

She had not expected that response. He could tell from her widened eyes. "But, surely, Deoradhan, by right of his kingship alone... He's been placed there by God."

"I am not overly fond of your God either, Fiona, as you well ken," he replied. "Thus, I give little heed to His supposed wishes regarding who should rule as tyrant over the Britons." Deoradhan stood, eager to see what Weylin wanted with him. "I will act according to my own benefit, my lady, as your father has done to me."

"Then how are you any different from him, my lord?" the young woman asked, coming around the table to him. "You are the same kind of man."

His hand rose to strike her. She didn't flinch, and the pity in her eyes weakened him. Deoradhan's hand dropped back to his side. Robbed of his fury, humiliated that he would have hit her, he could only turn his bitter soul toward the door without another word. His dying conscience told him what his mind denied:

She is right.

CHAPTER TWENTY-EIGHT

Camelot
503 A.D.

The late March wind cut Tarian across the face. Folding her arms tightly around her, she turned her feet back toward the main hall. *Lord, please get me back home soon, back to Deirdre, back to Oxfield.*

She tired of the endless revelries and outings that her ladyship planned and executed with equally eternal enthusiasm. But Drustan had insisted that they remain through the winter at Camelot. "Great changes may be ahead," he intoned, "and great opportunities for a flexible man."

You are so flexible, Drustan, that one day, you may never regain your proper shape at all.

As Tarian stepped up the stair into the back corridor, she collided with a dark-cloaked figure. She staggered backwards, and the person caught her by the arm, his hood falling away from his face. His face was only inches away from hers when she regained her balance.

"I'm sorry, my lady. I didn't see you."

She recognized that face, though she hadn't seen it for months. "Deoradhan," she greeted. "I didn't know you had come to Camelot."

The auburn-haired former messenger looked at her uneasily as he pulled up his heavy hood. "Aye, my lady, I've just arrived." He paused, then spoke low. "Tell me, my lady, is Lord Drustan about?"

Why was he acting so secretive? "Aye, he's here. Did you want to speak with him?"

Deoradhan gave a vigorous shake of his head. "Nay. Nay, but will you impart a favor to me, my lady?"

"What is it?"

"Do not tell my lord that I'm here."

"Alright, if you wish."

His eyes stared into hers. "Promise me that you will not tell anyone that you saw me, my lady."

"Alright, I promise. But why?"

Deoradhan hesitated. "I just need it to be so for now, my lady. Please?"

"I've already given my word, Deoradhan."

"Thank you, my lady." With a kiss to her hand, the young man rushed past her.

What was that all about? Fear crept around her heart. *I hope I didn't promise something I will regret.*

Summer Country

He saw her everywhere he looked. Every dry leaf on the ground, every birdsong in the frosty evening sky murmured Cairine's presence. Calum had not meant to come this way at all. But the past drew him back straight to where he had not wanted to tread.

His beard had grown, covering his smooth, scarred cheeks with golden brown fleece. It had given Calum additional protection from the cold, which struck at him continually throughout the long winter, despite his heavy fur cloak and woolen trousers. Yet his spiritual misery was so acute, the elemental sufferings held little annoyance for him.

Do I dare enter the village? Do I walk the same roads, see the same faces? They would not recognize him. It had been nearly eighteen years since he had last moved through the hamlet he now approached. Eighteen years since he had seen mother or father, brothers or sisters.

His feet trembled in their leather boots as the small gathering of cottages came into sight. Frozen fields stretched out as far as he could see on either side. *Just as I remember it. But I can't go back in time. I can never take back what happened.*

Camelot

Deoradhan ducked into a recess in the corridor. He had not expected to meet with Lady Tarian here. Usually, the lord of Oxfield and his household arrived just in time for the Feast of the Nativity and stayed for only a month or so. Never into March.

He smiled without joy. March was a historical month for assassinations. "And you, too, my son?" he murmured aloud, realizing how well Julius' words fit his own actions. *That first Brutus was a patriot, too.*

I was as a son to Arthur and now I am to be his demise? A soft-bladed knife?

He shook his head. *Arthur has done much to destroy me. He deserves no less than what I am prepared to do.*

But am I prepared to do it? He closed his eyes and pictured himself creeping up behind the heavily-sleeping king, plunging his dagger between the Pendragon's ribs. The job would require more than one thrust. Again and again the knife must do its work. The blood would splurt and pump from the gouges in the king's flesh. *Will he die quickly, or like most men, will he awaken and perish knowing that I betrayed him?*

And why was Drustan still here? Did he suspect…? The whole court whispered with supposed scheming. A man could not reign for two decades without developing a few enemies. *But the king little surmises how far the frustrations with his rule have run,* thought Deoradhan as he turned his feet back into the dimly-lit corridor.

Never mind the emotional pull of childhood attachments. First Arthur must go; then Weylin would follow. And his way would be clear to take back what belonged to him rightfully. He had business to do tonight.

No one must ever know I've come.

Oxfield

"When do you expect Garan will come fetch you?"

Bethan looked up from plucking the feathers from the chickens laid out on the table. She met Deirdre's eyes with a smile and shrugged. "I don't know exactly when."

"Possibly within the month?"

"I can hope." Bethan picked up a sharp knife and slid it across the fowl, the edge pulling out the quill remnants.

"True." Deirdre gave a sigh. "Sometimes, 'tis hard to hope, though, I admit. Life seems quiet here now that everyone is gone…Meghyn, now Calum, and Lady Tarian."

"Is she really a believer, Deirdre?"

"Aye, she is, but I think sometime 'tis harder to count the costs when you come into privilege, you ken. For years, she fell away from the way." Deirdre smiled. "Finally, she came to realize again that only Christ could satisfy her."

Only Christ… Does He alone satisfy me? Or do I follow Him because my Papa did? Bethan batted the thought around in her mind. Wasn't she prepared to give her life as a missionary to the heathen north with Garan, especially now that Papa had never returned?

But the idea continued to skulk into her thoughts. *Do I love Christ or only the things He gives me? Would I be content with Him alone?*

Bethan was not foolish enough to ignore the query completely. She didn't pray about it; she didn't dare to. But she allowed it a little room.

Summer Country

The dawn stained the sky with deep winter pink mingling with orange. Calum crunched through the remnants of the last snow, his boots breaking through the fragile ice coating. The wheel tracks in the road had frozen still, like miniature red sea partings. Nearby, possibly from the clustered evergreens growing close to the lane, Calum heard a strange bird call, melodic and gurgling with joyful expectation.

His eyes fixed on the thatched roofs ahead of him, Calum placed one heavy foot in front of the other. There, that first building housed the knife-sharpener. How well he remembered watching the man's skillful fingers work, bringing each blade to razor-sharpness. Aye, and there was the drinking-house, where his own father spent many hours after plowing. Here, on the right…

Calum shuddered. The druid priest's home. How strange, though. Usually, few visitors wanted to step into that abode. Yet as he approached it this morning, a dozen people flocked around its open door, despite the early hour. Puzzled, Calum paused a few feet away.

"Greetings, laddie," a man called out from the doorway. His face wore a graying red beard lit by a nearly toothless grin. "Are you coming to meeting? 'Tis the Lord's Day, after all."

'Twas Sunday, Calum realized. *I must play the part of a stranger.* "And is this where the Lord's people meet, man?" he said, mustering most of his strength to appear happy. *As a good Christian should be.*

"Aye, 'tis. And are you one of us?"

"I am." Calum strode forward toward the low doorway. *That my shaking limbs would not betray me. Why do they meet here, of all places? He must not live here any longer.*

The man grasped Calum by the forearm and then pulled him into a hearty hug. "Welcome, friend," he said. "Come inside. We're about ready to begin."

Inside, more than twenty people of various ages sat clustered on the fur rugs and perched on long hewn benches. A few younger men stood, leaning against the walls, some cradling children in their arms. Calum recognized one among them almost immediately.

'Twas Kieve. *My younger brother.* He had been but ten years old when Calum had left the village. Now he must be…Calum calculated his age. *Twenty-eight.* And was that his little son that he held in his arms? The toddler was the very image of his father.

Kieve's glance rested for a moment upon the stranger, and Calum turned his face away, not wishing to be recognized or acknowledged. He took a seat beside the man who had welcomed him inside.

"So who leads the mass?" he asked in a low voice.

"The priest does," replied the man. "Or his son sometimes now that the priest is so old. Here he is."

Calum shifted his eyes to an interior doorway, leading to the other room of the house. A man in his forties stepped through the humble archway. Gray wove through his black beard and hair, and the wrinkles around his eyes and mouth ran deep. Almost two full decades had passed, but Calum knew who this was.

Heddwyn. Calum remembered the man as a cocky twenty-something-year-old, bent on avoiding responsibilities and enjoying pleasure. As a boy, he had thought the young man could not be any more full of himself without bursting like an overripe Roman grape.

"Greetings in the name of our Lord," Heddwyn murmured, coming to the front of the room. Peace illuminated his countenance.

Calum had never felt so perplexed. How had everything changed from black to white, from ugly to beautiful in the years since he fled? What had happened in this village where Cairine had been put to her gruesome death? Aye, under the eyes of this very man, through the power of his father?

Through all the singing, the scripture recitation, the sermons, Calum sat and stood, stood and sat, participating as if through a dream-self. All around him, he recognized those whom he knew as opposed to the gospel when the preacher had come through the village all those years ago. Yet, here they worshipped the Lord with willing tongues and joyful hearts.

What happened?

CHAPTER TWENTY-NINE

Camelot

"Nia, where is my shawl? You know, the orange silk one." Tarian rustled through the messy trunk. "I must find the time to organize this. Before we leave for home," she added, smiling up at the middle-aged maidservant.

"I believe you left that shawl in my lord's chamber, my lady. I saw it there when I went in to make the bed this morning," replied the woman, kneeling to help Tarian neaten the trunk's contents.

"Don't worry about this, Nia. I'll see to it. Just fetch my shawl if you would. I wish to wear it to supper tonight. The queen wants all of her ladies to match, and—"

"And orange is her favorite color right now, aye?" the servant grinned. "Alright, my lady. I'll get your shawl."

Nia left the room, and Tarian continued with dressing for supper. *This constant bustle and excitement gladdened me when we first came, but I sicken of it now, especially with this child coming.* She dropped a hand to her waist, not noticeably thickened yet. *I must tell Drustan when we arrive back at Oxfield.* Spring was nearly upon them. Surely Drustan would wish to be home for the rest of the lambing season. Unless something more important loomed politically for him.

Poor Arthur. Sleep appeared to have forsaken him and worry to dog his heels. Gwynhwyfar half-loved and half-loathed him. Men hounded him for his attention to their petty problems while denying him the authority he needed to accomplish anything of value. Not an empty-pated woman, Tarian had observed these things while at the queen's side each day.

She looked up when the door opened. 'Twas Nia, without the shawl.

"It wasn't there? I wonder where it could be," said Tarian.

The maidservant didn't move from her place near the half-open door. Tarian glanced at her again and found the woman's face filling with anxiety. "What is it, Nia?"

Nia bit her lip. "I...That is, I wasn't able to look for it in my lord's chamber, my lady."

"Why not, Nia?" questioned Tarian. Drustan usually walked the archery fields at this hour of the day.

"I...It was occupied, my lady."

"Occupied? What do you mean, Nia?" The maid's voice held such strange fear that Tarian let the sash fall from her waist untied.

Tarian headed for the doorway, but the maid grasped her arm. "My lady..."

Tarian pulled away from the woman's hand. "Nay, Nia. If there is someone in my lord's chamber, I must see who 'tis."

As her feet moved down the stone corridor, she felt she did not wish to know what in Drustan's room had made her servant upset. Yet something else compelled her to look anyway, to put to rest Drustan's secrecy and know this man beneath his smooth surface. The incident last autumn in the stables came to her mind, and her spirit shrank away.

It would be easy to just walk away. Go back to your chamber and forget about the shawl.

Tarian stood before the door and placed her hand on the latch. Pausing for just a moment to take a breath, she heard it.

Giggling. Whispering.

Her stomach turned. She forced her hand to lift the latch. It was unlocked. Pushing it open on its silent hinges, Tarian stumbled into the antechamber, lit by several wall torches. On the desk across from the doorway, Drustan's writing implements and parchments stood, just as they had last evening when she had left this room.

Unblinking, Tarian moved to the open archway connecting the rooms. The smell of expensive perfume met her senses as the sight of Lady Seren, dressed only as Nature could dress a woman, met her eyes. Her only artificial ornament, an orange shawl draped over her hair.

Drustan stood from where he reclined when he saw her. "Well," he stated, iron in his voice. Lady Seren stepped toward him, and she stared at Tarian, chin raised, as if she had the right to be where she was.

Tarian was aware of the silence, waiting on her reaction. Gathering her courage, she walked forward until she stood before the two. Without looking at the woman, she plucked the orange shawl from her head. Her eyes met Drustan's.

"I was looking for my wrap," she stated. "You left the door unlocked."

He raised a derisive eyebrow. Numbly, Tarian turned and exited the room, waiting to run until she could be certain her footsteps would not be heard by her husband and his lover.

Summer Country

The priest's son invited the newcomer for supper.

"A homely affair 'twill be," admitted the man, "but as the Scripture says, better a dinner of herbs."

The man's wife, also a homely affair made beautiful by love, served her husband, their six children, and Calum a meal of bread and thick hare stew. Delicious though he knew 'twas, Calum hardly could eat it. Too many thoughts and emotions mixed in his mind and heart.

"My father can't join us this evening. His old bones are racked with arthritis." Heddwyn informed Calum, who felt profound relief but tried not to show it.

His host dipped into the stew with a scrap of bread. "Tell me, do you come from these parts?"

"Aye, from nearby. But I haven't been back since I was a youth," answered Calum.

"And do you find things much changed?" smiled the man.

"Aye, I do." Calum paused. "When I was a boy, 'twas pagan country. Now I see only hints of the old religion. Why is that? What happened to cause it, if I might ask?"

"You may, and I'll tell you what I know of it," answered the priest. "My short answer is: the Holy Spirit came down upon it."

"And the long answer?"

"When God's Spirit comes and breathes new life into dead bones, lad, 'tis difficult sometimes to trace His ways. But I believe it goes back to when we made a human sacrifice nearly twenty years ago, when my father was a leading druid here."

Calum drew a breath. "Aye?"

Heddwyn leaned back. "The victim was one of a few new converts to Christ, and the most persistent in the faith. My father despised her for her decision. He said 'twould be an end to the old ways, that the fields would die, that the rivers would run dry. And you ken, they did for awhile. So, the village leaders decided to offer the gods a sacrifice. And this girl was offered. She went willingly, without any resistance. I was a young man of twenty-seven or so at the time, and I can remember her eyes brimming with forgiveness and compassion for us as she died."

The man stopped for several moments. Calum finally prodded him on. "And so?"

"I was plagued with strange visions after her death. Distraught because even my father couldn't work an incantation against them, I went to a monastery for help. A last resort, believe me," added Heddwyn, smiling at Calum. "I lived among the brothers for a time, and they prayed over me, and now I know, for me. The visions faded, and how can I explain it? I felt my heart awaken as if it had never beaten before. I suddenly knew that Jesus was the Son of God, that the gods of my fathers were only stone and wood. I knew 'twas

Jesus who had given me the visions and He who had taken them away. I repented and fled to Him for mercy. And He gave it to me richly."

"And you returned here?" Calum asked, hardly believing what he heard.

"Aye," answered his host, dipping his bread into the communal bowl of stew again.

"And God gave the people ears to hear," piped up one of the little children. "That's what you always say, Papa."

Heddwyn reached over to tousle the lad's hair. "Aye, I do." He turned to Calum, narrowing his eyes in thought. "Calum…Calum…that name sounds familiar to my ears."

"Aye, it does," Heddwyn's wife agreed, sipping her ale.

Calum swallowed. "I'm sure 'tis familiar to you, Heddwyn. I…grew up in this village."

"You don't say!"

"Aye." Calum met the man's eyes as guilty tears rose into his own. "I fled on the day you made that sacrifice. I am Cairine's brother."

Silence. Calum was sure he could hear the mice making nests in the meadows outside.

Then rejoicing. Heddwyn gathered him into a bear hug, knocking over his stool as he did so. The children joined in, piling around Calum, kissing his shoulders, face, head, hands, anywhere they could reach. Finally, they drew away from stunned Calum.

"What…Why…" he stammered.

"You are the lost talent," explained Heddwyn's wife, a smile illuminating her countenance. "You are Jacob come back to your inheritance. Do you know how long we have prayed for you?"

"But…I aided in her death."

"How?" questioned Heddwyn.

"I didn't stop them from killing her. I didn't even protest. I am guilty of that. I've carried the guilt of it with me always." Calum stopped, sure that they would understand now that he was a curse, not the blessing they thought him to be.

Heddwyn gave him a quiet smile. "Well, lad, you know what the Lord says to that, aye?"

Calum gave him a questioning look. "What?" he gulped.

"'Surely he has borne our griefs and carried our sorrows.'" The man of God laid his veined hand on Calum's. "You know, whatever burdens we bear, Jesus would bear them for us. He already has, to Calvary."

Have I carried this too far, too long? Have I not given up this burden that Christ would bear for me? The tears brimmed in Calum's heart before they ran over the rims of his eyes.

"May I pray for you, laddie?" Heddwyn asked, his voice quiet as a mother bird's towards her downy chicks.

Calum barely could gasp it out. "Aye," he muttered, his head bowing to his knees. "Aye."

Heddwyn laid a hand gently on Calum's shoulder. Calum felt the man's children cluster around his knees, looking for a way to love and serve Him who upheld them all by His grace. The stew sat forgotten, the bread uneaten.

And in that soft evening twilight, in a humble cottage, Calum felt the fetters begin to crumble away from his soul.

CHAPTER THIRTY

Camelot

The pain flooded through her too heavily for her to care whether anyone saw her sobs. Tarian fled through the torch-lit corridors, almost colliding with a guard at this corner, running into a group of court boys at another. Her gown hung loose; she had not bothered with the sash when Nia came back to her chamber. She kept tripping over the hem, sometimes falling to her knees, rising again, her hands scraped.

You knew he was unfaithful.

Her tears poured out of her eyes swiftly as she remembered the wanton clinging to her husband. *Was I not enough? And what about this child within me?*

Finally, her feet could carry her no farther. An open doorway stood before her, dimly lit within. The king's chapel. No one would disturb her open-sored misery here. She stumbled inside the small room, falling prostrate before the stone altar. There she lay, weeping until the tears would no longer come.

My God, my God, why have you forsaken me?

As she lay there, quiet at last, she knew Jesus was there with her. Yet, she knew also that He would not take away the pain that caused her heart to throb. *Man of sorrows... Is this what You mean when You say that the cost is high?*

Fresh sobs shook her body. She heard footsteps behind her but didn't turn and rise to see who had entered the chapel. She suppressed her crying as much as she could, hoping that whoever 'twas wouldn't come to the front of the room.

But the person did. What was more, when he saw her lying there abased, he knelt beside her, his hood falling away from his face. Through blurry eyes, she recognized Deoradhan once again.

"My lady, are you…well, 'tis obvious you're not alright, but are you unhurt in body?" His hand went to her shoulder. In the torchlight, she saw the compassion surfacing in his eyes.

Tarian struggled to sit up. "Aye," she whispered. "In body, I'm fine."

Kneeling there, surrounded by the few polished benches, Deoradhan studied her. Under his kind gaze, she felt tears brimming at her eyes again.

Deoradhan gathered her in a gentle embrace. "'Tis alright, my lady," he murmured. His touch held no sensual connotations, and Tarian wept freely against the front of his cloak. *Why couldn't Drustan have been like this man, who is also not a believer? How will I raise my child under that pagan roof?*

She didn't know how long Deoradhan comforted her, but they still sat in the dimness when another entered the small chapel, his boots scuffling on the stone.

"What's this, Tarian?"

At the sound of her husband's voice, Tarian felt Deoradhan freeze. His hands dropped from her shoulders, and he pulled up his heavy hood. With a bound, he departed through another door near the altar. Tarian turned to face her husband alone.

Drustan stood there, sarcasm plating his smile. "Who was that, Tarian?"

Promise me that you'll tell no one I'm here. Tarian hesitated. Then she spat out, "How dare you ask me that after what I witnessed in your chambers this afternoon?"

Drustan approached her. "How dare I? How dare I? What I just saw, wife, could be construed as adultery, if I chose." He took her chin in his hand, forcing her to look him in the eyes. "Now, tell me who your secret comforter is."

She wrenched her face away from him. "Nay, I'll not. He's a friend, that is all."

Drustan raised his eyebrows. "Tell me your friend's name."

"Nay. I...I cannot."

His hand struck her cheek so hard she thought her teeth might come loose. Stumbling back, Tarian fell against one of the benches. *Lord God, keep my child safe!* "Now tell me his name, or I'll name him your lover," Drustan repeated calmly.

"My...?" She shook her head, her nose and eyes running. "Nay, you know you speak lies."

Drustan nodded slowly. "Nay. Well, Tarian," he spoke, gripping her forearm, "We must see what the king thinks on this matter." He strode toward the door, pulling her along with him.

Tarian couldn't believe this was happening. Wordless, she stumbled along behind her determined husband.

~ ~ ~

In the twilight, Deoradhan mounted his gray horse, Alasdair. *By the good will of the gods, Drustan did not see me. He will help Tarian.*

There had been too many close encounters on this trip for Deoradhan's liking. Besides, he had heard much to his advantage while at Camelot, much that told him he might not need to kill Arthur by his own hand. Many whispered of treachery in dark corners, murmured discontent at the king's table, and wore weapons belted beneath their tunics.

Just yesterday, he had overheard a gristled advisor to the king ask a young guard if he wished to come to a special meeting in the night. When the young guard had refused, the advisor warned him to keep his mouth shut if he knew what was good for him and his. Deoradhan saw the guard's face blanche, then set in determined silence.

Arthur will not live out the year. In a way, Deoradhan was relieved that this was happening. *I could not have killed Arthur by my own hand. He is not Weylin.*

The critical nobles, including Weylin, would get rid of Arthur in their own way. And then there would be retribution from the majority. In the resulting upheaval, Deoradhan would have both his revenge upon Weylin and his reward as a loyal subject.

Now to Oxfield, to retrieve Aine for a spring marriage, as he had sent word at the beginning of winter. *Aine, my delight.* She seemed all around him in this quiet dusk, her image ever-present in his mind. Hair black as the night sky, eyes as dark as an evening pool, skin white as the still-remaining clumps of snow. A flowering spring tree, promising to bear delectable fruits for him, only for him. Nature's goddess incarnate, with no tricks to play upon him.

She is waiting for me, he thought, his heart beating along with his horse's hooves.

CHAPTER THIRTY-ONE

Oxfield

Bethan knelt beside the stream within the fortress' walls, enjoying the warm morning sun. The water had thawed now 'twas April, and she didn't fear for Enid's safety. The young girl's laughter mingled with that of another little servant. Looking up, Bethan saw the two of them playing with their rag dolls on the opposite bank. She smiled. How sweet and carefree they were. How long ago her own childhood seemed, though she had turned only sixteen this winter.

"Bethan."

She startled at the fluty voice. *Garan.* She turned, rising to her feet. "You've come," she greeted him with a smile, hoping he would see and return her delight.

"Didn't I say that I would?" he frowned slightly.

He has grown taller since I last saw him, if twenty-two-year-old men can grow taller. Bethan was at a loss. "Aye, you did, but..." she trailed off under his penetrating gaze. "I'm very glad to see you," she finished. Perhaps now he would smile at her, bathing her in his approval.

Garan nodded and remained silent.

"It's my morning off," added Bethan. "Let me call Enid. She'll want to greet you."

Before she could call, he stopped her with a hand to her shoulder. "Nay, I'll speak to her later. Let me tell you my plans. We'll sit." He waited for her to sit and then perched by her side, his sandaled feet stretched out awkwardly, as if he were more used to manmade chairs.

"Now, I wish to leave tomorrow," he stated.

"Tomorrow?"

"Aye, tomorrow afternoon. I've come with a small party of like-minded men and women. We'll be traveling toward the northern border. We, however, will go across alone after we have been married. The rest of the party will spread out along the southern part of the Lothian border. 'Tis an area already evangelized sparsely. I wish to go where none have gone before. Are you prepared to do this with me, Bethan?" His eyes bored into her. She felt as if he could divide her soul and spirit with that gaze.

"Aye," she managed after a few moments. "You ken I gave you my promise."

He stared at her. "Good," he answered, a slight smile emerging at last. "I shall need a virtuous helpmate."

Will he come to love me? The thought came into Bethan's mind, but she dismissed it quickly. *Isn't it better to be valued than loved?*

Camelot

"My lady, the queen wishes to speak with you." Nia stood waiting for Tarian's approval.

Tarian raised blank eyes to Nia's face. "Show my lady in, Nia."

Nia nodded. "Aye, my lady." The maidservant opened the door and admitted the king's wife.

On shaky legs, Tarian stood as the high noblewoman entered. "My lady," she murmured, lowering her eyes.

Gwynhwyfar rushed forward and took Tarian's hands in hers. "Oh, Tarian, Tarian. What a terrible thing to happen!" She drew Tarian toward the chairs near the hearth. "And to happen to you, the most virtuous of us all! I envied you your goodness to such a wicked man, when I am so wicked to such a good man as I have."

Tarian merely nodded and looked toward the fire. "And do you know what the king has decreed, my lady?" she asked, hardly caring.

Gwynhwyfar bit her lip. "I came to bring you news before the message came, Tarian. I thought it would be better from a friend. And I do count myself that to you still, Tarian. A friend." She looked earnestly into Tarian's eyes.

"I know you do, my lady," Tarian replied. "So what does the king say?"

"He says," Gwynhwyfar began, "that there is no evidence against you that can convict you of...adultery."

Tarian let out a sigh of relief. *Not the death sentence, then.*

"But," the queen went on, her green eyes troubled, "your husband has declared that he has found you unclean in his eyes. And, as you probably know, Tarian, that is enough cause to force the king to grant a divorce."

"A divorce?" The word was terrible to her.

Gwynhwyfar nodded. "Aye. 'Twill be as if your marriage had not occurred."

"But I have done nothing wrong, my lady! He, he has been unfaithful to me!"

"I know. But the law and custom favor Drustan. Arthur has tried to be as lenient as possible. You take back with you your dowry."

Tarian shook her head. "My dowry will return to the king of Cantia." She raised tear-filled eyes to the queen. "And I? Where will I go?"

The queen was silent. Tarian knew where she must go. Back home, back to her uncle, back to her mother and father, to Cantia. The shunned former wife of a respectable lord, who had accused her of adultery.

No one will take me for a wife. All will view my child as the result of fornication. I will be a shame to my father and mother. My uncle will despise me. The king of Cantia may exile me, if he is very angry. Why, why did this have to happen, O Lord? I tried to obey You. And now what future will I have?

And commonsense answered her: *No future at all.*

CHAPTER THIRTY-TWO

Summer Country

Calum breathed deeply. His legs took long strides across the newly-greening meadow. *I feel like I'm living for the first spring in my life. Lord my God, thank You.* In his scrip, he felt his small volume of Scripture bounce against his leg.

But I have trusted in your steadfast love; my heart shall rejoice in your salvation. I will sing to the LORD, because he has dealt bountifully with me.

Ah, here was the place. Just a stade or two away from his borrowed cottage. He knelt down, setting to work immediately. Smiling, Calum remembered his brother Kieve's words yesterday regarding this house and tract:

"'Tis yours as long as you wish, brother." The younger man paused. *"Indeed, the whole of our family's land is yours by birthright."*

Calum had shook his head. *"I've no wish to take it, Kieve. It's yours and your family's. I have received more in this visit than I ever thought I would. But I will take up your offer to let me stay in that cottage."*

"Good. For long, I hope?"

"I don't know. I will help you with the sheep, if you'll let me. And I have a little money from my previous work. I need time apart."

Calum gave a heavy last blow to the wood so that it would stand firmly. He raised his eyes up to the oak tree, still wreathed with mistletoe. Cairine had died in this place. And another man, Heddwyn had received the first pangs of life here.

Her death birthed his life. Calum stood, a joy so deep running through his soul that he could not smile. *'Tis all a mercy. 'Twas always so, but I didn't see it.* The tears ran down his cheeks as he knelt on the grass, thanksgiving bubbling through his heart. *Thank you, Lord Jesus.*

After a few moments, he looked up at the waist-high cross he had just planted in the earth. Deeply carven into the wood, its letters read in Latin, "Absorta est mors in victoria."

Death is swallowed up in victory.

Oxfield

It would be as if they'd never parted. He was sure of it. Being with Aine would help him wait out the short time before he could claim Dunpeledyr as his own. Riding toward the closed gates, their iron shining in the noon light, Deoradhan inwardly raced through them, into the courtyard, to the kitchen where Aine would stand. Her arms would open, ready to receive him.

We will marry immediately, he decided. Smiling, he remembered how he had pressed Aine to accept his ever-more-warm embraces last autumn just before he'd left. At last, she'd pulled away from him. He'd questioned her, but she'd said that she wished to wait to be fully his until they married.

"Why?" he had asked. "*The ancient customs do not dictate that. 'Tis only the Christian way.*"

"*Aye,*" she'd replied in her only moment of rebellion against him, "*but I wish to wait. For my mother's sake, Deoradhan. Please.*"

And he'd agreed, though he desired her so. And had been faithful to her since. *Now at last I shall drink my wine with my milk, as Solomon says.*

He drew his gelding up before the gate. "Deoradhan, long-absent, requests entrance," he called out.

The gates swung wide. He barely greeted his old acquaintances, seeing none of their faces. Handing the reins over to a stableboy,

Deoradhan found himself running toward the kitchen door. He thrust it open and came face-to-face with Deirdre.

"Deirdre," he greeted, breathing to calm himself. "Where's Meghyn?"

Deirdre's mouth fell open, and Deoradhan felt dread begin to steal away a little of his excitement. "What is it, Deirdre?" he said, looking her straight in the eyes.

She swallowed. "Come in, Deoradhan. And welcome back. Aine will be glad to see you, I know."

Deoradhan stepped into the entryway. A couple stepped in behind him, and he turned to see who 'twas. Oh, that country girl of whom Calum was so fond. And a tall, pale man with her. What was her name? Oh, aye. "Bethan, hello," he said.

The brown-haired girl smiled. "Hello, Deoradhan. Welcome." She glanced at her companion, and they moved ahead of Deirdre and Deoradhan into the main room.

He followed Deirdre over to the hearth, noting that Meghyn was nowhere to be found. "Have a seat, Deoradhan," Deirdre invited, her long fingers motioning to a chair.

"Tell me at once, Deirdre," Deoradhan ordered, sitting on the edge of his chair.

The young woman sighed. "She's dead, Deoradhan. She died months ago. I thought you might already know."

A blow, indeed. Meghyn was no more than forty-five. And so dear to him. *Dear as a mother to me.* Tears came to his eyes, and he found he couldn't speak.

"She wanted me to tell you, Deoradhan, that she loved you no matter what has happened. And that she will meet you in the kingdom that never ends." Deirdre raised her eyes to meet Deoradhan's. "She loved you dearly, you know."

"I know." *Everyone I have loved has been taken from me. Except for one.* "Where is Aine?" he asked, rising to his feet and blinking away his tears with a shaky breath.

"She is resting in the next chamber."

"Resting?" Deoradhan had never known the lively girl to nap. "Is she ill?"

Deirdre gave him a quizzical look. "Women do rest when they are like this, Deoradhan." She rose. "I will go get her."

Aine must be ill. Deoradhan stopped Deirdre with a hand to her arm. "Nay. I will go." Heart pounding, he stepped toward the archway separating the rooms.

He did not need to enter. Apparently, the one for whom he longed had already risen from her sleep. She came to the doorway as he approached. He had never felt such shock as he did in that moment.

The girl who stood before him was not the Aine he remembered, the one whom he had dearly held in his waking dreams. *Who is this?* His mind blanked, and he thought he would be sick.

She stood there, stringy hair hanging around her thin white face, the only familiar part being her huge dark eyes, begging him, pleading with him.

Pleading with him to do what? Accept... that? That swollen belly that could give testimony to only one thing?

Treachery.

Deoradhan stumbled back, head spinning

Aine—for he must call her something—heaved her way toward him, hands outstretched. He drew back as if from an asp. "Don't touch me," he gasped, feeling as if her leprosy would spread to him. "Get away from me."

Aine's dry lips fell open. "Please, Deoradhan. Please, let me explain."

He blinked. "Explain?" he said, staring at her, his eyes avoiding that burden at her waist.

She looked around, obviously uncomfortable that others were in the room. "I...I didn't mean for this to happen."

He snorted. He couldn't help it.

Tears rose in Aine's eyes. "Please, Deoradhan, forgive me. 'Twas sin, but—"

"But what?"

Silence. He waited, bitterness quickly turning any love he had for her into hatred. "Cannot you forgive me, Deoradhan? 'Twas not all my fault. If you knew…"

"I don't care how it happened," he finally burst out. "It happened."

He saw that his words broke her and was glad, feeling the hatred saturate his spirit. "Can you change it, Aine?" he demanded. "Well, can you?"

She shook her head.

"'Tis over, Aine," the words poured out of his mouth like poison. "I never loved you. I only thought I did. I will not be a cuckold nor a husband to a woman who thinks so little of her promises."

Aine stared at him, then glanced at those around them. A sob burst up from her, as Deoradhan had never heard from her before. She rushed past him, past them all, out into the courtyard.

Woodenly, he moved to sit back down before the hearth again.

"Deoradhan," Deirdre spoke after a long time of silence. "We thought 'twas your child she carried."

He shook his head. *I have nothing left. Nothing but sorrow, pain, and my own hatred.*

Camelot

"'Tis the last of it, my lady."

Nia's voice cut through Tarian's thoughts. "Thank you, Nia." *All is ready to go with me. If I had given into Drustan's wishes, life would have been simpler. I would be packing to go home to Oxfield, not to Cantia.* She forced a smile. "I appreciate all that you've done to help me."

The servant woman shook her head. "Nay, my lady, 'tis the least I can do." Impetuously, it seemed, she picked up Tarian's hand and kissed it. "May the Lord bless you for keeping His ways, my lady. May His goodness and mercy follow you all the days of your life."

Tarian stared at her. "Thank you, Nia," she stammered, pulling

the maid toward her in a fierce embrace.
It was the will of the Lord to crush me...

CHAPTER THIRTY-THREE

Aine fled through the forest, tripping over roots, falling on her face in the mud. Finally, she stumbled against a huge oak, its trunk rippling brown in the slanted afternoon sunlight. Her mind aware only of pain, she huddled against the tree, shaking with tears.

I never loved you.

"What value do I have, then?" she moaned.

I never loved you.

Where could she go? Never back to Oxfield. Aine could not face her accuser again. *I would die of grief.* Deoradhan's angry face had told her that she would never receive forgiveness from him.

And if she would not receive it from him who had said he loved her so much, how would she receive it from anyone?

"Who will welcome a harlot?" she mumbled, scratching her face against the bark. At least the physical pain drew her concentration away from the emotional agony.

Though he seduced me. Forced me, really. 'Twas not all my fault. If Deoradhan knew…

No, even if he knew, he would reject her now. Yet again, after the brief respite of Deoradhan's worshipful love, Aine knew her own inadequacy.

I cannot measure up. I cannot, no matter how I try. The sobs poured out. *All I want is to be loved. But I'm not worthy to be loved.*

Groveling at the tree's roots, she remembered the words of the village priest…

And sin when it is fully grown brings forth death.

"Help me." The whisper came to her lips, directed to whom she knew not. Perhaps to the God whose voice her mother heard in the song of the robin. After a time, Aine stood upright again, wobbling under the weight of her too-heavy burden, shivering in the cold April wind. She directed her feet west. She didn't know where she was going, but she knew she could not return to the house of her judgment.

~ ~ ~

The shavings dropped one by one around Bricius' feet, curling into little heaps. The cottage trembled a bit in the blowing gusts, but here by his fire 'twas warm and cozy. He glanced up from his whittling and caught a smile from Lydia, who sat across from him, sewing patches on a pair of trousers. Their old dog lay panting at her feet.

An impatient knock interrupted the comfortable silence between them. Bricius rose, groaning a little. "I'll get it, my dear." He limped over to the door.

He knew his surprise must have shown when he opened it. "Deoradhan, isn't it?"

The young man smiled politely, but Bricius sensed the worry underpinning his expression. "Aye, you remember me."

"Please, come in." Bricius held the door open wide. Deoradhan hesitated and then entered, knocking the mud from his boots on the doorframe.

"I don't wish to intrude," he said. "I'm looking for Calum. No one seems to know where he went. I didn't know if you…"

Tenderness flooded into Bricius' heart at hearing Calum's name. "Aye, he's left Oxfield, lad."

"Do you know where he's gone?"

Bricius frowned. "Nay. He had some things to sort out, to pray over. 'Tis all I know. But God knows where he is. And that's enough for me."

Deoradhan snorted. It took Bricius by surprise. "I'm sorry," the young man said when he saw the startled look on Bricius' face. "It's just that everything seems to go back to this unrelenting, unfathomable God. No matter how I try to escape, He always comes back to dog my steps." He turned away, facing the fire.

Bricius sat down to ease his bones. *Lord God, give me the words to say to this young man, so bewildered, so angry.* He glanced over at Lydia, who continued sewing, her eyes lowered. *Praying.* Finally, he said, "I don't know what's at the root of your troubles, lad. I can only say that whatever 'tis, God will help you, if you ask Him."

"I don't want to ask Him. I don't need His help!" the visitor burst out, turning wild eyes to Bricius. "All I want is what is mine by right of birth."

"By right of birth?" At Deoradhan's nod, Bricius raised his eyebrows. "You ken what is yours by right of birth, lad? Death, that's all. Judgment. A pretty inheritance, aye? Yours by right of birth as Adam's son."

"That's not what I mean." Deoradhan turned his eyes back to the fire. "If I had what was stolen from me, I could have peace, at least, instead of this unending knowledge that someone else has what is mine."

Bricius rose to his feet and placed a hand on the younger man's shoulder. "You want peace, lad, but you'll never get it by holding onto things, whether it be the past or the future. We must lay all that down at Jesus' feet and follow Him if we would have peace."

"I don't understand that."

"I'm sure you don't, because it goes beyond understanding." Bricius gazed into Deoradhan's face. "I see in you the marks of the Creator, lad. But if you go on rejecting Him, I fear what will become of you."

Bricius was sure that the young man's eyes glinted with troubled tears. Yet after a moment, Deoradhan pulled away from Bricius' gentle touch. "I must go," he stated.

"Alright." Bricius paused with a sudden thought. "If you still seek Calum, you may find him in Summer Country."

"Summer Country?"

"Aye, he grew up there."

~ ~ ~

From her seat behind Enid, Bethan surveyed the small group travelling with them. Five men, mostly in their thirties and forties, and a few older women. She and Enid were the youngest members of the band, and what Garan lacked in years, he made up for in fervor. They had been traveling for a few days now together, but Bethan still felt like an outsider. Her father had not spoken of unbelievers as these people did, as if they were some kind of mysterious wild animal that needed to be tricked into a trap.

Yet they are sincere, she admitted. *And kind, especially among themselves.* Bethan glanced toward Garan riding to her right, and he met her eyes with a smile. *Everything he does is done purposely,* she realized. *Even that smile. I believe he thought it through before he allowed me to have it. But he is a good man, and I am blessed to have him.*

Her thoughts turned to Deoradhan and Aine. Aloud, she mused, "Deoradhan could have been gentler with poor Aine."

Garan's head swiveled toward her. "What do you mean? He was right."

His voice allowed for no question on the matter. But Bethan felt she could not agree, at least not completely. "But, Garan," she began softly, not wishing to seem contrary, "Deoradhan didn't know the whole of the story. To be honest, none of us did. We only assumed."

Garan frowned, as if she were a disagreeable little girl. "Bethan, the facts are these: an unwed lass is with child. Her promised husband doesn't acknowledge the child. Therefore, she has been unfaithful to him."

"But, Garan, others have not been unfaithful but have gotten in the same way as Aine. The Virgin herself—"

"As far as I am aware, there is only one virgin birth promised to the human race, Bethan. Or do you contradict the Scriptures now?"

Bethan blushed. "Nay. I didn't mean that Aine…I meant only that we don't know all the circumstances, Garan. She may have been forced."

His face softened the tiniest bit. "Perhaps. If so, I pity the girl. But the child is still the child of sin."

Bethan could not believe he had said that. "What did you say?"

"The child is one of sin. Deoradhan is right to reject it."

Bethan felt such indignation that it overcame her awe of Garan. "But the child did not sin, Garan. Surely, the Lord has compassion—"

"'Behold, I was brought forth in iniquity, and in sin did my mother conceive me.'" He glanced over at her. "I think that should answer your questions, Bethan. God, not man, always has the final word."

But you are not God, her heart rebelled as she looked at him in silence.

CHAPTER THIRTY-FOUR

Summer Country

In the nearby fields, Calum could hear the sheep bleating. 'Twas lambing season, and his brother owned dozens of sheep, many of them about to lamb. Their soft murmuring usually soothed him to sleep, but tonight he found that rest eluded him.

I'll walk the fields awhile. He sat up, throwing back the light wool blanket. How different this life was from all those years as a guard! How restful this country existence was. Each day, his soul healed from within, the sores closing up as with ointment.

His feet took him outside, where the stars sprinkled the sky like jewels across a peerless dark queen's brow. *How beautiful. Lord, You have set them in place.* A light wind rustled the grass, silvery with moonlight. Calum strode toward the oak on the hill, outlined black against the late night sky. *Someday, all the stars will sing together again, as they did at Creation.*

He walked up the incline slowly with the step of one who does not hurry anymore. He was just a little way from the wooden cross and decided to brush his fingers and eyes over the carven words once more. Moving toward it, he saw some kind of large object at the cross' foot.

A stray sheep. He approached it quietly, not wanting to startle it into fleeing. A few feet away, however, Calum realized with surprise that a small woman, not a sheep, lay facedown and curled up on the ground. Kneeling in the sparse grass, he reached out and touched her shoulder. 'Twas warm, so she still lived. But she didn't respond to his hand.

"Hello," he spoke aloud. "Lass." The person didn't turn over or show any sign of having heard him.

Calum gently rolled her over. *What in the world? She's heavy with child,* Calum thought with alarm. He brushed back the snarled mass of dark hair from her face and was so startled that he fell back on his heels.

Aine.

So many thoughts rushed into his mind. Where was Deoradhan? How did Aine come to be in Summer Country? He shook her shoulder again, but she still wouldn't wake. With the tenderness of a herd with a broken-legged lamb, Calum took her crumpled body into his arms and rose. *O Lord, show me what to do. Show me how I may care for her.*

~ ~ ~

He laid her on his bed. Aine's body shook with cold, and Calum covered her with as many blankets as he could find in the little shepherd's cottage. Still she trembled convulsively. Calum threw his eyes around for something to add to her warmth.

The heavy fur rug. He snatched it up and placed it on top of all the other layers. Turning to the hearth, he added more fuel to the dying fire and water to the pot hanging above it.

Lord, what has happened here? How did this come to be? he questioned, sitting by the young woman's side as he waited for the water to boil. Looking at her, Calum saw that her lips scaled with dryness. He jumped up from his stool and fetched a cup of water. Raising her up a little, he put the rim to her lips. He breathed when she swallowed. And swallowed again. Without opening her eyes, she reached out her small, soiled hands limply toward the cup. After a few gulps, she fell back, unresponsive again.

Should I go for someone? But for whom would I go? Not Kieve or his wife, two miles away, surely asleep at this hour. Not to the village, nearly four miles distant. And Calum had nursed many a sick man after battles. He could nurse a woman just as well for tonight.

His gaze rested on the girl's scratched, hollow face and then her swollen stomach. *Her soul needs healing as much as her body, I would guess. O Lord, help me.*

CHAPTER THIRTY-FIVE

Dunpeledyr

"Welcome. 'Tis not often that we receive messengers from our Lord Arthur," greeted Lady Seonaid, trying to appear calm. Two stern men backed by several armed guards had arrived without warning, bearing the Pendragon's banner. She had received them, as Weylin had taken a horse up to an estate farther north.

"My lady, we come with ill news for you."

"Whatever word the king sends, I am ready to hear."

"I'm glad of it, my lady. We've come to take your husband into custody."

'Twas utterly unexpected. "What do you mean?" she questioned, sure that she had misunderstood these solemn strangers.

"Just that, my lady. Your husband has been accused of treason."

Seonaid drew in her breath. "By whom? Who has accused him?"

"The king, my lady."

Summer Country

Deoradhan pushed his mount to move faster. The road over the hills flew under them, but he still could not shake the feeling that something—Someone—tracked his soul. He felt a Presence like some great red sun, born from the foundations of the world. 'Twas burning, beating, unrelenting in its effort to win him over, to force his acknowledgement.

He resisted, cowardly, willfully. Tears sometimes rose to his eyes, but he blinked them away. He drove his horse faster, determined to get away. *I own myself at least, do I not?* Was he not at any rate the ruler of his own heart, though a kingdom of darkness it might prove to be?

Summer Country

Aine woke fully on the second day. When her eyelids trembled open, Calum sat very still, anxious that she stay quiet. She stared up at the ceiling for long moments, blinking slowly as if it caused her pain, before turning her head to look at him.

She was surprised 'twas he. He could tell from the way her dark eyes opened wide in her thin face. *Like living tombs with the dead staring out.*

"Hush, don't speak, lass," he murmured, drawing the blankets up to her chin. She shivered down into the mattress. "Do you want some milk?" he asked, and when she nodded, he fetched it.

The girl swallowed eagerly but stopped when she met his gaze. At that, tears came into Aine's eyes. She began to weep as one who had no comforter.

"Lass, lass, 'tis alright." Calum clasped her hands in his, eyes trained on her face. She looked lighter than any woman should, except for that heavy weight at her middle. He felt alarm race through his heart. "Don't fret now. You're safe here with me. Do you remember me?" He felt relief at the bare nod. "Good. I'm glad that the Lord has brought you here."

At that, Aine began shaking with sobs. "How…can you…say that?" she gasped.

He frowned. "Say what, lass? 'Tis true. And when you feel better, I can send word to Deoradhan or—"

She stopped him with a violent shake of her head. "Deoradhan doesn't want me anymore. I have no one."

Deoradhan had done strange things in the past, but he was generally a faithful man, true to his promises. "I know he is away right now, but surely when his child is born—"

"'Tis not his child!" she interjected. "'Tis not Deoradhan's. This child will have no father, as his mother will have no husband." Her weeping increased. "I am a sinner, you see, Calum. Unloved. And now do you want to take care of me? A woman without a husband and her child of sin in your house?" she cried out, crumpling over his hands.

Calum was silent for moment, stroking her dirty hair with his callused hand. Finally, he spoke, "'Father of the fatherless and protector of widows is God in his holy habitation.'"

His words seemed to calm her a little. "And He will cover you with His feathers, Aine, if you will take refuge in Him," Calum added softly, feeling her heart beating rapidly against him.

Aine sighed. "I wish God really was like that." She looked up into his eyes. "I wish He was like you, Calum."

Humbled, Calum replied slowly, "It took me a long time to learn it, Aine, but God is merciful. He longs to take us under His wings, if only we will let Him." He smiled down into her hollow eyes. "He is far better than we could imagine Him to be. More good, more holy, more loving, more pure. So pure that He can purify the filthiest sinner. So holy than He stops at nothing to make us like Him. So loving that He encloses all Creation in His Father-heart. So good, He never harms without need."

She lay against his arm, quietly crying. "But not for me now," she whispered. "My poor mother…I have shamed her so with all I've done. And I don't mean only this," she said, indicating her belly. 'Tis the least of my sins. How selfish and foolish I've been, all my life. I see it now that I'm going to die."

"Hush, you'll not die," answered Calum, pressing a kiss on her hair. He felt the Spirit urge him to speak. "But if you do die, Aine, and we all do at some point, you can go into the loving arms of Jesus. Death can be another birth into life."

"Can it? Will He have mercy for such a one as me?" She smiled weakly. "I thought 'twas reserved for such as Bethan and Deirdre.

They are so sweet and deserving and I—"

"He who has been forgiven much, loves much." Calum laid her back so that she could rest. "Fly to Jesus, Aine," he murmured, brushing her hair back from her moist forehead.

The young woman closed her eyes. A few moments later, she opened them again, and Calum saw peace dwelling there at last. "He has," she whispered. "He has mercy."

Dunpeledyr

"Seonaid, I must tell you something."

Seonaid looked up from her weaving. For the past few days, she had done whatever she could to keep her hands occupied and her mind and heart praying. She smiled to welcome Fiona.

Weylin's daughter crossed the threshold and sat beside her stepmother. Seonaid could see something bothered the girl. "What is it, Fiona?" she asked, placing her hand on the young woman's.

Fiona was silent for moment, obviously gathering her thoughts. "Seonaid, do you know what happened to your son?"

An old pang seized Seonaid, but she smiled anyway. "You mean my firstborn, aye?"

"Aye. The one called Padruig."

Seonaid shook her head. "Nay, I do not. Maybe he died all those years past, when I sent him away from the fortress with one of our warriors. Maybe he survives still but doesn't know who he truly is." She paused and patted Fiona's hand. "If that is how God wants it, I am content. Content but broken-hearted. My prayer, Fiona, is that my son would come to know his Savior. Then we would be assured of an eternal meeting."

Fiona nodded, her gray eyes thoughtful. "Seonaid, I know who your son is."

The weaving stood still. "What do you mean, dear?"

Her stepdaughter licked her lips. "The horsemaster, Deoradhan. He is your son. He is Padruig."

Seonaid gripped the arms of her chair, white-knuckled. "How

do you know this?"

"I saw him first at Camelot, where I mistook him for Solas. Then, I pieced it together from some hints he dropped, though I'm sure he didn't mean me to find out." Fiona sighed. "Finally, when I confronted him months ago, he told me the truth."

Seonaid couldn't sit any longer. Rising from her chair, she paced the room. Deoradhan's face appeared in her mind. "No wonder he looked so familiar to me," she muttered. "He is the image of his father and brother." She stopped and stared at Fiona. "But why do you tell me now, Fiona?"

"I thought you should know because of what…may happen to Father," the girl replied. "Your son desires more than anything to rule Dunpeledyr again. I am sure he will try to find a way if Father…" She trailed off. "I thought you should be prepared."

Lady Seonaid nodded. "I see."

CHAPTER THIRTY-SIX

Oxfield

When morning came, Aine had grown feverish but was coherent. A girl from the village arrived shortly after dawn to change Aine's bed linens and wash her. Then, after a breakfast of bread and milk, Calum sat by her bedside once more, opening the small volume of Scripture that Bricius had given him.

"What's that?" Aine asked, turning her eyes toward the book.

"The Holy Scriptures," he replied, smiling at her.

"Will you read it aloud?" she asked in her mossy voice.

"Gladly." He bent his gaze to the page. "'He will tend his flock like a shepherd; he will gather the lambs in his arms; he will carry them in his bosom, and gently lead those that are with young.'"

Aine let out a sigh, and Calum looked up to see tears in her eyes again. "God has been so good to me." She looked up at him. "I can sense His love. That's what I always wanted, you ken. To be loved, to be held important to someone." She smiled. "I have found out how low I truly am, yet God holds me dear anyway, aye?"

His heart embraced this sweet sister. "Aye, Aine."

She turned her eyes up toward the ceiling. "I know that God will be a father to my child, but I wish…I wish I could have provided one for it in a human person." She smiled at him a little sadly. "But God knows best, aye?"

There 'twas. The sheepbreeder had said that the cottage was his brother Calum's abode. Deoradhan nudged his horse down the rocky path to the broad door. At the bottom, he dismounted quickly.

I will tell Calum all about my troubles. He will understand.

Calum answered his second knock. His face showed him changed somehow, more restful, no longer tormented. He immediately gripped Deoradhan's forearm in friendship. "Are you here to see Aine?" he asked, eyes meeting Deoradhan's.

Deoradhan stumbled back. "What?" Surely he had heard wrong.

Calum furrowed his brows. "Aine is here. Isn't that why you've come?"

"Nay!" He turned and staggered away across the grass. Calum followed him.

"She is with child, Deoradhan."

Deoradhan laughed mirthlessly. "I know it. I hope she didn't tell you 'twas mine."

"Of course she didn't."

They walked side-by-side silently. Calum was first to speak again. "Do you still plan to take Aine as your own?"

"What, are you mad?" Deoradhan couldn't believe his friend would suggest this. "After what she's done?"

"She's repented, man, and found forgiveness from God. If you love her-"

Deoradhan shook his head, knowing the ploy at work here. "Is that it, Calum? The prostitute plays her bit, repents of her folly, and the hero puts up with the fruit of her misdeeds?"

Calum's fierce grasp on his elbow forced him to halt. "She is more worthy of you than you are of her, Deoradhan. At least she admits that she did wrong. You cannot even admit that."

Deoradhan felt the old anger rise in him. "And where have I done wrong? In what way am I so evil?"

"Every time you reject the living God as your Master, you sin against Him and the universe, against all that is right and true."

"Is that the way you see it?"

"Aye."

The two stood there silently tense for long moments, Deoradhan's mind whirling into thicker and thicker knots. At last he looked squarely into Calum's eyes. *I'll catch him in this game. I'll show his Christianity to be weaker than a child.* "If Aine is now so virtuous and good, my friend," he smirked, "you marry her. Take her as your wife and her illegitimate babe as your son or daughter."

Now let's see him squirm.

But Calum gazed back at him, nodding. "Aye," he replied. "I will." The older man turned to walk back toward the cottage. Stunned, Deoradhan's eyes followed him.

A few steps away, Calum faced Deoradhan again. "I had planned to marry her anyway, Deoradhan, but I wanted to give you the opportunity to do right by the girl."

"Do right by her? I tell you, 'tis not my child. This 'right' that you speak of does not exist. She has no right …" Deoradhan trailed off, seeing Calum shaking his head.

"The only right any of us have," he said, "is the right to forgive, Deoradhan. The right to have mercy. 'Tis time you learned that, lad."

Deoradhan watched his friend disappear into the cottage.

~ ~ ~

Aine opened her eyes to see Calum enter, his brow serious. How good he was! "What is it, Calum? Who was at the door?" she asked, raising herself on her elbows.

He smiled. "Nothing is wrong, Aine. Don't worry." He approached the bed and sat on its edge. Looking at her, he spoke, "Aine, I have something I must ask you."

He wants me to leave. She swallowed. "What is it?"

Calum took her two hands in his. "I want you to be my wife. I will take your child as my child. I will love you…"

His words faded in the sweet joy that overwhelmed her. *He will take my shame on himself. He loves me despite what I have done, who I am.* The tears prevented her from speaking. She looked up into her protector's scarred face and realized, *I love him.* Not with the romantic love that flushes youth, but with a love pure and growing. And as he met her eyes, she understood that his love for her was of a yet more profound nature, needing no return to continue giving, requiring no consummation to be satisfied in the one he loved.

Gratefully, Aine leaned toward him, and Calum kissed her with a joy that went even beyond the sensual.

CHAPTER THIRTY-SEVEN

Upper Logress

"This is the last morning our whole party will be together," announced Garan at breakfast.

Bethan nodded and continued braiding Enid's golden hair.

"The rest of the group will gradually disperse," added Garan. "'Tis time, Bethan, you know."

"Time for what?" She finished Enid's braid. Her sister ran off to pet the horses.

"Time to put Enid away somewhere safe."

"What...What do you mean?" Bethan was sure she had misheard him.

Garan smiled sympathetically but with iron. "She can't come with us to Lothian. Surely, you understand that."

"What do you mean? She's my sister and—"

"And I'm your husband." His smile revolted her. "Or will soon be. Enid must be put away in a convent. As soon as possible. There is one a few miles from the Lothian border, and-"

"Nay." Bethan heard the word come out of her mouth before she thought it over. "Never."

She had surprised him. His pale eyes stared at her unblinking. Trembling inside, she reiterated, "I will not leave my sister behind."

"You will if I say you must when I marry you."

"Then I won't marry you," Bethan gasped.

Garan smiled, shaking his head. "Come now, Bethan. You know you must. Your father is gone. You have no other option."

"I wouldn't want to be that if I were you," she thought aloud, seeing him as if for the first time. *This is who he always was. I knew it but didn't want to admit it.*

"What?" he frowned.

"My only option. Don't you want to be loved?"

Garan arched his brows. "Affection has nothing to do with it, Bethan. This is God's will."

Bethan stared at him and finally shook her head. "'Tis God's will that you have compassion and love, Garan. And I realize now that you have neither." She stood from her seat on the boulder, looking into those eyes that never warmed. "I wonder if God truly lives in you. Your Christianity has none of the Christ I know."

"I see." His face showed no melting. "So you wish to break off from our holy mission? You wish to go back on your promise?"

"Aye," she managed, realizing the whole course of her life would change. *What will I do? Where will I go, so far from West Lea? So distant from Oxfield? And with Enid, too?* She closed her eyes. If only Papa were here to advise her.

"Alright. 'Tis probably for the best." He gave a sniff. "I could not have had a wife whose heart was divided from the Lord anyway."

She stared at him. Who was this man that she would have married? She swallowed as she thought about her predicament. "Is…Is there a village nearby where I could…?"

Garan nodded brusquely. "A small town sits a few miles nearer the border, I'm told. You will likely find some kind of work there." He rose to his feet. "If you've finished breakfast, you should prepare your things. We leave shortly." He moved off toward the horses, leaving Bethan to damp the fire.

God of my father, direct my steps, she pleaded.

Summer Country

Their marriage took place very quietly, with only Kieve and his wife Eilley as witnesses. Aine lay back against her pillows as Heddwyn bound her and Calum's hands together with a cord. *They have asked us no questions. They assume that I am his wife already in fact, though not in name.*

Her gaze turned to Calum, who returned a smile to her. *'Tis like the Scripture my mother used to murmur, "Surely he has borne our griefs and carried our sorrows."* Tears rose to her eyes. Calum had insisted that the child she carried be known as his. *'Tis no lie, lass. 'Tis a mercy, that's all.* A great mercy for him to bestow, she knew, for all the time she had known him at Oxfield, no word of reproach had marred his character.

As Heddwyn pronounced his blessing, Aine felt a little ashamed that she'd not heard two words of the ceremony. She had been concentrating too hard on Calum, whose presence perfumed the air with inexplicable peace.

What have I done to deserve this? Nothing.

Camelot

Deoradhan slowed to a trot as he rode through the heavy gates. Immediately, he sensed something had occurred to stop the usual merry bustle of the capital. The guard had been doubled, and the gatekeeper had requested full identification from Deoradhan. *What has happened here in the short weeks I've been gone?* he wondered.

As he mounted the wide stone steps to the main hall, a familiar king's attendant burst from the doors. He grasped Deoradhan by the arms. "The king has been waiting for you to arrive."

Deoradhan frowned. "But I came of my own accord."

The attendant raised his brows. "The Pendragon has sent letters to Oxfield, to Lothian, even Summer Country when word reached him that you might be there. When he heard that you had been seen riding through the gates, he sent me to fetch you immediately."

"Yestin, what has happened here?"

The attendant glanced around him nervously. "Treason. A trial is in progress already."

"Who has been accused?"

"The guard Rhun and Lord Ilar, both. But the one masterminding the plot from afar was found to be none other than Lord Weylin." Yestin cleared his throat. "Since you have been employed by Weylin at Dunpeledyr these past months…"

"Am I suspected?" Deoradhan felt his heart thud against his chest in fear even as his mind raced regarding the consequences of this charge for Weylin.

Yestin shook his head. "Nay, there is no evidence to convict you as part of the plot to kill the king."

"To kill the king? Did they actually attempt anything?" Deoradhan inquired, his voice low so that any passerby would be unable to hear their conversation.

"Aye, two weeks past the king rode out, and Rhun was with him, as well as some of the nobles at court. Sometime in the morning, Rhun shot an arrow—he said at first 'twas at an animal, but 'twas aimed toward the king."

"Was the king hurt?" asked Deoradhan, surprised at his own anxiety.

"Nay," answered Yestin, leading the way through the thick double doors. The four guards stood at sharp attention. "But one of the nobles attending him took the arrow instead. Riding too close to the king, he was. Lord Drustan of Oxfield."

"Lord Drustan…" 'Twas such an odd turn of events. "How did the plot come out?" Deoradhan asked, his words echoing a little in the torch-lit corridor.

"Under questioning, Rhun admitted others had appointed him. He named Weylin as the chief conspirator." Yestin stopped before the king's chamber door and knocked. "My lord king, Deoradhan has come."

CHAPTER THIRTY-EIGHT

Southern Lothian

"Come, Enid. There will be work for us here." Bethan took her sister's dirty hand and set their steps toward the large cluster of cottages ahead. Nearly a fortnight had passed since she and Enid had parted ways with Garan. Bethan had chosen their road with little thought toward direction. *We need work and a place to stay, no matter where 'tis,* she reminded herself whenever her thoughts turned toward the south.

And no work could be found. Thus far, their path had wound through eight hamlets and small towns, filled with mostly Britonic inhabitants, poor and roughly clad. Many nights, someone took pity on the two travelers and offered them a meal and shelter in their cowshed in exchange for a little washing, cooking, or sewing. But Bethan knew that she must find a permanent position if they were to survive. As she and Enid walked, her mind returned to the words Papa had spoken some dark nights:

> *Because you have made the LORD your dwelling place,*
> *The Most High, who is my refuge –*
> *No evil shall be allowed to befall you,*
> *No plague come near your tent.*
> *For he will command his angels concerning you*
> *To guard you in all your ways.*

Did I ever make You my dwelling place, truly, Lord? Or did I just walk in the footprints of my papa? The thought unsettled her. *If I have taken Your grace for granted, Lord, may it not be so now. May it not be only because now I realize how much I need You.*

As they moved into the main, muddy street of the village, Bethan and Enid drew stares from the natives. Her arm around her sister, Bethan hurried toward the door of the first neatly-kept cottage. *I've done this a hundred times already, and each time the answer has been nay.* She sighed and raised a fist to knock. *Let it be an "aye" this time, please, Lord.*

Before she could rap on the door, they heard someone say from behind them, "May I help you?"

Bethan and Enid turned. A dark-haired woman stood in the path, a basket full of herbs on her arm. She smiled and came toward them. "I live here. Did you want something?"

"My sister and I are looking for work, ma'am. Do you know of anything around here?" Bethan held her breath.

"Nay, not in this village, I would say," answered the woman. Bethan let out a sigh. "But," the woman continued, "if you're seriously in need of work, Dunpeledyr's not twelve miles from here. They've always work available, especially with summer coming. Lots of young people from this village find positions there."

"Thank you, ma'am! And what road would we take there?"

The woman pointed northwest. "There's a Roman-built road—or what's left of it—that will lead you nearly to the gate. But 'tis too late in the day to go now. Stay for the night and start your journey in the morning. 'Tis only me and my dogs here. We could do with a bit of company."

The weight of worry slid off Bethan's shoulders. "If you're sure it wouldn't impose on you…"

The woman shook her head. "Nay, of course not. I wouldn't have offered it if I hadn't meant it, dear. Now come inside, lay aside your things, and have a good supper. I've brought some fine herbs for a stew."

CHAPTER THIRTY-NINE

Camelot

He looks like he is dying from the inside out. Deoradhan's eyes pondered the Pendragon as the man rose from his couch and moved across his chamber.

"My lord king, if I have disturbed your rest—"

Arthur held up a hand, weariness lining his eyes. "Nay, nay, my son..." He stopped. "I'm sorry. I know you don't like me to call you..."

A pang drove through Deoradhan's heart. *I love this man. I love him...despite everything that is past.* He cleared his throat. "Yestin said you wanted to see me, my lord."

He saw Arthur's lips tighten. "Aye. I did. I do." The king gestured toward one of the alcoves. "Come and sit with me, Deoradhan."

Deoradhan nodded and followed Arthur into the dimly-lit alcove. Arthur drew a curtain across the opening. "No one will hear us here," he explained, sitting down. He looked into Deoradhan's face for long moments. "You know what has happened with Weylin."

"Aye, my king."

Arthur paused, then said, "I am not a fool, Deoradhan. I'm sure you must have known that Weylin plotted against me."

Deoradhan nodded. *I will tell him the truth.* "I did, my lord."

"And did he ask you to help him?" Arthur looked away.

"He did, my lord," Deoradhan said quietly. "But I could not go through with it."

Arthur met Deoradhan's eyes again, probing his soul. "Why not? Do you not hate me?"

Deoradhan's heart felt like it would break. "Nay, my king, I don't," he whispered. "I...thought I did. But I cannot."

Arthur let out a heavy sigh. The sigh sounded like it had been locked away twenty years. Finally, he murmured, "Good. I'm glad." He reached out and laid a hand on Deoradhan's. "Thank you, my...Deoradhan. You will never know how much your kindness means to me."

They sat silently for a long moment. Then the king stood. "You know Weylin will be convicted, Deoradhan. He will die a traitor's death."

Deoradhan's head snapped up. *At last. Can it really be so?*

"His lands will pass to Solas...unless you wish me to charge Weylin with an additional crime." The king paused.

"What do you mean, my lord?"

"Disobedience to the crown during the siege of Dunpeledyr. I ordered him to manage the matter justly, letting your father live if possible. Convicted of this crime as well, Weylin and his house will forfeit their status as nobles of this land. Every stade of his property will be available for me to redistribute as I please, if you understand me, Deoradhan."

He means he will give Dunpeledyr to me, Deoradhan realized. His spirit bubbled with excitement. The goal of his life was within his reach. "How will you accomplish this, my lord?" he breathed.

"As a living witness to his actions, you must charge him publicly."

"But...but I was just a lad. I don't even remember the siege of Dunpeledyr except as if in the dream of a dream."

"I will accept your testimony as valid."

"When, my lord?" Deoradhan breathed.

"Tomorrow morning."

Deoradhan stared at the king, then nodded and stood. "I will do it, my lord." His blood pummeled through his body with excitement.

As he turned to go, Arthur stretched out his hand. When Deoradhan looked into his eyes, he saw them beseeching, seeking some proof of reconciliation.

'Tis a peace offering, he realized. The Pendragon didn't need an additional charge to convict Lord Weylin; the man's treason condemned him already. *He's doing this for me, to atone for the past.* Slowly, Deoradhan reached out and grasped Arthur's forearm.

Years rolled off the king's face. "I cannot help what has gone before, lad," he whispered, "but I will try to repair what I've broken down."

Without comprehending it, Deoradhan felt his heart soften like snow under a spring rain. He nodded again, unsure of what to say, bowed, and turned to go.

As he pushed back the curtain, his eyes fell on a small book, lying open on the table. Someone – the king, he supposed – had tattered its pages by extensive use. Curious, though he didn't know why, Deoradhan paused to scan the contents. In darkly-inked words, he read,

> *Therefore I will divide him a portion with the many,*
> *And he shall divide the spoil with the strong,*
> *Because he poured out His soul to death,*
> *And was numbered with the transgressors;*
> *Yet he bore the sin of many,*
> *And makes intercession for the transgressors.*

The book of Isaiah. Deoradhan felt his spirit bitter and harden in the old familiar way. *Arthur has become more religious and thinks he can get ahead with his God by giving me Dunpeledyr. But he cannot give me back my father, nor take away the stain Weylin has put on my mother. A God without justice may accept such a sacrifice, but I shall never. I will not forgive him, for neither he nor his God can erase the past.*

Summer Country

Aine's pains began without warning, deep in the night. Calum woke to her hand pushing at his shoulder along with her frightened voice whispering, "Calum, Calum, wake up."

He rose from his pallet on the floor, shaking his head to clear away the sleep. He had been up most of the past nights with his brother, helping with the lambing, and his drowsiness drugged him now. "What is it, Aine?" Calum mumbled, kneeling at the side of her narrow bed.

She had risen to her elbows. "The child…It's coming, Calum." In the moonlight streaming through the small window, he saw her face ashen and perspiring. "It's too early," she gasped.

He kissed her forehead and tried not to let his own anxiety show. "I'll get Eilley," he said. "'Tis probably only a false alarm." He was glad his brother's house stood only two miles away. Kieve's wife had offered to help with Aine's delivery, though it hadn't been expected for another month or so.

Aine held tightly to his hand, her eyes filled with terror. "I am so afraid, Calum."

He swallowed and drew her close to himself. "Perfect love casts out fear," he murmured, holding her to his heart. He felt her trembling. *O Lord, help her. And me.* Calum closed his eyes and let her go. "I'll be right back," he promised. "I have to get Eilley."

Aine nodded and another pain wracked her. She gripped the mattress with white fingers, biting her lip until Calum could see blood staining it. *O Lord, be our Help in this hour.*

He turned and exited, closing the door softly behind him.

CHAPTER FORTY

How I wish for a mount now, Calum thought as his feet flew over the heavy spring grass, laden with dew. He didn't stop running or praying until he reached Kieve's house, tucked between two hills.

Kieve's middle daughter answered his pounding. "Mama has gone to help our neighbor with a birthing," she explained.

"Where's your Papa, Bronwyn?" he gasped.

"In the fields with the sheep, Uncle," the seven-year-old replied. "He left the dogs with us."

What am I to do now, Lord? "Bronwyn, your aunt's pains have come. Where is the nearest midwife besides your mama?"

Bronwyn squinted in thought. "I think old Dilys helps sometimes. She lives in the village."

Two more miles away. He'd already been absent fifteen minutes at least. *I can't go two more miles and then hobble four more back with an elderly woman in tow.* "Tell your mama that Uncle Calum needs her, whenever she returns. Alright, Bronwyn?"

The little girl nodded. "Alright, Uncle."

Lord, help me, Calum pleaded as he came to a halt before his own door again. He'd delivered lambs, calves, even foals, but never children. *But I have to do this. There is no other way.* He opened the door slowly, hesitant to tell Aine that no midwife had come.

Aine had kicked off her blankets and curled up in a ball of misery in the middle of the bed. Calum walked forward. A sick feeling came into his chest as he realized the mattress wore a wide circle of blood.

Camelot

The hills rose up all around him, sloping green mounds speckled with the white primroses. 'Twas Lothian in the spring, Deoradhan recognized. His bare feet felt the cool earth, and his nostrils breathed in the fragrant wild scents around him.

A man stood in the sunlight as well, apart from him. Deoradhan knew that the stranger was his father, appearing just as he had always thought him to be. Righteousness, courage, selflessness all shared the throne on Lord Eion's countenance. His father waited there as though expecting another. Deoradhan called out to him, but the lord either couldn't hear him or wouldn't respond.

Turning his eyes, Deoradhan realized another person had entered the valley. Weylin, he thought and tried to warn his father. But his father had already seen the intruder and faced him as Weylin drew a sharp knife. With relief, Deoradhan saw that his father was well-armed, far better than his opponent. Weylin drew close, and Deoradhan watched for Lord Eion to draw his own blade and hack his enemy to pieces.

Yet his father didn't defend himself. Horror filled Deoradhan's breast as he saw the attacker plunge his dagger into his father's heart. Over and over, the knife entered his father's chest until the blood ran over the valley grasses, rushing to Deoradhan's feet in a river. Looking up from the red pool, he saw his father wither and fall to the earth, still.

Anger burned in Deoradhan. Able to move at last, he ran to his father's side and found him dead. He drew his sword. He would have no mercy on the killer. He turned and faced his enemy, staring into his face with prepared hatred.

But Weylin had disappeared or morphed somehow. Deoradhan blinked in utter dismay at the man standing there, bloody knife in hand, fresh from the killing. 'Twas not Weylin.

'Twas himself.

"How can this be?" he cried out. Shaking, his eyes went back to the corpse lying at his feet. No longer did his father's face look back. 'Twas the Lord Christ. He knew it, though he could not tell how or why this change had occurred...

Deoradhan woke, shaking. Slowly, he realized he lay in his old room at Camelot. But a Presence had come with the dream, so real to him that he couldn't dismiss his vision. He knew that the Lord stood in this chamber with him, and he heard a Voice in his heart, whispering uncomfortable things, things he could not dismiss.

Unable to roll over and sleep, Deoradhan rose from the feather mattress, pushing aside the yellow sheets. He must move, must do anything but lay here under this torrent of thoughts that threatened to drown him. With trembling hands, he slipped a mantle over his sleeping tunic and stepped into the corridor. Unthinking, unseeing, his feet found their way to the king's private chapel where he had comforted Lady Tarian some weeks ago.

Silently, he moved toward the front of the room, the thoughts of all the years pouring through his mind. The bitterness against Arthur. The hatred toward Weylin. The sense of self-righteousness coloring his every scheme. *Yet I rightfully felt that. They deserved it.*

Like a flash of summer lightning, his mind recalled how he had killed the Lord Christ in his dream. *But I didn't really do it. 'Twas only a night vision. That passage in Isaiah I glanced at in the king's chamber poisoning my thoughts. The Jews, the cursed Romans, 'twas they who killed Jesus. Not I.*

But the guilt increased, pressing unwanted reflections into his soul, as though from some outside Source. *Have you not killed Him in your heart?* The Presence had followed him to this quiet room and demanded answers from him, answers to questions he sweated to ponder. *Have you not forsaken His ways to follow your own wants?*

Deoradhan thought of Dunpeledyr. "'Tis my right!" he addressed the Presence aloud, hearing his voice echo through the chapel. "I only required what was rightfully mine. What You had taken from me." He raised his chin. "If anything, 'tis You who ought to ask my forgiveness, like Arthur, like them all!"

Silence. Then...

Do I not have the right to do what I wish with My own things?

Deoradhan found no reply to this in his mouth. He stood before the stone altar, helpless, feeling his heart thud against his ribs.

As though a curtain had been pulled away from his mind, he suddenly knew that if he rejected this God now, he would be exiled from Him forever. He would no longer be able to hear the Voice that both drew and repulsed him. Long moments passed. He felt his soul tense and rebel against this Invader.

If I give myself to You, what will become of me? Would he become forever a slave to this God who could do as He pleased? The pull was irresistible, for Deoradhan sensed that the Source of life called his life back to His own. Yet Deoradhan knew that the Presence would not constrain him to lay down his arms, would not tear open his soul and force His way in. He could say nay...and yet he could not.

Finally, with a deliberate movement, Deoradhan bent his knees and knelt on the wide stone flags. His head dropped to his chest, his hands fell to the floor, and he prostrated before the Presence.

Long moments later, he rose, the manacles he had not known enslaved him fallen off his shoulders. With open eyes, Deoradhan breathed. "I am free," he said aloud.

I expected to stand up a bondservant. But I find I am a son, liberated at last... from myself.

CHAPTER FORTY-ONE

Summer Country

She is going to die. I am going to lose her. The child would not come, no matter how Aine groaned and strained, her frail limbs shaking with effort.

Calum wiped the sweat off Aine's face and forced himself to reassure her with a smile. He must be strong for her. She had lost consciousness once in pain already. *She has no strength left, Lord. Please let the child come.* He kissed her brow tenderly. Such love had entered his heart for this woman in the few weeks he had known her.

"Water," Aine moaned. "Please."

Calum rose and went to the water bucket once more. *Do not take her from me,* he pleaded. He turned with the cup of water, and his heart ached again at the sight of his wife writhing, powerless against her agony.

Please, Lord, do not take her from me. Take the child, take anything, but not her.

Camelot

'Twas dawn. Feeling the cool darkness lift around him, Deoradhan turned his steps toward the fortress again. He had spent the remainder of the night walking the fields, remembering, repenting, submitting. 'Twas a new sensation, having a lord other than himself to rule his thoughts, actions, and feelings. So many faces came to his mind, so many people he had wronged. Meghyn, Arthur, Aine. So much to make right.

Never had the grass appeared so alive, never before had his heart rejoiced to see squirrels and birds scurrying and swooping in the faint morning light. Joy flooded him in great throbbing pulses. *I am free from my old desires,* he realized. *Free to do as 'twas meant for me to do and, what's more, at liberty to become who I was meant to be.*

He broke into a run and entered the fortress gates gasping for breath. The guards admitted him with strange looks, but he grinned back at them and continued on his way.

"Where is the king?" he asked a familiar attendant to the Pendragon.

"At breakfast," the man replied, "in his chambers."

Deoradhan grasped the man's shoulder. "Thank you." His feet flew over the stones, and he arrived at Arthur's rooms at a sprint.

I must calm myself, or he'll think I've gone mad. A chuckle burst from Deoradhan. *He'll think it already when I say what I've come to tell him.* He raised a hand and knocked quickly.

A servant opened the door a crack. "The king is at breakfast and won't be dis—"

"Tell him 'tis Deoradhan. He will see me," interrupted Deoradhan with a smile.

The young man raised his eyebrows but retreated to do as Deoradhan asked. A moment later, the servant had returned. "The king will see you, my lord."

Deoradhan nodded and entered behind the servant. Arthur sat at a low table, eating cheese and bread.

"Deoradhan," he greeted. "What is it? I didn't expect to see you until the trial this morning."

Deoradhan sat down opposite the king. "I've come to speak to you about that, my lord," he began. "I cannot testify against Weylin."

Arthur sat silent. Stunned, Deoradhan knew. "What has brought about this change of heart, lad?" he finally asked.

Deoradhan smiled. "I realized, my lord, that I could not accuse another of the same sins of which I am guilty."

Arthur did not understand. Deoradhan could see it in his face. Gently, he knelt beside the king. "My lord, you have been very kind to me in offering this. Despite my ingratitude over the years, you have always held out your hand to me. I'm sorry for the wrongs I've done you."

'Twas obvious he had baffled the king. Arthur slowly answered, "You do know, Deoradhan, that if you don't bring these charges against Weylin, his line will retain his lands. Weylin will receive the death sentence, but Dunpeledyr will go to Solas, his heir." He paused. "You will have no claim on it nor the chance of a claim once Weylin is dead. Dunpeledyr will be lost to you forever."

With fresh joy, Deoradhan realized he felt no regret. "Then it is lost, my lord." He smiled thoughtfully. "I think I have had enough of houses and lands to last me for one lifetime. I have spent too much time trying to gain them, at any rate. From now on, by God's grace, I will be content with what He deems right."

Arthur nodded. "Alright, lad."

Deoradhan looked the king in the eyes. "I do not mind, my lord," he said softly, "if you call me your son."

Summer Country

Eilley had come at last. Calum had seen the apprehension grow on her face as she examined Aine.

"You did everything that could be done, Calum," his brother's wife murmured. "Let me help her for a bit. Take a breather outside."

Calum knelt beside the bed, his eyes locked onto Aine's countenance. Her eyes had been closed, but she opened them at Eilley's words.

"Go ahead, Calum," she whispered. "But don't be long."

With a gentle touch from her rough-hewn hand, Eilley guided him toward the door. He stumbled outside into the light of early morning, nearly blinded after the cottage's dimness. It seemed so strange to him that the sun had risen as usual, that the sheep bleated in the nearby fields, that bees flew past on their way to pollen-rich flowers. So strange when inside Aine lay…

He shook his head and slid to the ground. *Lord, let her live.*

~ ~ ~

As though from a far-off distance, Aine felt the woman's hands smooth back her hair, wash her arms, adjust her pillows. The pain had continued and increased until Aine could no longer think. *Let it be over soon,* she pleaded. *And please let this child live.*

In the midst of the pain, she felt Jesus' presence more intensely than she had before. 'Twas as if He sat by her as the pains came. Sometimes, Calum's face seemed to become His, his eyes flooded with sympathy and sweet comfort. Once, she began the question in her spirit, *Why…* But His face came before her again, and her question faded in the brightness of His countenance.

If you will take me, my Savior…and the child…watch over Calum. Don't let the grief overcome him, her heart asked, sure that the request would be granted.

Another numbing pain poured through her body. Eilley's form grew dark. *'Tis the end,* she realized, and her eyes slid shut as her senses faded. *O Lord, be with me.*

CHAPTER FORTY-TWO

Cantia

Tarian was weeding in her parents' garden when the messenger came. She stood up quickly at the sight of the royal crest on his tunic and wiped her hands on her simple garment. She saw the messenger's eyes narrow and his hand hesitate over giving her the scroll.

"You are Lady Tarian, aye?" he questioned.

What noblewoman would weed a garden? A disgraced one who has nothing to offer her family but what her hands can do. She gently took the sealed scroll from him. "Aye, I am. Do you...Do you wait for a reply?"

"I do."

She nodded and dropped her eyes to the scroll. Her fingernails, chipped and stained green and brown, peeled back the wax seal. She skimmed the document; then, only half-believing what she read, went back to the beginning:

Arthur, High King of all Britain and High Judge, to Lady Tarian, formerly of Oxfield. Greetings. Drustan, lord of Oxfield, advisor to the king, sleeps. The king requests your immediate attendance upon receipt of this letter.

"Drustan...sleeps?" she wondered aloud, knowing 'twas a euphemism for death. "How?"

"Protecting the king, my lady," the messenger answered, his face unemotional. "He was related to you?"

"Aye," she breathed. "Aye, he was."

Summer Country

Calum felt someone shaking his shoulder. He lifted his head from where it rested on the edge of Aine's bed. Blearily, he looked up to see Eilley gazing down at him, tears in her eyes. "'Tis over," she whispered, wiping the moisture from her cheeks.

His eyes turned toward Aine's still, white face supported by the pillows. The sorrow rolled over his soul, and he began to sob great cries that wracked his shoulders. Eilley wrapped her arms around his head, drawing him to her. *Your will be done,* his heart wept. *Your will be done.*

Rising to his knees, he reached a hand to stroke Aine's hollow cheek. "She is at rest now," he murmured, his tears dropping on the woolen blanket.

"Aye, she is at rest, Calum," replied Eilley.

He leaned forward and kissed her pale lips. Slowly sitting back on his heels, he looked into that face full of a serenity derived from the Prince of Peace alone. "She has more life now than ever before," he said, not caring that his tears ran unchecked.

"I don't know about that, Calum," he was surprised to hear Eilley reply. He turned, and she gave him a smile. "She has a long recovery ahead of her. She'll need many days to regain her strength. And the child's a small one, though hearty."

Stupefied, Calum could only stare at his sister-in-law. "What do you mean? I thought she was..." He couldn't finish.

Eilley chuckled. "You thought she was dead? Well, then, the Lord has given her back to you from the dead. Like Lazarus, aye?" She couldn't stop giggling, and Calum slowly joined her, tears mixing with his laughter.

"Where is the child?" he finally managed.

"Beside her mother, sleeping."

Calum rose to his feet and moved back the blanket ever so

gently. There, nestled beside Aine, he saw a tiny swaddled bundle, soundly sleeping. "May I hold it?" he asked Eilley.

She smiled. "Of course, if you don't wake her. 'Tis a little daughter you have."

Delicately, feeling like one who is about to smell a precious rose, Calum lifted the infant and held it to his chest, filled with gratitude.

"What will you name the child?" questioned Eilley.

Calum lowered a kiss to the small reddened brow. "Mercy," he said. "We will call her Mercy."

CHAPTER FORTY-THREE

Dunpeledyr

"And what kind of work have you done?" the gracious auburn-haired woman asked.

Bethan smiled back. "I spent half a year in Oxfield, in Southern Logress, my lady. I worked as a kitchen servant there, but I'm able to do any kind of household work as well."

Lady Seonaid nodded. "Good. Well, Bethan, I think we could use your services here. And your sister's as well. Generally, we move servants from one kind of work to another at Dunpeledyr, and I doubt that will alter under my son's leadership."

Bethan cocked her head. "I'm sorry, my lady. I didn't know your husband had recently died."

"Aye, while at the king's house." The noblewoman stood, quietly thoughtful, as if she'd forgotten Bethan waited for direction. "For yet a little while and the wicked shall be no more," Bethan heard her murmur, her eyes turned away.

After a few moments, she seemed to remember Bethan and Enid. "Oh, aye. My daughter Lady Fiona will determine where you are needed at present. Meanwhile, Lorna will show you where you will sleep," she said, nodding toward a woman near her side.

Bethan's eyes followed the elegant lady as she moved from the hall. "Come along, lassies," the servant woman Lorna interrupted. "There's plenty of room above the stables."

Bethan put an arm around her sister's shoulders and walked after Lorna. *Lord, You have been gracious to us. Be gracious also to my Papa, wherever he is.* And she knew that He would be.

Summer Country

Five days after Aine gave birth, Calum heard horse's hooves trotting down the lane outside his cottage. Moments later, a soft knock came to his ears. "I'll be right back," he promised Aine, putting aside his little volume.

She smiled, propped up on her pillows. *Every day she improves.* He laid a tender hand on her cheek and moved to the door. Opening it, Calum saw Deoradhan on the other side. He glanced back toward the bed. Aine had closed her eyes, dozing, Mercy cuddled beside her.

"Deoradhan," he stated quietly. *What does he want? Lord, help me to love him.*

"Calum, I need to speak with you."

Calum nodded and drew the door closed behind him. From a tree by the lane, he heard a songbird let out its melodic laughter, and he smiled, thinking to himself that winter was indeed past and spring had come.

Deoradhan led him toward the cross up on the hill, not speaking until they had arrived. Calum watched the younger man gazed at the wooden memorial. He smiled. "'Death is swallowed up in victory,'" he murmured and then turned his eyes toward Calum. "That has become true in me as well, Calum." He sighed and ran his fingers over the carved words. "After all those years of shaking my fist at Heaven, He has conquered me at last. And I can't say I'm sorry for it."

This was unexpected, to say the least. Calum felt his mouth drop open. He was about to speak, but Deoradhan went on. "I've come back to apologize for the things I said and did. They were awful wrongs toward you and especially toward Aine." His eyes, clear of bitterness at last, grew tender mentioning her name. Calum tensed. "May I speak with her, Calum? Is she still here?"

Calum swallowed. "Aye, she is, Deoradhan. I must tell you... I...I've married her." *O Lord, may he understand!*

Deoradhan stood still for a long moment. Then he nodded. "'Tis as it should be," he murmured.

After a moment, Calum laid a hand on his friend's shoulder. "Come into the house, Deoradhan."

Camelot

"The king will see you now, my lady," the attendant directed his words toward Tarian. Arrayed in her finest, she nodded and moved through the open doors to the hall.

Arthur rose from his throne when she entered. She curtsied low, and he took her hand, raising it to his lips. "Lady Tarian, you are welcome. Thank you for coming."

She nodded. "My lord," she greeted. "I trust you are well."

He smiled, the weariness retreating from his face like the gloom when the sun appears. "I will get to the point quickly, my lady. As you know, your husband, Drustan, is dead. He rode too near my side, and a traitor's arrow took him rather than me." He paused. "I don't know whether this news brings you grief or not."

Tarian remained silent.

"However," continued the king, "what concerns us today is this: Your husband was rich in lands. His wife should inherit those lands until her death, when they will pass to his nearest male relative, whether that would be his son, cousin, nephew."

Tarian felt that the king wished for a response. "But, as my lord knows, I am no longer Drustan's wife by law. You judged me yourself, my king, and decreed the divorce," she said quietly, hands folded before her.

The king nodded. "Aye, I did. Yet I did not believe nor do I now believe the charges laid at your feet by your husband. I said that at the time, didn't I?"

Tarian nodded. If he hadn't, she may have been executed for adultery rather than merely dismissed as an unsatisfactory wife.

Arthur moved over to the table near his throne. Tarian saw a parchment lying there. He picked it up. "This is the single document that declares you divorced from Lord Drustan, my lady."

What is the purpose of this? Did I come from Cantia for this? Patiently, she nodded again. "Aye, my lord."

He stepped to the huge hearth, blazing to keep away the spring chill. Without any hesitation, the king tossed the document into the flames. Startled, Tarian met his eyes.

"Oxfield is yours, my lady," he stated. "There is no existing record of your marriage coming to an end. As far as I am concerned, you are the lady of Oxfield until your death."

Tears rose to Tarian's eyes. "Thank you, my lord," she choked out. "May God reward you for dealing righteously with me."

CHAPTER FORTY-FOUR

Arthur met him with an embrace. "Deoradhan," he smiled.

"My lord king," Deoradhan acknowledged. The submissive title no longer grated on his spirit.

Arthur held up a scroll. "A letter has come for you. From Dunpeledyr."

Deoradhan met the king's eyes for an instant, then took the scroll. He pried off the seal and ran his gaze over the words. "They wish me to return there," he said, looking up. "They want me to come back to Dunpeledyr." Joy filled his heart. "Does my lord king mind?" he asked.

Arthur smiled and shook his head. Deoradhan saw a wistfulness pass through the king's blue eyes. "Nay, lad, go with my blessing," he murmured.

Deoradhan clasped Arthur tightly to him. "Thank you, my lord." He paused, then decided to say the words swelling up in his heart. "I love you, my lord, as a son loves his father. I was a fool to feel and think otherwise before."

Dunpeledyr

Solas walked through the guardhouse, his hand on Fiona's arm. She whispered descriptions to him as they went, becoming the new lord's eyes.

'Twas an awesome responsibility, this being master of the fortress. At times, Solas felt like Solomon when the kingship of

Israel fell upon his shoulders. *Aye, I am like a little child, Lord. Give me wisdom to govern well, to please You,* he prayed daily when he woke.

He and Fiona had finished their survey of the guardhouse, finding it in good order to the best of their knowledge. They stepped out of the cool building into the bright midday sun, and Fiona stopped short. "'Tis Deoradhan," she said. "Padruig, I mean."

"Where?"

"He's just riding through the gate," she answered. "He's seen us now."

Solas felt his heart speed in excitement. "Let's go to meet him, Fiona."

She led them forward across the wide courtyard. "Padruig," she called out.

They halted. Solas stretched out his arm and felt a strong grip on his forearm. "Brother," he greeted. "I am glad you've returned home."

"Solas, Fiona. Thank you for asking me to come."

Solas kept his hold on his brother's arm. "Will you speak with me apart a moment, Padruig? You don't mind if we call you by that name, do you? That's how Mama always speaks of you."

"And you're an exile no longer," added Fiona.

"You may call me what you wish. And I will speak with you, Solas, for as long as you'd like."

Solas smiled. "Come, then. We'll walk in the fields."

~ ~ ~

That evening, just as dusk kissed the earth with her soft darkness, Deoradhan—*Padruig,* he reminded himself with a smile—strolled through the courtyard once more. His mind repeated the conversation with his brother, and he marveled at all that had occurred:

"Dunpeledyr is yours if you want it, brother. I am only the second-born to

our mother," Solas said. "The estate is yours by birthright."

Padruig had thought for only a moment. Then, he knew what he must say. "Nay, Solas. God has chosen you to lead this people, not me." He sighed in relief. "There was a time when I would have leapt at the words you just spoke. But now I find I'm content wherever God places me. What do the Scriptures say? 'I would rather be a doorkeeper in the house of my God than dwell in tents of wickedness,' aye?"

Slowly, Solas nodded. "Alright. Let it be so, then."

Padruig let his steps take him into the stable, warm from the animals' heat. He moved over to Alasdair's stall and picked up a brush. He'd not had a chance to groom the horse himself after their journey here. He knew a stable lad had done it already, but the horse welcomed his master's company.

A little loose hay sprinkled down from the rafters above him. Padruig looked up. He knew servants slept in the loft. Humming an old hymn, he went back to brushing the gray horse.

Movement to his right, outside the stall, caught the corner of his eye. He turned his head to see a girl slipping by, a cup for water in her hand. Thinking nothing more of it, Padruig returned to grooming Alasdair.

A little later, the same girl walked by again on her way back to the loft, he surmised. With this second glance, though, he thought she looked familiar. *Odd.* Padruig gave Alasdair a last pat, then moved out of the stall.

She had reached the ladder, but Padruig could see her profile in the dim light entering the open stable doors. "Bethan, is that you?" he called.

The girl turned, the cup full of water in her hand. "Aye, 'tis."

He took a few steps toward her. "What are you doing up here in Lothian, lass?"

She stood there, unease written across her face. "I... came with a larger party but decided to travel with them no further."

That man, Padruig remembered. *The one at her side in Oxfield.* He *must have misled her...* Aloud, he said, "So you are working here then?"

She nodded. "Aye. My little sister works here as well."

"With no plans to return south?"

She shook her head, and they stood silently for a moment. Then Padruig said, "You don't seem surprised to see me here."

"News of your arrival traveled quickly, my lord." She paused. "I must go to sleep, my lord. I rise early."

Padruig nodded. "Alright. Good night, Bethan."

~ ~ ~

Padruig rose early as well. Dawn found him walking through the yellowing fields, seeking the Lord's face in prayer. *Once I thought myself so strong, so independent. Now I know how weak I am, how helpless.*

He turned his feet toward the fortress, growing high from the hills. *Dunpeledyr ... Place of Spears. But You have turned it into a place of mercy for me.*

His mind and heart still engaged in prayer as he went, and he came across Bethan suddenly. Her brown hair loose around her shoulders, she knelt in a little hollow in the grass, evidently praying. She hadn't heard him approach, and Padruig stood, watching her lips moving silently. He meant to move on before she finished, but the sight of her devotion so transfixed him that she opened her eyes and found him there.

"I'm sorry," he said. "I didn't mean to spy, Bethan. 'Twas ... so lovely."

He hadn't meant to say that. She gave him an inquisitive look and rose to her feet, brushing off her long tunic. "I can remember a time when you found prayer useless and foolish, my lord."

Padruig nodded. "You have a good memory, Bethan. But 'twas I who was useless and foolish."

"Is this change of heart recent, my lord?" Bethan asked, walking toward the walls.

Padruig fell in step with her. *She remembers my behavior to Aine not three months ago.* "Aye, Bethan, 'tis. And 'tis nothing of me, but all of Christ." He stopped, and she did as well. "When I saw you last, I said and did terrible things. Not to you, I know, but to one whom I vowed to hold dear."

Bethan bit her lip and nodded. "We all do things we ought not do, my lord. Do you know what has happened to Aine?"

He was glad to feel no pain in his reply. "She has married Calum and given birth to a sweet daughter. I saw them both not a month ago."

Surprise flickered in Bethan's eyes, and she walked in silence for a moment. Finally, she said, "I'm sorry, Deoradhan—or should I call you Padruig? I know you loved her."

"Either name is fine, lass." He shook his head. "And nay, lass, don't pity me. I rejoice with Calum and Aine. To tell you the truth, Bethan, Calum loves her more than I ever did. He has more capacity for loving others."

"Because he loves his God so well," Bethan commented, plucking a wildflower as they walked.

"Aye," Padruig agreed. "How I wish I could love so well as he. Calum understands something so simple, yet so difficult for us mortals to grasp."

"What is that?"

"He knows that real love satisfies itself through giving, not taking. He chose to love Aine when, by my worthless standard, she was unlovable. I think of all the times when…" He trailed off, and then took a deep breath. "Let us say that I am determined that the next time shall be different, by God's grace."

His eyes were drawn to her face as they walked. A maturity he had not seen before rested there, integrity made strong through obedience to the living God. Her quiet strength pervaded the atmosphere around them, in a way similar to Fiona. *Yet unlike, too.* Her nature held rare sweetness.

"God will help you love as well as Calum, Padruig. 'Tis not what we are that matters, but what He is making us to be." Bethan answered. "You've come to know the Truth, Padruig. 'Twill set you free, you ken."

Free from the past. Free from wrongs done and received. "Aye," he agreed. "It has, lass."

They walked a few steps in silence. "So," Bethan said at last, "what will you do now?"

"Solas has asked me to stay here and advise him. I will act as his ambassador and the manager of his affairs." Padruig paused. "So I hope to see you often, Bethan."

He risked a glance at her face and saw her lips quivering at the corners. "I hope so, too, Padruig." Her smile blossomed. "And I am glad you've come home."

Finis

Made in the USA
Charleston, SC
10 November 2013